Haunted by the Fire

BLOOMSPOONS ADVENTURES BOOK TWO

ROSA LEE JUDE

ISBN-10:1-942994-06-0
ISBN-13:978-1-942994-06-0

Rosa Lee Jude
Visit my website at www.RosaLeeJude.com

Books by Rosa Lee Jude

Contemporary Romance
I STILL DO
UNTIL INFINITY

Urban Fantasy
The Enchanted Journey Series:
TREMBLE
JASMINE
NEVERWRONG

Time Travel/Historical Fiction
BloomSpoons Adventures Series
THE LEGEND OF AMBURGEY GIBBONEY

The Legends of Graham Mansion Series:
(with Mary Lin Brewer)
REDEMPTION
AMBITION
DECEPTION
SALVATION
REVELATION

Haunted by theFire

Chapter One

"WE HAD ALREADY PASSED our first anniversary before Tyler told me he was from another time. I was pregnant with Amburgey. I got in my car and drove to West Virginia where I stayed with one of my sisters for a week."

Symphony Wallace listened to her grandmother, Nadia French, talk about her grandfather. Since moving to Wytheville, Virginia, Symphony's life was a whirlwind of discovery learning about her time-travelling birth mother, Amburgey Gibboney. She also experienced firsthand that the time travel gene ran in her family. Symphony took her own sudden trip that landed her over sixty years in the past during the town's polio epidemic.

In the days since Symphony returned from 1950, a sizable portion of her free time was spent with Nadia. The ruse of Symphony being a house sitter fell away and she moved her remaining belongings into her grandmother's home. Evenings together always began in a conversational manner with the chitchat of a normal day. This particular one did not take long, though, for the topic to turn to time travel and those who had taken such journeys.

"From another time? That must have been shocking."

"Shocking. I suppose that is an accurate word in retrospect. Terrified is how I felt. I was carrying a child who was fathered by someone from another time. I could not imagine what that might mean for the baby."

Sitting on the back deck of Nadia's home, Symphony watched her newly found grandmother stare into the distance. Symphony could not imagine the level of worry Nadia must have endured. She wondered what she carried in her genes that were a byproduct of her time-hopping ancestry.

Symphony chose to remain silent and allow Nadia a quiet moment of reflection. The evening was the end of a series of busy work days as she helped with last minute plans for the Museums' activities that were part of Wytheville's annual summer festival— Chautauqua.

"I'm surprised that you are not at the balloon glow tonight." Nadia's sudden change of subject caught Symphony off-guard. "Since this is your first summer living here, I thought you would want to experience each night's festival events."

"I had every intention of doing that until I fell in the grocery store parking lot." Symphony shifted her weight in the cushioned lounge chair she was sitting in. "My tailbone had a talk with me on the way home and convinced me that an evening of non-physical relaxation might do both my body and my pride some good."

"I wondered why you were moving awkwardly when I got home." Nadia smiled. She reached over to pour Symphony another glass of her special punch. Her grandmother would not reveal the concoction's ingredients, but Symphony was certain that it had medicinal value. "Are you sure you don't need to seek some medical care? Asphalt is quite a hard surface to fall on. Is that why the eggs were missing from our grocery list items?"

"Yes, I managed to break my fall with the eggs, ungracefully too." Symphony saw Nadia was trying to hide a smile. "You go ahead and laugh. It's exactly how you are imagining. That cute little pink skirt you complimented me about this morning is now on the delicate cycle in the washing machine trying to get the eggs out."

"I'm sorry, dear. I'm glad you weren't seriously injured." Nadia chuckled.

"It's my penance for not waiting to purchase the eggs at the farmers market tomorrow." Symphony paused and looked intently at her grandmother. "Tell me more about Tyler Gibboney."

Nadia took a deep breath. Symphony watched as a dreamy look changed her expression. It was like someone poured love into her eyes. They danced and glimmered with light from a hidden source.

"He was the most unusual man I ever met, my Tyler. I believe that Millie told you the story. I met him in Atlantic City while I was representing West Virginia in the Miss America pageant. He liked to tell the story of how he became instantly smitten when he saw me walk across the stage. The truth of the matter is that I felt him long before I saw him. I felt his presence at that very moment before I ever even knew he existed."

Nadia's eyes went back and forth in rapid succession before a smile appeared. She bit her bottom lip and shook her head before she started talking again.

"There were hundreds of eyes on us when we walked across the stage during the opening introductions. At one moment, I could almost physically feel someone watching me. It was like an electric charge was coming from somewhere in the audience. I paused for a few seconds too long and was pushed by the girl coming up behind me. It was such an incredible feeling; I had to stop walking, to know where it was coming from. I found out soon enough."

"Did Tyler feel it, too?"

"I think he did. He was sending the signal to me. I never stood a chance. He could have revealed later that he was from Mars. It would not have mattered. I loved him the moment our souls met that night."

"Your friend, Millie, told me that the relationship progressed quickly. Did his being a time traveler make him have some sort of power over you?" Symphony wondered if her journey created any special abilities she might use later.

"There's obviously some sort of magical force that allows a person to be able to travel through time. I've heard about time portals and tokens more than I would like, but those are just enablers, I think. It is still some force of nature that gives certain people the ability to sidestep time and gain some level of control over it."

"Sidestep time. That's an interesting way of describing it."

"One morning, I was feeding Amburgey breakfast in her high chair at the kitchen table; Tyler strolled in from what I thought was an early morning run. He nonchalantly told me while he drank his orange juice that he had just travelled to the twenty-first century where everyone carried a phone in their pocket."

"Well, that doesn't seem so farfetched."

"Not now. We are living in a time when it is commonplace. This conversation occurred in the early 1970s. Some people had mobile phones, but they were in big bags and they cost a lot of money." Nadia took a deep breath and shook her head. "He was so casual about it. Tyler talked about time travel like he was going to see a movie. I always felt that he didn't treat it as seriously as he should. Maybe I was right."

"What time period was he from?"

"Tyler was born in 1900. He was in his early twenties when we first met."

"Do you know what he used for a time travel portal? I've wondered if he had any connection to the grandfather clock in the Rock House foyer."

"No. Tyler and I never lived in Wytheville together. He must have used some other portal. We lived in several different places. He must have had more than one portal, or else he had a way of getting to the one quickly. It may be more complicated than I want to know."

"So you made up the story of him being on a business trip when he failed to return home?"

"No. He really was on a business trip when he left. He was on a plane flight, at some point, during his trip. I do not think he died on the plane. The business trip was a convenient story to help declare him dead. He had a friend that helped me with the legal stuff. I'm sure he knew about Tyler's other life."

Nadia fingered the necklace around her neck. Symphony had noticed she frequently wore it.

"Did Tyler give you that?"

"Yes. It was his mother's. He actually went back to his own time to get it for me. It's quite unusual."

Nadia leaned toward Symphony and held the pendant out for her to look closer.

"It's a pearl with a slipper on top of it. It's like a Cinderella slipper."

"Yes. Apparently, Tyler's father made it. He was a jeweler. She was his princess. That's what Tyler used to call me."

Symphony noticed that tears were forming in Nadia's eyes. The woman held on to the pendant long after she leaned back onto her lounge chair.

"So, Tyler was travelling into the future when he met you."

"Yes. Tyler had no real interest in travelling to the past. He was a futuristic type person. He wanted to know what was ahead. He told me that one of his first trips was to the past and he had witnessed something tragic. He was more excited about seeing into the future."

"Why did Amburgey go looking for him in the past then?"

"It was the past in reference to her time, not his. When you met her in 1950, it was the future in relation to Tyler's original life."

"Could you show me some photos of him?" A mental image of the man Symphony saw in the hotel lobby in 1950 flashed before her eyes.

"That look that just crossed your face. You remembered something. Do you think you saw Tyler in 1950?"

"You may not have time travel abilities, Nadia, but I do think you possess the ability to read minds though. This isn't the first time I've experienced such an incident with you."

"I think I am just suspicious by nature. It's been an earned attribute in my life with the Gibboney time travelers." Nadia rose from the lounger and picked up the pitcher on the table. "If we are going to shake the dust off all my Tyler memories this evening, I'm going to have to have more punch."

"What's in that stuff? It's quite tasty."

"You have your secrets, I have mine. It's healthy, mostly. Lots of fruit juice. Lots of natural ingredients."

"Something Cybelee would like."

"There's another mysterious person."

"Did she have some connection to Amburgey? This pendant

looks a lot like the ones she sells. It obviously has some sort of power in relation to travelling in time."

"Amburgey was very secretive during the time she was going on her journeys. Unfortunately, I didn't realize what she was doing until she was too deep into it. I thought she was just being a teenager. I was caught up in my life with Nathan. I was trying to have something different. That pendant fell under my radar. I don't remember hearing about Cybelee until several years later. I don't see how the timing would be right for this to be one of her creations. Maybe she copied the work of another."

"I don't think I'm brave enough to suggest that Cybelee copied anyone on anything. She's rather formidable."

"Now who's the one with the interesting word choice? Will you feed Psycho while I go upstairs and get some photo albums?"

Symphony followed her grandmother into the house with Psycho, her grandmother's golden retriever, close on her heels. Previously, Symphony was told that Psycho was originally Amburgey's dog.

"Do you know what time period Psycho came from?" Symphony began opening a can of wet dog food.

"He came back with her after her first trip. I thought he was a local stray for the longest time."

"Do you think that was her trip to 1950?"

"I really couldn't say for certain. Amburgey did not share many details about her journeys. I've never found any writings or journals about her trips. She has stacks and stacks of diaries in the attic. I never read them while she was growing up. But, after she was gone for a year or so, I poured through each of them. There was not even a sliver of mention of time travel in them, even when she wrote about her father. I did learn that if she ever does come home, I have lots to punish her for. From my reading, I now know that she had a habit of sneaking out of the house at night."

Nadia chuckled and headed for the staircase. Symphony looked out the kitchen window, watching the summer sun begin to set. The light dinner they ate earlier left a hungry spot. She quickly put together a plate of cheese and crackers with some green and red grapes.

A glance at her phone revealed a text message from her mother, Mariel, telling her that she and Symphony's father, Peter, had landed safely in California. Peter would be attending a meteorology convention there during the upcoming week. They would follow it with a week of sightseeing along the Pacific coast.

"I just heard from my mother." Symphony spoke when Nadia returned to the room.

"Have she and Peter arrived in California?"

Symphony revealed Nadia's identity to her adoptive parents, Peter and Mariel Wallace, when Nadia first offered to allow Symphony to stay in her home. It had prompted them to make a brief visit to Wytheville to meet her before Nadia departed on her extended vacation.

"Yes. They landed about an hour ago and were on their way to their hotel when she texted. It's been a while since they have taken a real vacation. I hope they will relax once Dad's conference is over."

"I hope to have the opportunity to get to know them better. I'm so grateful that you were placed with such wonderful people. It has been a persistent worry all these years. I wondered how you were being raised."

"I know that this may be hard for you to hear, but I cannot imagine being raised by anyone else. I felt nothing but love and encouragement. No one tried to hide my beginnings. I was always made to feel that it made me special, rather than anything less."

"It is a great comfort. Now, I look forward to making up for lost time with you. If I can get you to stay in the present."

Symphony let Psycho back outside and took the plate of food to where they were sitting on the back deck. When Symphony returned to the kitchen, Nadia was giving the punch a final stir with a wooden spoon.

"I missed seeing all the ingredients again."

"My secret recipe."

"'The 'recipe' like the Baldwin Sisters made on *The Waltons?*"

"Not as potent, my dear. I'm surprised to hear that you know that TV show."

"Oh, yes. It was one of my mother's favorites. She has family who live near where the show was based. I've been to Walton's Mountain."

"Interesting. If you will carry the pitcher, I will bring these photo albums."

A HALF-HOUR LATER, after Nadia and Symphony had delved through the first collection of photos. Symphony saw the irony in how Nadia appeared to be showing her life in reverse, starting with her trips around the world and her years with Nathan, her second husband. It seemed as if Nadia was stalling for some reason.

"This is my Tyler." It was apparent from the creases on the edges of the cover that the burgundy album was faithfully looked at for many years. "I'm not sure who has poured over these photographs more, Amburgey or me. Of course, it's been many years since her fingers have touched these pages."

Symphony watched Nadia's fingertips slowly touch the black and white photograph on the page in front of her. Four little black corner holders held the photo in place.

Nadia's eyes glistened with emotion and a faint smile appeared when the woman's fingertips lovingly caressed the face in the photo that was smiling back at her. Symphony turned her attention to Tyler's face. Studying it closely, she had no doubt. It was the man she saw in the hotel lobby just before both she and Amburgey left 1950.

"He was there." Symphony's words broke the silence.

"I'm sorry, what did you say?"

"He was there in 1950. I saw this man right before I came back."

"You saw Tyler? In 1950?" Nadia's hands went to her face. Her eyes showed shock.

"He was in the lobby of the hotel right before we found the clock. Amburgey ran through the lobby so quickly, I doubt she saw him. He was standing at the desk. He had on a trench coat. I thought it was strange in the heat of a dry summer."

"Tyler loved trench coats." Symphony saw a loving smile return to Nadia's face. "I have no idea why. I used to joke with him about his obsession with them. He said it came from his youth. I suppose the garments became more popular in this country during the post-World War I era when he was becoming a man." Nadia covered her mouth for a moment as she choked back tears before she moved her hands away and revealed a smile. Tears spilled from her eyes.

"Nadia, he stared at Amburgey. I think that is why I noticed him. It was like he was locked on her presence. A few minutes later, I was back in the present. I have no idea what happened to him."

"It must have been one of the time periods she thought she could find him in." Nadia put the fingertips of each of her hands on the sides of her temple and stared down at the photograph. "Why did you have to tell her those stories? Why did you have to go on those jaunts yourself? Wasn't staying with your family enough?"

"The journey he was on when you two met would have been a trip into the future, right?"

"He liked the idea of going ahead of his lifetime. He said that he had only travelled to a time before his birth once and it did not turn out so well. He liked the future."

"You said he took several trips while Amburgey was growing up. Was he searching for something or someone?"

"I think he mostly missed his family. Once, he tried to convince me that all three of us should make a trip together so that Amburgey and I could meet his mother. It was the worst fight we ever had. The next trip he took was the one he did not come back from. I've felt guilty ever since that he was angry with me and might have not been focusing on what he was doing."

"You're afraid he had an accident?"

"Yes. I guess so. Maybe something went wrong and he got stuck somewhere."

"You weren't living here when he was taking these trips, right?"

"No, we lived in New Jersey for a while after we were first married. We moved around a lot when Amburgey was young."

"Did you ever come to Wytheville?"

"No, I barely knew that Wytheville existed before Tyler left. I didn't even know he had an inheritance here until many months after he was gone."

Nadia did not know that Symphony had investigated into Tyler Gibboney since she had arrived in Wytheville. The investigation led to some interesting questions and maybe a revelation.

"Please don't be angry at what I'm about to tell you, Nadia. It's just all part of my way of piecing together this puzzle of my heritage."

"Spit it out. I understand your desire to know the truth."

"I did a little investigating into the deeds to this property before it passed to you and Amburgey."

"And?"

"Amburgey Gibboney was put on the deed in 1924."

"What? How can that be? It must be another Amburgey Gibboney. Tyler couldn't have possibly known—"

"Long before I came to Wytheville, I began researching the name 'Amburgey Gibboney.' It was all I knew about my heritage. My research showed only four Amburgey Gibboneys in the last two hundred years. One of them was noted on a deed to this property in 1924. Who chose Amburgey's name?"

"I did." A look of acceptance crossed Nadia's face. "I had a teacher in elementary school that I adored. Her name was Miss Amburgey. The name stuck with me. I named our daughter. Tyler agreed to my wishes." Nadia reached over and took hold of Symphony's hands. A huge sigh left her lungs like it was being pushed out by an unseen force. Her shoulders slumped in resolution. "It was not some distant bachelor uncle who left this house and property to Tyler. He wanted us to come back here after he was gone."

"He loved his wife and daughter and wanted them to be provided for." Symphony squeezed Nadia's hands. "He did what any good husband and father would."

"A good husband and father would not have gallivanted through time, putting his life at risk and creating some attractive scavenger hunt for his young daughter." Nadia stood up and walked to the edge of the terrace. "I loved Tyler with all my heart and soul. It did not blind me to his weaknesses. A part of me knew that he would always take those trips. I never allowed myself to truly imagine that he might not return. I never dreamed that my daughter would follow him into that black hole of time."

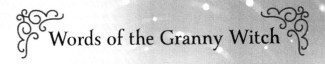 Words of the Granny Witch

"Anyone who has an ounce of adventure in his or her heart cannot deny it. As natural as the blood coursing through their veins is the desire to chase the unknown.

"The mother who gave birth to the child was pulled into the life of her ancestors. She could pretend that she was searching for an absent father. The truth is she would have gone even if he had tucked her in bed the night before.

"I dream of wedding flowers burning and a child falling from the sky. One wiser than me said that the burning flowers foretold of the heartache that would befall the union. The child falling symbolized a loss. I grieved for the death of a child I had not birthed until the Granny Witch told me that death was not the only way to lose someone."

Chapter Two

"THERE WERE MULTIPLE FIRES in the history of Wytheville that had devastating effects on the town." Allison Emerson, Director of Museums and Symphony's supervisor, began the staff meeting. "But the fire that occurred on the morning of March 8, 1924, is called the 'Great Town Fire.' We will open our fall exhibit in early October to honor this significant event. Does anyone know why it will be in October?"

Symphony glanced around at her coworkers. They all seemed to be pondering Allison's question. All of them, except one. Symphony's new best friend raised her hand.

"Yes, Marcella. Go ahead and tell them."

"October is National Fire Prevention Month."

"Exactly. We are going to have an incredible exhibit about this major moment in local history, and we are going to work with the fire department to promote fire prevention and safety."

"Will this include education programming in the schools?"

"Great question, Symphony. Yes, it will. Some of the firefighters will be accompanying our staff on those classroom presentations. Guess who is going to get to research the 1924 fire?"

"That's no secret, Allison. You've already given me that assignment." Symphony pulled out a large folder of research documents.

"Shocking." Marcella's tone was sarcastic when she saw the folder.

"Excellent, Symphony. I'm glad you took the hint and ran with it. I'm sure you have combed the research library for what you have there. There is more information about the fire than what you can find in print."

"Oh, I know what you are going to say. I forgot about that." Marcella spoke when she made eye contact with Allison. "That will work quite nicely. And, Symphony will get to work with Garon again. That will be delightful." Marcella gave Symphony a wide-eyed look.

"Garon?" Symphony's eyes darted from Marcella to Allison.

"Garon has been a supporter of the Museums and the Historical Society for many years. Long before he retired and left Hollywood, he made monetary donations and was even involved one summer in the collection of some oral histories." Allison opened up a box in front of her. "These audio recordings were originally on cassette tapes. Some of you may remember that while our spring intern, Drew, was here, I had him make CDs from several boxes of the recordings. These are some of them." Allison held up a sizable stack of CDs.

"I remember the summer that Garon came to town to work on that project. I was a reporter at the newspaper then. It was quite a big deal for a movie star to come and interview people. There were even a few national news stories about it." Marcella picked up the notebook that Allison had set on top of the stack of CDs. Glancing over Marcella's shoulder when she opened it, Symphony could see handwritten notes in beautiful penmanship. "That was the first time I met Garon. I interviewed him and did a story. It was quite fun."

"Excuse me, Allison. What was the topic that the project focused on?" Symphony continued to look over Marcella's shoulder while she flipped through the notebook.

"That was the neat thing about this project. Garon offered to come and spend a summer and interview as many of the older community that he could. We knew there were tons of great stories lurking in the memories of the seniors in the area. I had not been in this position for long at that point and had zero staff." Allison sat down opposite Symphony. "Fortunately, there were several students who wanted to do summer internships to help gather these oral histories. Unfortunately, many of the seniors seemed reluctant to share their stories with the students. Garon was the one who provided the funding for the purchase of the recorders and supplies. When he heard about the dilemma of getting the seniors to share their stories, he decided to come here himself and assist with the project."

"People lined up to tell their stories to Garon." Marcella chuckled. "We published a photograph on the front page of the newspaper that literally showed people standing in a line outside of the Rock House waiting to get inside to be interviewed by a movie star."

"It was really something." Allison continued. "We had a list of topics that we were especially interested in hearing further information about. These included the polio epidemic, the building of the interstates, local citizens who served in the military, and the significant events in our community. The interviews were conducted in the summer of 1995. We never dreamed we would talk to people who remembered the Great Town Fire in 1924. It was almost seventy years later by then. A couple of people who came to the Rock House to share their stories were children at the time of the fire. Those stories led us to a few older family members with amazingly vivid memories of seeing the after effects of the fire. One person was found who was living in the downtown area when the fire took place."

"My goodness. That's what I'm going to hear on these CDs?" Symphony reached over and touched the stack in front of her.

"That and a whole lot more." Allison looked at her watch. "We've covered enough of our planning for the next few weeks. I know that everyone has extra duties associated with our activities for Chautauqua this week."

While most of the other staff left the room, Symphony, Marcella, and Allison lingered around the table. Marcella still looked at the folder of research.

"It's amazing how quickly we can forget the things we do. I do not remember writing that story." Marcella pointed at a newspaper clipping that was on the backside of one about the fire. "I remember this story that another reporter wrote looking back on the 1924 fire. I do not remember writing the one that's on the next page."

"How long did you work at the newspaper?" Symphony took the folder that Marcella handed back to her and then put it in the box with the CDs.

"Too long." Marcella laughed. "I worked at the newspaper here and the one in Marion for a total of fifteen years. I was a mere child when I became a reporter. It was an adventure." Marcella's tone was dripping in sarcasm.

"Then, she came to work here, and the rest is history." Allison laughed heartily at her joke. Marcella and Symphony remained silent. "I know; I should not quit my job for a life in comedy."

"I've got to say, Allison, giving me this stack of CDs during the week of Chautauqua is rather mean."

"Mean? I don't understand, Symphony." Allison furrowed her brow and tilted her head.

"You know that I am going to want to start listening to them immediately. There's entertainment every night in the park. I'm going to be torn."

"Oh, don't worry about listening to them this week. Enjoy the events. Remember, we are not planning to open the exhibit until the first week of October. You have plenty of time."

"Besides, Chautauqua is a Native American word that means 'week of rain.'" Marcella picked up her papers from the meeting.

"What? Don't try and fool me. I'm a researcher by trade. I was not familiar with the word 'Chautauqua' before I came here. When I heard about the festival, I looked it up. It is an Iroquois word meaning bag tied in the middle or two moccasins tied together. Neither of which have anything to do with the festival." Symphony narrowed her eyes at her friend before smiling. "You are messing with me."

"Yes, Marcella is giving you a hard time. Unfortunately though, it does seem to rain quite often during this week each year." Allison began walking toward the door. "It's the curse of having an outdoor festival, I suppose. Anyway, rain or shine, go enjoy your first time at the festival, Symphony. The CDs can wait. It would also not be a bad idea to talk to Garon about anything that he might remember that was not captured in the recordings."

"Another adventure with Garon. Who knows where that might lead?" Marcella winked, closing the door behind them.

"I WAS SURPRISED that you were able to be here tonight." Symphony looked around the area while she and Jason waited in line for food. "Most Wednesdays you are at the brewery."

"Well, it's festival week and my girlfriend has never attended before." Jason put his right arm around Symphony while waving at a passerby with his left. "Besides, it's beach night. This may surprise you, but I can shag." Jason raised his eyebrows and smiled.

"This may surprise you, but I cannot."

"Not yet."

"Hmmm, I don't think there's a 'yet' for me."

Symphony shook her head and returned to studying the menu posted in front of her. She was determined to try all the food vendors before the week was over. Tonight's choice was Greek food.

"Oh, my darling, there's lots of 'yets' in your future."

Symphony saw an older gentleman walking toward them and waving. Jason returned the gesture.

"Okay. You have about five seconds to come up with a story, if you need one. My Uncle Belcher is walking toward us."

"WHAT?" Symphony quickly covered her mouth. "He still attends festivals? How old is he?"

"He's eighty-eight and very active. He's also sharp as a tack, so get ready." Jason squeezed Symphony's arm. "Uncle Belcher, how are you?"

"I'm fine, Jason. I talked to your mother this morning. Isn't it a beautiful night?"

Symphony held her breath. She had not worked up the nerve to turn around and face the man. Her heart beat grew faster with each passing second.

"Uncle Belcher, you haven't met my girlfriend."

Symphony could feel Jason tugging on her arm. Taking a deep breath, she slowly turned around. She knew that she needed to maintain control of her reaction to Belcher. Jason's uncle was one of the people who Symphony met on her journey to 1950. Young

Belcher was quite smitten with Symphony. Maybe by now, she was a blurry memory in Belcher's life. The man met her gaze with a smile and an extended hand.

"This is my Uncle Belcher." Jason winked at her, before turning back to his Uncle. "This is Symphony."

Symphony smiled while slowly making eye contact with the man. For a split second, she felt relief. There did not appear to be any recognition in his eyes. He gripped her hand in a strong handshake and tilted his head to study her more closely.

"What did you say her name was?"

Symphony could hear Jason letting out a sigh.

"Her name is Symphony."

"Forgive me for staring, young lady. You are the spitting image of a girl I knew many years ago." A faraway look appeared in Belcher's eyes. "Her name was Symphony Wallace, I believe. What's your last name?"

"Well, isn't that a coincidence. My last name is Wallace, too. What are the odds?" The nervous giggle that escaped from Symphony probably sounded strange to Jason. She hoped that Belcher would not think so.

"Indeed. Despite my fuzzy old man memory, standing here gazing at you is like travelling back in time."

Symphony heard Jason gasp but did not dare look in his direction. The pendant that hung around her neck—her time travel token—was feeling quite heavy in the summer sun. An awkward silence hung in the air before Belcher spoke again.

"Perhaps it was your mother or another relative I met all those years ago. Is Symphony a family name?"

"I wouldn't know, sir. I was adopted." Symphony turned to see where they were in line. "It looks like we are next to order. It was really nice meeting you, sir. I hope to see you again." Symphony kept her tone friendly, yet formal. She turned around, pretending to becoming engrossed in the menu board. She knew it was rude, but she could see his expression grow more suspicious the longer he looked at her.

"Take care, Uncle Belcher. I'll come see you sometime soon."

Symphony heard the old man mumble a goodbye. She could feel Jason staring a hole through her.

"That adopted thing really came in handy, huh?"

Symphony could feel Jason's breath in her ear from the whisper.

"I'm sorry, Jason. I know I was rude." Symphony turned to face him. Over Jason's shoulder, she could see Belcher walking away. She quickly hid behind Jason when Belcher glanced back in their direction. "I didn't know what else to do. He was staring so intently at me. I thought I would die when he spoke of travelling back in time."

"You're not the only one. I can't even imagine what my expression looked like."

"Will he tell your mother I was rude? I would hate for that to be her first impression of me."

"My mother's first impression of you came straight from me. Her second impression of you was on the night of the symposium."

"What?"

"Yeah. I've been trying to think of a way to break that to you. We haven't had too many face-to-face conversations since you returned from your trip." Jason rolled his eyes and shook his head. "For the record, I didn't know she was going to attend. I think she was on a fact-finding mission."

"And?" Symphony was afraid to hear his answer.

"Mom said you were very pleasant and professional. She loved your retro outfit. Allison spoke highly of you."

"Allison knows your mother?" Symphony shook her head and threw her hands up in the air. "Does everyone know your mother?"

"A lot of people do. She's worked in Wytheville most of her life. You would have met her already, but I wasn't sure where our relationship was going. I didn't want her to scare you off." Jason chuckled, stopping as he saw the expression on Symphony's face. "She's anxious for all of her sons to be married and giving her grandchildren. I am the final holdout. She was beyond thrilled when I told her about you. I don't tell her about women I date." Symphony remained silent. "I haven't wanted her to get attached to anyone." Jason pulled Symphony into an embrace. "Until now."

"Thank you, Jason." Symphony smiled. "That would simply be wonderful to hear, if I hadn't had that awkward encounter with her brother."

"Don't worry about that. Remember, he saw you here in the present. The awkward is really all on him. He's living up to his reputation of being the crazy uncle."

"The trouble is that he is not crazy. He's quite sane. He did meet me in his youth and I am here now." They moved to the front of the line.

"I'm quite glad that I met you first." Jason whispered in her ear. "If you are this concerned about him, he must have reached your heart."

"He reached my heart because it was like having a little of you with me there. It made me feel safe." Symphony looked into Jason's eyes.

"I'm glad. I'll have to thank him for that somehow. I'd say we could name our son after him. Belcher is an unfortunate name though."

"Yes."

Symphony watched Jason give his food order at the window. Her mind drifted to what he said.

"Our son." Her voice was not quite loud enough to be a whisper. "I like the sound of that."

Words of the Granny Witch

"The old ones used to say that every time you felt a shiver, it meant that someone was walking on your grave. It's a twist on time when the present meets the future and the receiver feels the destiny. I've often wondered if the past and the future aren't guests at the same dinner table. Maybe they reached for that bowl of potatoes that you took a serving from and wondered why the bowl slipped right out of their grasp. Maybe you felt the brush of foggy fingertips and wondered what you imagined.

"The Queens of Appalachia used midwifery as their trade and would brand a child either an old or young soul when he or she cried the first yelp. The most experienced of them took the prophecy deeper saying that a child is born with the memories of its ancestors right there in the same string of genes that makes locks of hair blonde and eyes blue.

"If you skip through time, what carries forth to your descendants? The time which was rightfully yours or that you borrowed from another?"

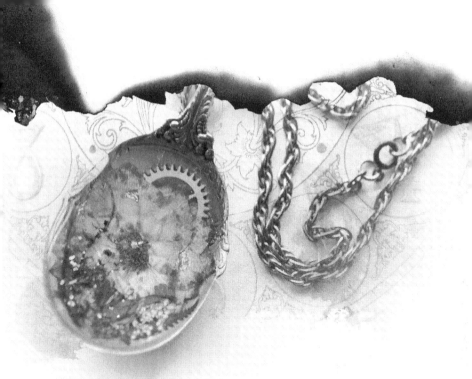

Chapter Three

"THAT'S AN IMPRESSIVE COLLECTION of movie posters."
Symphony walked around the large, high-ceilinged room
in Garon's Withers Road home. She imagined that the room in
the pre-Civil War mansion-like structure would have been used
as a large dining hall in its earliest years. Mammoth floor to ceiling
windows graced the largest wall on the eastern side of the house. She
looked closer at the windowpanes and frames, and the baseboard
and crown molding. It appeared that all such components were
original. When Symphony shared with Allison about her upcoming
visit with Garon, Allison said that Garon had spared no expense in
the restoration and renovation of the historic structure.

"I have an original from each of my movies in this room." Garon
raised his hands in a sweeping motion. "There's another room on the
south side where I display posters from my favorite movies. All of
those starred other people."

Without standing and counting, Symphony estimated that at least fifty posters hung on the walls of the room. The framing alone might cost more than she made in a year.

"Is this a room in the future Garon Fitzgerald museum?" Symphony laughed, making her way to the sitting area in the middle of the room where Garon was already seated. "I'd like to be the curator."

"Actually, it is. I have a trust set up for that precise purpose. It includes this house and its contents. Upstairs, I have archived many of the costumes and props from my movies as well as tons of personal items. I also purchased the house across the street where I was born and grew up."

"Your own version of Graceland in Wytheville."

"Elvis Presley Enterprises set the bar for legacy preservation and monetization. I've suggested in the trust documents that they be consulted on the operation."

"You are serious."

"I am, or will be, dead serious. I want my hometown to profit from my spot in the stars. Forget the curator position; I might amend the documents to name you the director. Allison will be retired by then, hopefully."

"Hopefully?"

"Hopefully she gets to retire, and I have a few more years to inhabit this side of the ground." Garon poured Symphony a glass of lemonade from a sparkling crystal pitcher. "Enough of that. You are here to discuss the 1924 fire. I am here—"

"Because you live here?" Symphony winked and smiled.

"You have been hanging around Marcella too much. Her quick wit is rubbing off on you. It's charming on her. I'm not sure about you." Garon raised one eyebrow. With her Grammie Wallace,

Symphony watched him make the gesture many times in his movies. It still amazed her that she was seeing it in real life.

"I'll have you know that I came to Wytheville with my own level of wit from its own natural source."

"Yes, I'm familiar with that source."

"I've been meaning to talk to you about that. Why didn't you tell me that you had met Amburgey, and me before, for that matter?"

"I've been waiting for you to bring this up." Garon took a deep breath and leaned back into the couch where he was seated. "Time is a powerful thing. The brain is the center of our existence. Through my many years of life, I've realized that we think we are in control. Our brain decides what we know and when we know it. Time has its own way of interceding and serving like a sieve. I've thought about my encounter with Amburgey many times over the years. It was one of the reasons that I began researching her when I moved back to Wytheville. I can honestly say that I did not remember meeting you until after you returned from your journey. It's like someone dropped the memory into my mind. I remember it now as you described it. I can't say for a certainty that I ever knew it before."

"My entire body is one big chill right now."

"That's an understandable reaction, Symphony. My feelings are not far from it. I've experienced some amazing occurrences in my life. I've been blessed to live out my wildest dreams. This connection I made to Amburgey, and to you, it's unlike anything else. It's in a class by itself."

"When did you remember your encounter with Amburgey?" Symphony stared intently at Garon. Everything he was saying was putting into words how she had been feeling since her return from 1950.

"Another excellent question. My mother passed away in 1984,

and I returned several times to Wytheville around that time. I had moved her to live with me in California after my father passed in the late 1970s. I kept our home there. I recently closed it up and hired someone to maintain the property. I brought her back here to be buried with my father in East End Cemetery. Everyone knew I was in town, so I granted the newspaper a rare interview. They did something interesting and brave, quite frankly. They sent a recent high school graduate that was working with them for the summer prior to going off to college. Her name was Amburgey Gibboney."

"Oh my."

"Oh my indeed. Your mother was serious and professional with her tape recorder and small notebook. Watching you interviewing Cybelee was like travelling back in time myself. She was also animated and full of excitement. Amburgey was a breath of happy air in my summer of sadness." Garon grew silent for a few moments. "All the while she was interviewing me, I kept feeling like there was something familiar about her. I couldn't put my finger on it. At that point, it had been decades since I spent any significant time in Wytheville. It was far easier to send my parents plane tickets to visit me than it was to come home. I shook off the feeling. I thought it was impossible that I could have met her before. If you want to think about it in the most complicated way possible, I hadn't met her yet, in her time scheme."

"This has to be one of the reasons why time travel is so dangerous. It messes with our truth." Symphony rose from the couch and began pacing around the room. Her eyes took in the many different movie posters. Her mind was, however, a considerable distance away.

"It does indeed. It bends our personal truth. I daresay it is the reason why some people go mad. It could drive one crazy with only the consciousness of it." Garon cleared his throat and took a drink of lemonade. Symphony turned and focused her attention on him. "You have to promise you won't tell Nadia what I'm about to say. She obviously knew that Amburgey interviewed me. I don't believe that Nadia knows about the final question Amburgey asked me."

"I promise." Symphony returned to her seat beside him.

"Amburgey had turned off her little recorder and then put her notebook back into her backpack." Garon stopped for a moment. "As she was gathering up her belongings, I asked her where she was going to college and what she planned to major in. We were chit chatting, or so I thought. I followed her out of the parlor in my parents' home. Before she crossed the doorway, she turned back to face me, and asked me a question. 'What advice would you offer to a small town girl getting ready to begin her life?' I replied, without hesitation, in a way I have countless times throughout the latter part of my career. 'Don't be afraid to allow yourself to take an adventure. You might meet your wildest dreams.' She seemed quite taken with what I said. When I read her article later, I was surprised she didn't use the quote."

"She felt it was her own personal message. Amburgey thought it was a sign."

"I believe she did. You can understand why I would prefer Nadia did not know that tidbit. I've felt a mixture of joy and sorrow in the years since I've learned the legend of her life. I never thought that I played a role in her decision-making process. In what I have learned about the timeline of her trips, our chance meeting might have been the nudge she needed to begin her dance with time."

"Oh, Garon. The layers to this story get deeper and deeper."

"Much like the vast seconds that click by on a clock." Garon reached over and picked up a folder on the coffee table in front of him. "Enough of that. Let's get down to business. Allison is eager for us to cover the great turning points in Wytheville's history in the special exhibits at the museums. Like polio was in 1950, the 'Great Town Fire' was another destructive force on this community."

"I hope you have more information than what I found thus far. While it obviously made an impact, there doesn't seem to be much record of what happened."

"You must have discovered in your previous positions that the further you journey back in history, the shorter the historical accounts become. With today's age of technology, a hundred years from now, I wonder how long it will take historians to research a topic. They will be combing through countless, accurate and inaccurate, records. There used to be two sides to every story. Now, there appears to be hundreds."

"All I want is one accurate description of this fire so that we can put together a special exhibit to depict what happened and align the topic with fire prevention today."

"That's precisely why Allison sent you to me. I believe I have what you need." Garon opened the thick folder. Symphony sat down next to him. "My family had a strong connection to one of the families who lived through that fire. It was a story I often heard recounted during my childhood."

"Allison told me about the oral histories that you helped collect. I haven't listened to them. I did not expect to find someone almost a hundred years afterward who would have such firsthand information." Symphony wanted to reach for the folder and look closer at the documents he was protectively holding. "You seem to have become my knight in shining armor."

"A role I never played. Sad, but true." Garon put his right hand over his heart. "I shall be your historian in argyle and loafers."

"What was the family connection?"

Since Garon wasn't handing over the folder, Symphony took her laptop out of the bag beside her and got ready to take notes while he shared the events.

"Let me tell you the story leading up to this family connection." Garon took another sip of his beverage, set the glass down, and clutched the folder to his chest. "This is an old Hollywood habit, my dear. When I was learning my lines for a movie, I would clutch the script in this manner. I felt I was absorbing the words."

Symphony laughed. Garon winked at her. Even in these rare personal moments of revelations, it was not long before Garon would return to 'performance-mode,' which she and Marcella named the action.

"It was the cold, late winter morning of March 8, 1924. A Saturday, as fate would have it. Herman Sollod was slumbering, it is presumed, in a second-story flat on Main Street that he shared with his sister, Fannie, her husband, Saul Alper, and their son. The apartment was over Saul Alper's Victory Merchandise Company and other businesses."

"Help me get my bearings. Where was this structure?"

"It was on the north side of Main Street in the two hundred block, about where the antique mall is today."

"Gotcha. Please proceed with your story." Symphony resumed typing.

"It is said that Herman discovered the fire around four-thirty in the morning. Apparently, the fire had already been burning for a while. When Herman opened the hall door, flames burst into the room and seriously burned him. Despite this, the brave man was able to fight his way through the apartment to where his sister and brother-in-law were sleeping and awakened them."

"I have always been afraid of fire. I'm not sure where it originated." Symphony paused a moment.

"As I was saying, the fire was burning for some time before it was discovered. The stairs to the apartment were already destroyed. Saul jumped from the second-story window. This is where the story begins to have 'versions.'" Garon made quotation marks in the air. "Some accounts say that Fannie Alper threw her baby to her husband, who caught it safely. Other accounts say that this scenario was not possible because her husband was injured from his jump. Both Fannie and Herman also jumped to safety. They were both injured."

"So, you are saying that jumping from the second story injured all three of the adults?"

"Yes. It would seem logical because, for one thing, they were the first ones to discover the fire. No one else knew, at that point. There was nothing below to break their fall—no net or mattress or anything we would associate today with such occurrences. I would think from that height it would be quite likely that they sustained a broken bone or, at the very least, a serious sprain."

"Do you think there was someone on the street who caught the child?"

"I think there had to be someone other than Saul who caught the child. All the accounts I read said that the child was completely unharmed, not a scratch on him."

"I don't suppose you learned who the person was."

"Sadly, no. But, one of the stories refers to the person as 'her.' I think it is a mystery that may never be solved. Interestingly, none of the accounts mention anyone else jumping from buildings that day or being injured. There had to be others living above the businesses at the time, but none of the documents speak of them."

"Where was the fire believed to have originated?"

"The most common conclusion seems to be that it started on the ground floor in either the Alper store or the one next to it. Either way, the fire started in the rear and from an unknown cause. The entire rear portions were ablaze by the time the first firemen reached the scene."

"Did Wytheville have a fire truck in 1924?"

"Yes. There was only one motor driven truck at their disposal. It was a Motel T Ford chassis with an American LaFrance commercial hose and chemical apparatus." Garon flipped through a few pages of his file.

"Is that the same one we have on display at the Boyd Museum?"

"Indeed. It was restored years later by members of the fire department. It has a legacy attached to it."

"Where was the water hydrant then?" Symphony looked up from her computer hearing Garon rustling papers. "What? You haven't memorized that part."

"I thought I was doing quite well, young lady. You like to throw curve balls. Here it is." Garon pointed to the sheet of paper. "The hydrant was on the corner of Main where Counts Drug Store now sits."

"That doesn't seem too far."

"I suppose not. It was a much different time though. Emergency services were not commonplace. Even the means of notifying the firefighters was complicated because all were volunteers. And, in this case, it was the middle of the night." Garon returned his gaze to his papers. "This report says that the fire truck did not have a pump. The firefighters were entirely dependent on the hydrant or plug pressure from the gravity flow of water from the reservoir. Since the fire continued to burn, additional plugs were used at other locations. It was the March winds that made the fire spread quickly."

Garon's house phone rang. He got up and while moving to answer it in another room, he handed the folder to Symphony.

"Why is it that I feel I will never get that back?" Garon winked releasing the folder, walking away and shaking his head. Symphony noticed he was moving slower than usual with a more pronounced limp in his normal agile stride.

Symphony continued reading where Garon left off. Then she began to flip through other pages in the file. It was a collection of newspaper clippings and historical society articles. The fire was documented and re-documented through the decades since 1924. Reading the articles, it became obvious to her the fire was a critical point for the small community. From the overall review of Wytheville's history that she read in the early days of her employment, Symphony sensed that fire haunted the town many times since its founding.

"Sorry to keep you waiting. It was a call from an old Hollywood friend. It appears that I shall be asked to present an award for his lifetime of achievements at the next Oscars."

"Oh my, how exciting!" Symphony gave Garon a wide-eyed look. "May I ask who that might be?"

"You may certainly ask, I will not answer." Garon took a long sip of lemonade and sat back down on the couch. "I really cannot reveal that, my dear. You would recognize the name, I'm sure."

"I understand. The Academy must keep their secrets. Can I be your date to the Oscars then?" Symphony giggled and returned her attention back to the file of papers.

"Why, my dear, that is a splendid idea!"

THE FOLLOWING MORNING, Symphony began her day at the Museums' main office filling Marcella in on her research meeting with Garon.

"Before I left, Garon gave me the file of research. I spent the rest of the afternoon and early evening reviewing it. It's amazing how such an account can bring a bit of history back to life."

"Hold on a minute." Marcella stopped what she was doing. "Garon said you could be his date to the Oscars next year?" She looked intently at Symphony. "That's Hollywood, you know. Red carpet. George Clooney, perhaps."

"I'm sure he was joking."

"I would not be so sure. You said he's been asked to present an award?"

"Yes, to one of his actor friends. He said I would recognize the name, so he couldn't tell me. Top secret stuff."

"I see a sequin gown and stiletto heels in your future. Jason better hope you don't meet George." Marcella had a devilish grin on her face. "I have a friend who would sell her soul to go to the Oscars."

"Who is that?"

"I can't say. Top secret stuff." Marcella rolled her eyes and laughed.

"Enough of that. Can I tell you what I learned about the 1924 fire?" Symphony stared at Marcella with the most serious face she could muster.

"Oh, yes. By all means, enlighten me with your findings."

"The fire started in the early morning hours of March 8, 1924."

"I remember reading in the walking tour that it was discovered by a man who lived above a store on Main Street. Wasn't there something about he and others jumping from the second story?"

"Yes. It was a man and his sister and brother-in-law. The brother-in-law owned the store they lived above. They also had a toddler son."

"I remember. The baby was thrown down for someone to catch."

"Garon seems to think that there is a little mystery in the facts surrounding who caught the child. The important thing is that while the adults were injured by jumping, they all survived the fire."

"Indeed. I don't remember reading about any lives lost in that fire."

"Correct. There were not any fatalities. I'm sure there were injuries suffered by the firefighters and smoke inhalation issues. It's incredible, in that day, that no lives were lost in a fire that started in the middle of the night."

Symphony paused and organized her papers while Marcella answered the phone. She needed to compare the documents with the notes she hastily took during her conversation with Garon.

"The fire started in the center of downtown. The building where it began was close to where the antique store stands today. Apparently, because of the March winds, it spread to the adjacent buildings on both sides rather rapidly."

"Those buildings were made of wood, right?" Marcella rose to put the message in Allison's box. "Some of the buildings are brick now."

"I haven't read anything about that yet. I would assume that they were at least partly made of wood. By six o'clock that morning, a neighboring community of volunteer firefighters had travelled to assist fighting the fire. The fire truck was positioned behind the building where the fire had begun so that it could draw water from the town branch, Cedar Run. That would insure that the town's reservoir would not be depleted or lessen the pressure on the plugs from which the local firemen were operating their fire hoses."

"There are records about Cedar Run dating back to the late 1700s. I believe it is two miles long, which I suppose is rather short for such a waterway. I think it is fed by twenty-one springs though." Marcella resumed her computer work.

"The articles and accounts indicate that the fire must have spread quickly. There is one business after another named as being engulfed in flames—a bank, drug store, jewelry store, millinery, pool room, doctors' offices on the second story of one of the buildings, and many others." Symphony handed Marcella a list of businesses she compiled the night before.

"This also lists a confectionery. You've put an asterisk beside it. What does that mean?"

"The George T. Beuchler Confectionery was apparently well-known at the time for its homemade bread. It was the last structure that was completely destroyed. Ironically, in later years, the Wythe Theater was built on the same spot. That theater was also destroyed by fire in 1960."

"Goodness. Do you have the address? I wonder what stands there now."

"I do not. I think I will investigate that though." Symphony wrote a note to herself. "One of the articles talked about how intense the heat became. This was after the fire jumped across the street."

"To the side where the Millwald Theater now stands?"

"Yes. Fortunately, the Millwald was not built until 1928. This article talks about the heat that became so intense that the windows of the buildings began to melt. How hot would glass have to be to melt like that?"

"I remember that story." Allison entered the room from behind Symphony, causing her to jump. "It was strange to hear some of the old-timers, when I was a kid, describe what melted windows looked like."

"Not as pretty as blown glass, I'm sure." Marcella handed Allison a stack of mail. "Professor Clancy, from Radford University, returned your call. He says that he will be sending you several links regarding the research you inquired about. More work for Symphony?"

"I'm afraid that it will be." Allison's expression changed to a pained smile as she made eye contact with Symphony. "This is about an exhibit I would like to unveil next year. It has a little mystery tied to it as well, and will honor the Father of Wytheville."

"Mystery, huh? Maybe I should change my middle name."

"Symphony Mystery Wallace. Doesn't sound bad." Symphony scowled at Marcella's comment. "Of course, many of us believe that Symphony Mystery Newberry would have a nice ring to it, too."

"Slow down there, friend. Let's not plan that far ahead. By the way, Allison, that reminded me of something. Jason says that his mother was at the polio symposium. Why didn't anyone tell me that?"

"You didn't know she was there?" Marcella shook her head. "You didn't recognize her?"

"I've never seen her."

"Oh, Symphony. You mean to tell me you haven't looked her up on social media?" Marcella continued to shake her head while she quickly typed on her keyboard. "If you are dating the son, you should be able to spot the mother in a crowd. Haven't you heard of Facebook?" Marcella turned her computer screen where Symphony could see it. "This is Alice Newberry, Jason's mother."

"I saw her that night. She had on a coral pantsuit. I remember thinking that my mother would love it. Coral is her favorite color and it's hard to find clothes that shade." Symphony put her head in her hands. "I feel so foolish. Marcella's right. I should have looked her up. It's a small town. It never even crossed my mind that I could run into her somewhere."

"'Marcella was right.' Did you hear that, Allison?"

"Yes, I did. I know that makes you happy, Marcella. I don't agree that Symphony should stalk Jason's mother." Allison began to walk toward her office. "I'm glad you were able to meet with Garon. I hope you can make that information into an exhibit."

"No one said stalk. I believe that 'become familiar with' is a more accurate term." Marcella moved Symphony's stack of folders to an adjoining table and resumed her filing work. "It's always good to be aware of those who are nearby. It's a safety measure."

"Exactly. I wished I knew that Jason's Uncle Belcher was walking toward us the other night at Chautauqua." Marcella stopped filing and Allison turned around at the door of her office. "Yes, I met Belcher in this century. It was delightful. The poor man probably thinks he lost his mind."

"I never thought about the possibility that you could still encounter someone from 1950 who would recognize you." Allison's eyes darted back and forth. "I knew you said you met Garon, but he didn't appear to recognize you when you first met, did he?"

"He and I had a similar conversation yesterday. It's more complicated than I want to ponder. It's almost like I wasn't in his conscious memory until now. Yet, I might have been in his sub-conscious all along. It's like the difference between the present-past and the past-past."

"That sounds like terms you use when you are diagraming sentences. I don't like it." Marcella stood up and walked into the exhibit area outside of her office. A visitor had entered a few moments previously and was looking at the displays.

"Symphony, it must be scary to think about what effect your presence in 1950 had on those you met. Do you think that Belcher recognized you?" Allison leaned against the doorframe, still clutching the stack of mail Marcella gave her. "It had to be an unnerving experience for the both of you."

"I'm sure Belcher remembered the Symphony he met in 1950." A nervous laugh escaped. "Listen to me, referring to that 'me' as being a different person. Belcher looked very confused. But his expression left no guessing, he remembered me. I was rather rude and curt in my responses to him. I did not want him to get any notion that I remembered him, too. It's going to be horrendously awkward if I ever see him again."

"If you keep dating Jason, you most certainly will. I think Jason has a fairly close-knit family on both sides." Allison tilted her head and smiled. "Chin up, it will pass. Maybe you can think of a way to make a joke out of it with him."

"I hope it doesn't make Jason's family suspicious of me."

"Just play your Nadia card. It will make any suspicions disappear. Nadia and Nathan were well-known and respected in this community. If you reveal that she is your biological grandmother, all other things will fade away."

"Until they find out about Amburgey's unusual mode of travel."

"Well, maybe you will be married to Jason by then." Allison put her hand over her mouth. "I know; I'm as bad as Marcella."

"I'm not going to lie and say that the thought hasn't passed through my mind. Jason is a wonderful guy. I'm leery to think that could even be possible." Symphony put down the papers and looked up at Allison. "When I came to Wytheville, I expected to dive head first into this job and maybe gradually find out something about Amburgey. I feel like I've done the opposite. It was not my intent. I hope I haven't let you down."

"Good grief, Symphony. That couldn't be farther from the truth. You've done an excellent job with every assignment. I've heard that from others as well. Despite your trip afterwards, I could not imagine the polio symposium going any better. A lot of that is because of the interview you did with Cybelee. It still amazes me that she was so willing to allow you to meet with her." Allison turned back toward her office, but then did another complete circle back to where Symphony was seated. "That reminds me. I almost forgot. Cybelee sent me an email the morning after the symposium. She really enjoyed it, and she said to tell you that she thought your outfit was a nice touch."

"Cybelee liked the symposium and my outfit? I don't understand. How did she see any of that?"

"Oh, I guess no one told you. We connected her to the symposium electronically. I don't know what the term is for the technology. It's sort of like Skype, but more advanced. She sent one of her technicians over to set up the equipment. I believe it gave her a complete view of the room."

"Really?"

"Yes, really. If it is cutting edge technology, Cybelee has it. Her world is probably years ahead of the one that most of us live in."

"Cybelee likes to travel to the future. How interesting! I guess that is a byproduct of having an international company. It amazes me that such a multi-dimensional business is located in such a remote location."

"I'm not sure that I would classify her section of these mountains as remote. From the highest of her buildings, you can see the interstate and all its hustle-bustle. The roads that cross this corner of our state bring tens of thousands of people through here each day."

"I understand that, Allison. It baffles the mind to think that she sat in her cabin in those beautiful woods and thought my outfit was cute." Symphony giggled and shook her head. "I never imagined that someone, besides those in the room, was watching. First, Jason's mother and now Cybelee, I must be more observant of what is going on around me. I might miss something important. In fact, I think I already did."

"It's been my experience that the mind can only grasp so much at a time, especially complicated parcels of information. Like with a good meal, we can only digest what our body can handle. With all that you have experienced, it's a wonder your brain doesn't have indigestion." Allison rubbed her head and laughed. "I think mine might, and I've just been an observer."

"Good point. I would like to slow down. It's a hard thing to do. I did manage to relax a little at the festival though. That was a good diversion to help me get over the jetlag of my travels."

"Travels, yes. Now, you can get fired up about your next assignment." Allison put her hand over her mouth. "Forgive me."

"Marcella is rubbing off on you. The 1924 fire is full of interesting tidbits. It's so amazing that no one perished considering the magnitude of the blaze."

"Amazing, indeed! That gives a special purpose to combining its history with a program on fire prevention. It will be an excellent opportunity for education. I've got to get to this stack of mail Marcella gave me. She appears to be in a deep conversation with those visitors. Before I go, I must also tell you that in the message Cybelee sent me she asked if I would send you back to see her soon."

"Why does she want to see me?" Despite the fact that Symphony's brow was furrowed, a little jolt of excitement passed through her. "Does she want to talk about my cute outfit?"

"I seriously doubt it. She told me that since the symposium, she's been thinking about adding a section to her website that discusses the strong local historical connection to polio. We would certainly welcome that level of publicity for our exhibit. She would like you to help her choose the content and blend it with her company's mission."

"I'm sure you are delighted to hear that she wishes to give the Museums this international exposure."

"I am. This is not common knowledge. She values her privacy in many ways. Cybelee is a strong benefactor for our programs. I would like for you to honor her request."

"Certainly. I will be happy to, Allison."

"Excellent. I will send her an email to confirm and copy you. Please adjust your schedule to her wishes. Cybelee does not like to be kept waiting."

"I'm already well aware of that."

Allison returned to her office moments before Marcella came back from speaking with the visitors.

"They were such nice people. The woman's mother was originally from here. The woman lives in Massachusetts and is researching her family history." Symphony remained silent. "Symphony, are you okay? You look like you are a thousand miles away."

"Allison just told me that I am going to be visiting Cybelee again."

"Yes, she mentioned that to me this morning. I thought you would be excited. You look a little sick."

"I'm happy to help her gather content for her website, especially since it will help to promote the Museums. I'm really nervous though. She has quite a forceful presence."

"That's true. You don't get to be the owner of an international company by being timid and laidback. I didn't find her to be overbearing though. Cybelee was friendly in her own stern way."

"You're right. I guess I'm just being silly." Symphony began to gather up the folders of information.

"Stop a minute." Marcella paused until Symphony made eye contact with her. "What are you afraid of? What's making you concerned about meeting with Cybelee again?"

"This pendant." Symphony pulled the necklace into view from beneath her blouse. "You know that it helped me go on the trip. You also know that it was left with me by Amburgey. I know that it is similar to the ones that Cybelee sells in her BloomSpoons line. That leads me to believe that Cybelee might have known my mother, or, at least, someone connected to Amburgey. There's a part of me that is tied up in knots thinking about it. I've had moments since I returned from 1950 that I wanted to put this pendant away in a box and never wear it again."

"And, yet, there it still hangs, close to your heart."

"Crazy, isn't it?"

"Not from my point of view. You wondered about your biological mother for your entire life. You have met her, in a way." Marcella shook her head and paused. "I understand why you feel hesitant to have that pendant nearby considering your recent trip. But, I also know that it is definitely a concrete link between you and Amburgey. I don't think you will be ready to put it away until you meet her in this time and make a real connection."

"I think you are right. I hope it is possible. It's troubling to imagine why Amburgey hasn't been in contact with Nadia all of these years. Nadia hasn't revealed anything negative that happened between her and her daughter. I think Nadia would support Amburgey in any decision she made, including helping to raise me."

"Do you wish that you were raised by Amburgey?" Symphony noticed the thoughtful, yet concerned, look that was on her friend's face. "That may be too private of a question?"

"No, it's not. I don't suppose that any adopted child would choose to be one. Yet, I cannot imagine having any better of a childhood than I had with my adoptive parents. I've often thought of the risk they took in taking me. Since I was left on the doorstep of a church, there were no records regarding my birth. My parents might be fugitives from the law. I could have had mental or physical health issues. My mother could have tried to find me and take me back at some point.

About a year before she died, my Grammie told me that Mariel, my adoptive mother, confided something to her during the first year after my adoption. She told Grammie that whenever she was outside with me, Mom felt like we were being watched. She never saw anyone. At some point, Mom stopped feeling that way. There's no way of knowing whether it was real or not. Since Grammie told me that, I've dreamed it was my biological mother making sure I ended up with good people."

"It's hard to imagine someone vanishing without a trace. Amburgey had a plan in place to become invisible." Marcella walked back to the lobby area, after the bell rang announcing more visitors.

"Or, perhaps, Amburgey went to another time where she no longer would be missed."

Words of the Granny Witch

"There are Granny Witches of this life who specialize in midwifery. They witness the miracle of birth. Many of them will tell you that the bond between mother and child within the womb is entirely different than the bond that occurs once the child is physically separated. An unborn baby is physically connected and utterly dependent on the mother for its entire existence. Once the child is born, the mother will forever feel it with her, even if it dies. The child does not form such a bond until it meets the mother face-to-face. Usually, the mother it knows from the inside is the same. If it is not, it does not hinder the bond. Love is the true bond. Biology is just an enhancement."

Chapter Four

MAKING HER WAY UP THE path to Cybelee's cabin, Symphony noticed that the gardens were even more beautiful than she remembered. After a few email exchanges, an appointment was set for Symphony to return to the remote location in the woods. She thought Marcella or Garon might accompany her. Both had previous engagements and Cybelee was not flexible with her time. Symphony dared not suggest alternatives. She was on her own.

The path she took from her vehicle opened up to reveal the cabin a few hundred feet away. Symphony's eyes were again drawn to the tall hollowed-out tree in the center of the open area. The unusual globe that was the centerpiece of the tree trunk glowed from the rays of sun streaming down into it. From a distance, it cast the illusion of movement. Drawing closer, Symphony realized it was the hundreds of pieces of cut glass that not only created the round shape but the illusion of movement.

There were so many different colors, it was mesmerizing. The countless different angles reflected light and made the color change in the blink of an eye. While she had not thought of it on her first visit, Symphony now realized what it reminded her of.

"It's like a kaleidoscope." Symphony whispered.

"You are quite observant, young lady."

Symphony jumped and looked around to see where the voice was coming from. There was no doubt whose voice it was.

"I'm sorry. I did not realize you were outside. I hope it is alright that I stopped to take a closer look at this work of art."

Symphony realized why she did not notice Cybelee while she was walking up the path. The woman had an almost chameleon-like appearance in a striking flowing kimono in varying shades of forest green. Studying the outfit, Symphony also saw small embroidered flowers of beautiful rich colors.

"Art is meant to be enjoyed." Cybelee walked around the globe to the side opposite Symphony. "I would prefer that you did not stare at me."

"I'm sorry. Your outfit is a work of art, too. The shades of color match your garden perfectly."

"You did not see me because I did not want you to."

Symphony did not allow Cybelee to see her reaction to the statement. She knew the woman could smell fear.

"The globe. It's as if it has every shade of every color imaginable."

"And, ones we haven't imagined."

"I noticed something hanging above it when I was here before." Symphony squinted to see. "I do not see anything now."

"That's part of the magic. It shows different people different things." Cybelee paused and Symphony waited for the next revelation. "Do you want to know how the globe came to be?"

"Yes. It's so beautiful."

"Interesting. I'm not sure that beautiful would be an accurate description nor would it be the adjective to use to describe the process." Cybelee moved her hands in front of her body. Her hands and arms were covered with long, tan gloves. Symphony's eyes focused on them, Cybelee gave her silent question an answer. "When you arrived, I was working in my herbs. I've been developing a new treatment. I must be careful before it is perfected."

"That's exciting." Symphony quickly refocused her attention to Cybelee's face. During their last visit there were only portions of her face visible. Most of it was covered with her long hair and large glasses. "May I ask what type of treatment you are working on?"

"I'm working on a treatment for age. Is that not a universal desire to conquer the aging process?" Cybelee laughed, causing Symphony to be reminded of evil stepmothers from a dozen fairytale movies. "Everyone wants a fountain of youth."

"That would certainly make you millions." Symphony thought for a moment about what she was told about Cybelee's international company. "More."

"Money is only useful for who it can help. All the wealth in the world could not satisfy my strongest desire."

"I remember from our last conversation that it would be unwise for me to ask you what that desire was."

Cybelee walked away from the globe and toward her cabin. The woman again began to fade into the foliage around her. The design of the fabric seemed to be made for that very purpose. Symphony was caught off-guard when she looked up and found that Cybelee had turned to face her and was smiling. It was a rare expression in Symphony's presence.

"You are sharp. I like that. I will tell you what my strongest desire is. It is not a rare one. I wish to be able to turn back time."

"I've heard it said that youth is wasted on the young." After taking one last look at the globe, Symphony followed Cybelee up the pathway.

"I have no interest in being younger." Cybelee continued to walk with her back to Symphony. "I do wish to avoid a mistake—a costly one."

Cybelee was already through the doorway of the cabin when she finished speaking. Symphony took her time to climb the steps, taking in the eclectic assortment of furnishings on the expansive porch. In her previous visit, Symphony did not notice a stringless guitar propped up next to an old chair. The chair looked like it might have sat in a fine dining room in its day. The guitar was painted with flowers on it and had long since quit making music.

"Come in and make yourself comfortable. I have my laptop set up at the table."

Having fallen under the spell of the beauty of the gardens, Symphony almost forgot why she was summoned to Cybelee's compound. Her task was to help the woman weave the local history related to polio into the portion of the BloomSpoons website that told the story of how Cybelee's post-polio syndrome treatments came to exist. It would provide a direct link to the exhibit featured about the time period when the disease devastated Wytheville in 1950. Despite the heat of the day, a cold chill ran down Symphony's spine remembering her time visiting that era.

"Did someone walk over your grave?" Cybelee's comment caught Symphony off guard.

"What?" Symphony placed her bag on the floor beside a seat at the table. Cybelee walked toward her. The woman was carrying a tray with a pitcher of a purple beverage and two glasses.

"You moved as if a chill had passed over you. Orenda used to say that meant someone was walking on your grave."

"I've heard the phrase. My grandmother used to say it. I was just surprised to hear you refer to it. Who is Orenda? I think I have heard that unusual name before."

"Orenda is the woman who used to live in this cabin. She was a legendary Granny Witch. I learned everything I know about natural remedies from her. I learned a great deal." Cybelee paused and placed the tray on the table.

"Now, I remember. Garon mentioned her." Symphony stopped talking. She realized she should not have revealed that piece of information.

"Yes, Garon knew Orenda when he was still Gary Moore. Orenda gave him the push he needed." Cybelee poured the purple beverage into the two glasses.

"Is that all she gave him?" Symphony accepted the glass that Cybelee held out to her, furrowing her brow. She looked at the liquid.

"You think she gave him some sort of magic to help him become famous. Orenda had magic at her fingertips, no doubt. She rarely used it. She preferred to give her customers the ability to use the magic that was already within them. It's a sense that few use and most possess."

"What do you call it?"

"Confidence. Belief. Esteem. There probably is not an exact word to describe it. I would liken it to a fire within. Orenda could see the spark of talent that burned within Garon. He needed a push. He needed someone else to believe."

"And the world would thank her for giving him that push. My Grammie Wallace would be first in line to thank her." Symphony looked back at the glass she was holding while Cybelee sat down next to her. "I am wondering what this beautiful drink is."

"I'm sorry. I should have told you. It's lavender lemonade. The lavender is from Beagle Ridge Herb Farm. Have you been there yet? I get all the lavender we use in our products from my dear friend, Ellen. She and her husband, Gregg, own the business."

"Lavender lemonade. It sounds delicious." Symphony stopped and took a big sip. "It is delicious. I'm not sure that I have ever tasted lavender. I've also been careful around it. I have a tendency toward being allergic to the scent."

"I understand. I think part of that comes from people being exposed to commercially created products that have lots of scents and ingredients going on at once. It's far rarer to be truly allergic to the pure plant."

"I have not been to Beagle Ridge yet. I believe I am scheduled to go there with Allison soon for a meeting of some sort. I tried one of the Beagle Ridge herbal products—the peppermint foot crème. Marcella gave me a jar. It is heavenly. I have also met Ellen, a delightful lady. I worked with her one afternoon while we were greeting travelers at the Visitors Center. She has quite an interesting background."

"It is interesting. She began travelling as a child because of her parents' life. I think it is a touch of serendipity that led her to these beautiful mountains to live out her passion. She is a kindred spirit." Cybelee took a drink and set down her glass. "I'm ready to get to work on this website. Then, as a reward for your efforts, I will tell you the story about how the globe came to be."

The next two hours flew by. Symphony helped Cybelee add information to her website. At first, Symphony thought there would be one of Cybelee's website teams on hand to work out the technical aspects. She soon discovered that a technician was indeed at Cybelee's disposal, her virtual disposal.

"I think it worked out quite nicely this way." Cybelee closed her laptop. "We uploaded the information to the Cloud. Then, Ron retrieved it and made the additions you suggested right before our eyes. This was fun."

For the second time that day, Symphony saw joy in the expression on Cybelee's face. It gave her a glimmer of what the woman was really like and what her face could reveal, if it came out from behind all the glasses and hair.

"You must be famished. It's almost three o'clock. Where are my manners?" Cybelee quickly jumped to her feet and walked to the small kitchen area in the back of the cabin. "I've prepared us a nice salad." Cybelee stopped in her tracks and suddenly turned back around. "Do you eat chicken? I should have inquired about that before you came."

"Yes. I eat chicken. But, you do not have to feed me. I came here to work." Symphony began to put her laptop and other belongings in her bag.

"Oh, but, my dear." Symphony turned to look at Cybelee. She had her right hand over her heart. Symphony forgot that Cybelee still had the gloves on. "A good southern woman is always the gracious hostess. A business or social occasion, it does not matter." Cybelee was exaggerating her southern accent. "There must always be some sustenance prepared to offer her guests."

Symphony giggled and shook her head. Symphony put her belongings next to the front door. Cybelee returned to the kitchen. It was only then that she took off the gloves. Symphony followed her into the kitchen and watched her go to the kitchen sink where she washed her hands.

"May I help you do something? My good southern upbringing dictates that I offer my assistance."

"Indeed. You were raised right. It is good to know." Cybelee turned around with two plates in her hand. "Everything is ready. I merely needed to assemble it. Please be seated."

While Symphony made her way back to the table, Cybelee placed a plate at each of their seats. A few seconds later, after Symphony sat down, Cybelee returned with a basket of rolls and a bowl of fresh fruit salad.

"The chicken salad looks delicious." A scoop of salad lay on a large lettuce leaf.

"It is a dear friend's special recipe—wild rice chicken salad."

As the two began eating, Symphony noticed Cybelee's hands. She remembered their first meeting and the feeling she got that Cybelee's hands looked older than the rest of her. With the opportunity to get a closer look at them, Symphony noticed that the skin on the tops of Cybelee's hands was thin and transparent. It reminded her of Grammie's hands before she died. Her grandmother was in her eighties when she passed. Symphony could not imagine Cybelee being even close to that decade of life. Her age was like most other aspects of her persona—a mystery.

So lost in thought Symphony did not notice Cybelee was staring at her. She stopped eating.

"You are wondering about the ring I am wearing."

Symphony's eyes went to the unusual piece of jewelry on the ring finger of Cybelee's left hand. It was the same one she remembered from her previous visit.

"It is beautiful. Is it an Essex crystal?" Symphony thought she saw a look of surprise cross Cybelee's face.

"Yes, it is. I'm impressed. How are you familiar with such?"

"I saw some similar pieces on a research trip while I was in grad school. I thought that I recognized it when I was here the first time. It's an amazing and meticulous process that goes into making such an intricate piece. Yours is simply gorgeous. I don't remember seeing one like it on the trip or through any online research I did later. May I look closer?"

"Certainly." Cybelee moved her hand closer to Symphony.

"It's a delicate bird with a flower in its beak and small flowers around it. The diamonds encircling the crystal are a lovely touch."

"Yes. The bird is a dove."

"The symbol of love."

"Yes." Cybelee moved her hand back to her lap and continued eating.

"A piece of antique jewelry is a prized possession. Do you know when it was made?"

"Not precisely. I believe it dates back to the mid-1800s."

"Such detailed craftsmanship is rarely seen today. As a society, our jewelry tends to shy away from one-of-a-kind pieces, such as yours, and more toward the mass-produced variety. May I ask if your ring is a family heirloom?"

"It is not." Cybelee's curt response told Symphony not to press her any further.

"Thank you for allowing me to get a closer look of it. The ones I saw before were under glass."

"Would you like some more chicken salad or fruit?" Cybelee's tone softened.

"No. I have had plenty. It was delicious. Thank you."

"Let's have another glass of lemonade on the porch, and I will tell you about the globe."

Cybelee picked up Symphony's plate and her own and set them on the counter next to the sink while Symphony refilled both of their glasses. Handing Cybelee her glass, Symphony allowed her to lead the way out.

"You may leave your bag there until we finish our beverages and my story."

Cybelee walked over the threshold and toward the left side of the porch. Symphony could see that the angle offered the best vantage point for a view of the globe. They sat down in two side-by-side rocking chairs with a small table between them.

"It's so peaceful and beautiful here. I don't think I would ever want to leave." The thought came out of Symphony's mouth before she realized. "I'm sorry if that was too personal of a statement."

"Certainly not. You speak truth. It is one of the reasons that I rarely leave my little piece of paradise. I have everything I need here to do my work. I have staff that can bring me anything that I want. I can reach out to the ends of the Earth in a virtual sense. I've long since given up travel and face-to-face interaction is a novelty to me."

"Given up travel? I cannot imagine. There are so many places I would love to go."

"The places I would like to go no longer exist for me."

Symphony started to respond after Cybelee was silent for a few minutes. She thought better of it.

"The creation of the globe was a turning point in my life. I moved to this place to live with and learn from Orenda. I'm sure you know of the Granny Witches, Queens of Appalachia as they are now called in reverence. Orenda was perhaps one of the most magical creatures to ever exist. And, yet, she was nothing more than a simple woman of these mountains who dared to allow herself to become one with all of the great elements around her. She drank in the essence of nature like a bee takes in the nectar of a flower. She opened her mind and heart not only to the cause, but also the cure, of any malady that crossed her path. Orenda looked deep inside the soul of someone. Even beyond where he or she would recognize, where the future was burning inside, waiting to be released."

A few minutes before, Symphony had broken her gaze into the landscape in front of her and was staring intently at Cybelee's profile whilst she described Orenda. Despite how the woman's long hair and large glasses concealed her features, Symphony could see a glimmer of the serene expression that occupied Cybelee's face. She was not talking only about someone she revered; she was speaking about someone she loved.

"She sounds wonderful."

Cybelee turned toward Symphony and lowered her glasses to look Symphony squarely in the eyes.

"Wonderful is too generic a term to describe Orenda. I believe that there may be a person or two in every generation of mankind whom by the sheer magnitude of their personality or talent are larger than life, like a god-like being walking among us. Most of these seem to attain some great celebrity or notoriety in this life. They seem to become exaggerations of themselves in the end. Orenda was one of the even more rare ones. She lived a simple life that never took her off this mountain. Yet, she touched lives around the world in her time and the times of others."

Cybelee's reference to time made Symphony's ears perk up and her heart race. She almost bit her tongue in two trying to hold in the question that was burning inside her. Symphony turned toward the beautiful view to calm herself. She did not have to exercise patience long.

"The pendant you wear. It was created for time travel."

With lightning speed, she turned in Cybelee's direction. In a split second of thought, Symphony imagined that she might have to visit a chiropractor to help correct the damage she did to her neck.

"Time travel?" Symphony tried to keep her voice calm. "What do you mean by that?" She swore she heard a chuckle escape Cybelee's lips.

"The necklace was created by Orenda and your birth mother. It was the piece that I have modeled all of the BloomSpoons jewelry from ever since. Your pendant is the original."

"The original?" Symphony's right hand grasped the pendant. "How do you know that?"

"It was created in this cabin. I was here when it was made."

"You know Amburgey?" Symphony did not try to conceal the emotion in her voice.

"I knew Amburgey." Cybelee's tone was solemn.

"Knew. As in, she no longer exists?" Symphony could feel tears forming in her eyes.

"Knew. As it was a long time ago when I last saw that young girl. She is a stranger to me now."

"Everyone who knew Amburgey says the same thing. I fear that she must be dead. How could she stay away from the people who loved her this long?"

"The Amburgey I knew was broken. Broken like the pieces of glass in that globe. She helped assemble it, all those years ago—broken soul. Orenda helped heal her." Cybelee released a deep breath. "All those pieces of glass were once separately something else. Together, they form something new. People are like that. Your existence is lots of broken pieces that together form your life. No matter what you think you may have left behind, you cannot shake the pieces of your life. They stay with you, regardless of how you try to change."

"It looks like you had a lot of anger within you to create all those broken pieces." Symphony could not imagine how many different objects were shattered to make the globe. "You seem so calm now."

"Calm?" Cybelee took in another deep breath and slowly released it. "I've spent the better part of my life trying to have calm in my life.

Trying to make sense of what my purpose is. Each person must find a purpose."

Symphony's hand grasped the pendant. It was a reflex for her.

"You say this was created to be used for time travel. What gave my mother the idea that was possible?"

"There is no need to play cat and mouse with me, Symphony. You know full well that it is possible. You know enough about your biological family to understand that time travel is in your genes."

"How do you know what I have learned?" Symphony turned to look at Cybelee, but the woman rose and began walking away from her.

"I see the talent of your skills in your work. You are one who has a hunger for answers, no matter the topic. You are living with Nadia French. She has no doubt told you many stories by now. I would not be surprised if you have already gained a little experience yourself, if you dare to be so brave."

"I'm not brave. It would appear that many decisions are made for me. This link to my mother has a mind of its own." Symphony stood up and followed Cybelee, holding the pendant in front of her. "If you knew her then, tell me what she was thinking to leave such a thing with a baby?"

"Orenda taught that we are more than just our physical selves. She showed that we could give a piece of our being, a piece of our magic, to another. Amburgey wanted to go with you."

"Then, why did she not keep me?" A stream of tears left Symphony's eyes. Before she realized what was happening her whole body was shaking and she was sobbing. "Why didn't she want me?"

Cybelee was standing in front of the tall tree trunk, gazing at the globe. Her back was turned to Symphony. Through her tears, Symphony saw Cybelee's shoulders rise and fall, like a great weight was on them. Slowly, she turned around.

"On the seventh day after your birth, Amburgey left you with Nadia for a while and came here to see Orenda. They spent several hours in these woods and within this cabin. Amburgey was afraid."

"Afraid of being a single mother? Nadia gave me every indication that she would have helped Amburgey any way possible. She said she was willing to raise me herself if Amburgey allowed her."

"I cannot reveal what was in Amburgey's mind and heart during those desperate days. That's her story to tell. I can tell you that she was not afraid of being your mother. She was afraid of *not* being able to be. Her fear of the unknown trumped her maternal instincts. It made her second-guess the simplest of decisions."

"You're talking in riddles." Symphony left Cybelee's side and began to pace. "You make it sound like she was running from something."

"She was."

"No one seems to know anything about my father. Was he who my mother was running from?"

"Amburgey did run away from him once. It was a foolish, impetuous act. But, she could never undo it."

"Never. You make it sound so final. Did he die?"

"Again. It is not a question I will answer. In her eyes, his location was worse than death. It sealed the fate of her heart."

"You are talking in circles again. It makes no sense."

"That's why she left you the pendant. Amburgey wanted you to experience it all for yourself. It is the only real way you could understand."

"This is the reason I am here today, isn't it? This visit was not really about your website. Someone else could compile the information." Symphony stopped in front of Cybelee.

"Amburgey knew you would one day seek to find out about your heritage. It was your destiny to come to Wytheville and meet the people who have now crossed your path. Amburgey knew that if she laid the groundwork, it would all fall into place. If good people who loved you raised you, you would someday have the confidence to find out where your past began. She thought that Orenda would be the one to have this conversation with you. Alas, it was not to be. You are stuck with me instead."

"Amburgey trusted you. I guess I have to then."

"Amburgey drew close to Orenda from the time she learned about her father's travels. Orenda gave her understanding that Nadia would not. It is not Nadia's fault. Her life was turned upside down by a force beyond her control. She lost the man she loved. Nadia's biggest fear was losing her daughter."

"Sounds like a self-fulfilling prophecy."

"Indeed. It would appear so. Amburgey was so afraid of what the future held. She was driven to sacrifice it. Orenda tried to squelch her fears. She was only able to keep Amburgey from ending her physical life. Amburgey still chose to give up all that her life held."

"I still don't understand why. What was she so afraid of?"

"You will need to read the words of Amburgey's father to understand what drove her fear. Has Nadia shown you the little cabin on her property?"

"Yes. She says it was where I was born."

"There is a diary hidden there. It belonged to Amburgey's father. It is the story of his travels and how they affected him."

"Do you know where the diary is hidden?"

"You will have to figure that out for yourself. I'm sure that Amburgey left you some clues." Cybelee looked down at her wrist. "I've enjoyed our visit and appreciate your help. I have a conference call in a half-hour. I need to prepare. Come and retrieve your belongings."

Symphony followed Cybelee up the path and then the steps to the doorway of the cabin. After Cybelee opened the door and walked through, Symphony reached inside to get her bag.

"You didn't finish explaining about the globe. What was the purpose of creating it?"

"Amburgey thought it would be a cathartic experience. It was after she had left you to be found by others. She tried to shatter the sadness with the breaking of the glass. For days thereafter, she travelled all over the place finding old bottles, glasses, plates, anything like that. For hours at a time, she would break one piece after another. When the madness was over, it was clear that the sadness had only multiplied. So, the globe was created to try to make her whole again."

Symphony stood in front of Cybelee for several moments trying to absorb what the woman told her. She rubbed her temple. Her head was pounding.

"Well, thank you for your hospitality. I knew you were a mysterious person. The information you have shared has made me understand better. Yet, I am even more confused."

"Confusion is part of the process. Even when all has been revealed to you."

"Why is that?" Symphony tilted her head and furrowed her brow.

"Because you did not live it. Some things cannot be fully understood from the outside. You have to be on the inside to grasp all of the meaning. You will understand enough to make your own judgment."

"Judgment? Why would I judge Amburgey's choices?"

"Amburgey's choices caused you to exist. For better or worse, they touched your entire life." Symphony heard the chiming of a clock. "I must go. Safe travels. I look forward to seeing you again."

Cybelee nodded and closed the door. Symphony stood there a moment before turning to leave.

"Safe travels. I wonder what she meant by that."

Words of the Granny Witch

"Each person lives as many lives as the people they know. Not one after another but lives together, one on top of another. Each of those people knows a different version of you. He or she perceives you differently than the one who is sitting right beside you.

"It's because of that and many other reasons that we never truly know a person. We don't actually know ourselves in all our versions. The whole concept of judging another person's life based on the version you've experienced is nothing but folly. It's like asking ten people to describe the sky. It looks different to every one of them.

"People come to this place searching for the meaning of their lives. They want to know where they fit in. How they should live. Every moment contains a decision that could change everything they've already known. Life changes in the blink of an eye.

"The man who drew his last breath probably did not know it was going to be his final one. Would he have made it last longer? The baby girl who entered the world a few seconds ago is crying for a life that could have been just as easily snuffed out when she entered into it.

"Granny witches wiser than me lived and died. There was no magic that made them immortal, no matter what the fairytales may say. You've got to use what you know to make the choices in front of you. That's the easy part. It's far harder to accept what's left over when you are on the other side of the one-way door of decision."

Chapter Five

SYMPHONY AWOKE IN A COLD sweat. For the third night in a row, her dream was the same. She was on a dark street, freezing in the cold air. A fog hung all around her, making it hard for her eyes to focus on her surroundings. Suddenly, she heard a woman scream. The sound was coming from above. She looked up and saw something falling toward her. At first, it looked like a bundle of something. She could not tell what it was. Then, a piece of material flew off and the object fell faster toward her. Each time Symphony awakened, the bundle was slipping through her fingers to the ground.

Sitting up in the bed, Symphony looked at her alarm clock. It was five in the morning—a Saturday morning. The long work week behind her could be rewarded with a few extra hours of sleep. That would be impossible. The haunted feeling left by the dream was stronger than a cup of coffee.

A few minutes later, Symphony stumbled down the stairs where she found Psycho, her grandmother's dog, sitting at the bottom step.

"I bet you would like to go out."

Psycho's long Golden Retriever tail wagged a reply, and he followed Symphony through the house to the kitchen. Symphony saw that a sprinkling of rain was falling when she opened the back door and stepped outside. The summer morning air was cool. In the direction of the lighted driveway, Symphony saw fog hanging in the air, reminding her of the recent dream. It left her with a feeling of foreboding, a dread that she could not explain. A few minutes passed before Psycho returned and led the way back into the house.

"Are you ready for your cereal?"

Psycho's tail wagged and Symphony went to the cabinet where the breakfast food was kept. She quickly learned when she first moved into Nadia's home that the canine companion liked a bowl of cereal with bananas and milk each morning. He would go psycho if anything else were served to him.

"I think it's a Cheerios kind of day. Would you agree?" Psycho wagged his tail and sat down at his food mat like a patron waiting for a server to bring his food. "You may have your traditional banana. I believe that I saw some lovely strawberries in the fridge that will be yummy on mine."

"The strawberries came from the midweek farmers market."

Symphony dropped the unopened box of cereal on the floor and it went sailing toward Psycho when Nadia spoke from behind her.

"I'm sorry. I didn't mean to scare you." Nadia laughed. She picked up the box from beside her dog and patted his head. "Psycho is not used to playing catch with boxes."

"I'm not used to you being up this early."

"I heard you two milling around down here and thought I better see what was going on. Are you up to stay?"

"Yes. A dream woke me up. Despite the fact that this is Saturday, I don't think I will be falling back to sleep."

"Then, let's get that coffee pot going. Even with the early hour, I think I could eat some breakfast. How about I whip up a quiche and some cinnamon rolls? Doesn't that sound better than cereal?"

"Absolutely. If you throw in some bacon, Psycho might even add a second course to his Saturday morning menu."

When he heard 'bacon,' Psycho rose from chomping on his cereal and looked up at Symphony.

"I think that was a yes." Symphony smiled.

"Sounds good to me. You get that coffee pot going and I will dig in the freezer for some of my homemade cinnamon rolls."

"They are delicious. I'm glad you make them in big batches and freeze them."

"The recipe came from the menu at the Trinkle Mansion B&B. Didn't you tell me that you stayed there during your first couple of nights in Wytheville?" Nadia opened the freezer door and began moving things around.

"Yes. It was wonderful. I remember having them for breakfast one morning. No wonder they are so good. Patti's food is amazing. I can't remember what Patti calls them on her menu."

"Mountain Man Cinnamon Rolls, one of Patti's specialties. She and Bernie are such good friends to me." Nadia bent down to the bottom shelf of her freezer. "I wonder if I have any left. I don't see them." A few seconds passed with Symphony hearing Nadia moving items around. "There they are. This must be the last of them. I'll have to make another batch soon."

"Yes. Please do. I would love for Jason to try them."

"Jason's already had them. I made him a big batch after he completed that special design project for the historical society." Nadia smiled. "He can certainly have more though." She set the container on the kitchen counter.

The coffee pot began brewing while Nadia assembled the ingredients for the quiche. After pouring both of them a large cup, Symphony sat down at the small table in the kitchen to drink her coffee and watch her grandmother prepare the food. It was these moments that made Symphony wish she knew Nadia earlier in their lives. She imagined that if her childhood had included this grandmother, the two of them would have spent many hours cooking together. Symphony had similar times with Grammie Wallace. They were cherished memories.

"I saw Allison the other day at a meeting, and she told me that you are deep into researching the 1924 fire." Nadia began cracking one egg after another into a large stainless steel bowl. "I don't know much about it, but what I know sounds quite tragic, in terms of the loss of businesses and structures. It was miraculous that no lives were lost."

"That's a good summation. I've only begun to scratch the surface in research. It is amazing, considering the time period that so much firefighting help was able to get to the burning site as quickly as it did. It's another good example of the resilience of this town. It literally rose from the ashes again."

"Again?" Nadia looked up from where she was cutting broccoli and onions to go into the quiche. "There was another fire."

"As I understand it, there were several fires in the 1800s in the downtown area that resulted in serious structural damage or total loss to many buildings. I suppose that all cities and towns, big and small, experienced a certain amount of that until we learned more about how to prevent fires from starting and also had trained fire fighters and good equipment to aid when fires did occur."

"I had not thought about that. I do remember hearing historic accounts about devastating fires in some of the large cities." Nadia motioned for Symphony to come to the counter. "You can help with this part. Get my deep pie dish from the cupboard behind you and place the crust in it while I finish the rest of these ingredients."

"Allison wants to tie the 1924 fire into an educational exhibit and school program with local fire fighters. I guess it is a way to show how far we have advanced in fire safety and prevention."

"Unlike the research you did for the post-polio syndrome, I doubt you are going to find anyone who can give you a first-hand account of the events." Nadia slid the quiche and the pan of cinnamon rolls into the oven. "Now, we wait."

"Yeah. The aroma is going to starve me to death." Symphony finished off her first cup of coffee as the sun's rays began to peek through the kitchen window. "I think I will save myself and go take a shower while your kitchen magic is working."

"When you come back down, I want to hear about your meeting with Cybelee. We've both been so busy during the evenings since then, I haven't had a chance to interrogate you about it." Nadia refilled her coffee cup and headed toward the back door. "Come on, Psycho. Let's go for a walk."

"Don't forget his bacon."

"Oh, goodness. I did forget. You remind me, buddy, when we come back in."

Psycho answered with a big wag of his tail, and then he followed Nadia out the door.

Symphony climbed the stairs back to her bedroom. Her mind wandered to the dream that woke her. It left Symphony with a feeling that she could not shake or explain. It felt heavy on her heart. If the dream had to keep repeating itself, she wished its meaning would become clearer.

Opening her closet, she looked for something comfortable and cool to wear. Symphony planned to spend most, if not all of the day, at home. Jason left on Friday evening for a weekend fishing trip with his brothers. Her parents, Peter and Mariel, were going to drive down from West Virginia to spend the day with her on Sunday on their way to her mother's college reunion. It would be the second time they met Nadia. Symphony hoped that it was more comfortable for all involved.

Reaching in the back of the closet for a well-worn soft shirt from her early college days, Symphony spied the suitcase that Nadia gave her when she first moved in. While she made an initial perusal of the contents in those weeks she was "house-sitting" for Nadia, Symphony had a feeling that the case was like a good book. Each time she looked in it, she would find something that she did not see before.

Taking the case to her bed, she opened it up, and began to look inside. The embroidery of a handkerchief caught her eye. Little purple and yellow pansies adorned the corner of the folded cloth. The detail was meticulous. The cloth looked quite old and slightly yellowed with age. She picked the handkerchief up. A piece of paper moved underneath. She remembered it was the schedule from a long ago show. Picking it up, Symphony noticed that the edges were scorched.

"An Evening of Entertainment at the Wytheville Opera House." Symphony began to read the cover content aloud. "March 7, 1924." Symphony turned over the cover to look at the back but quickly did a double take. "1924! That was the night of the Great Town Fire. No, don't tell me that Amburgey went back to that time, too. This cannot be happening. I will not let it happen."

Symphony put the program back in the suitcase and closed the two small latches. Picking it up by the handle, she saw the side of the suitcase that was singed.

"Amburgey probably left 1924 with flames falling down around her. Why was I born into a family of time travelers?"

"Because I was pretty and wanted to get out of West Virginia."

The suitcase dropped to the floor when Symphony jumped at the sound of Nadia's voice behind her.

"You are as bad as Allison about sneaking up on me. I've probably been scared out of a couple of years of my life already." Symphony picked the suitcase up. "What do you mean 'pretty and wanted to get out of West Virginia'?"

"That's why I entered the Miss West Virginia pageant. It got me into competing for the title of Miss America. If I wasn't on that pageant stage, Tyler wouldn't have seen me, and he wouldn't have become your grandfather."

"I suppose that is true. But then I would miss all this fun." Symphony rolled her eyes and gave Nadia a big grin. "Since Amburgey's name was put on the deed to this property in 1924 and this suitcase contains a program from the Wytheville Opera House from that same year, I would surmise that she went to 1924 to find Tyler."

"Unfortunately, that sounds quite possible. I guess that means you will be following them there as well. Why would your research into 1924 only be for an exhibit?"

"You sound rather resigned to the idea." Symphony returned the suitcase to the closet and closed the door.

"I've now been through it with three generations of this family. I hope and pray that I don't lose you, like I lost the other two." Nadia began to cry. "I don't think I can take another loss to this crazy travel business. I don't think I can take another loss, period."

Symphony moved toward Nadia and pulled her into a hug. They were slow, at first, to exchange physical affection. Since Symphony returned from her trip to 1950, Nadia hugged her almost every time they were together.

"You hugged me." Nadia pulled slightly away to look Symphony in the eyes.

"Maybe it's time that I start treating you like a grandmother, huh?" Symphony smiled and hugged her again. "I promise you that I will do everything in my power to not get lost. Maybe. Just maybe, I can find one of the lost ones and bring that person home to you."

"IT'S BREATHTAKING UP here." Symphony gazed in each direction and saw the beautiful vistas of the Blue Ridge Mountains.

"It's breathtaking alright. I hardly have any breath left." Marcella's hands formed a vice grip on the railing at the top of the tower at Big Walker Lookout. "I can't believe that you talked me into climbing up here."

"It was your idea for us to come here. You said I had to experience one of the oldest attractions in the area."

"Yes. I said drive up Big Walker Mountain and have some lemon ice cream in the Country Store. I did not suggest that we climb the tower." Marcella's eyes were as big as saucers as Symphony walked from corner to corner on the platform at the top of the tower. "You are making me nervous pacing like that."

"Is that the Seven Sisters mountain range that I've read about?" Symphony pointed.

"Do you see seven mountains?"

"Yes, I think so." Symphony squinted her eyes and counted.

"Then, I guess it is the Seven Sisters. Can we go back down now?"

"I never would have imagined you to be scared of anything." Symphony raised her eyebrows and walked past her friend again.

"I'm not scared. I'm just not comfortable with the wind blowing."

"Wind? The air is still." Symphony licked her index finger and held it up in the air. "Calm."

"Good grief. I've had enough. I am going back down. There's ice cream down there with my name on it. Mr. Abbey said so." Marcella started walking down the steps.

"Okay. You win. How high up are we again?"

"You'll have to ask someone in the store. I'm not answering any more questions until my feet are on the ground."

A few minutes later, once their feet were firmly on the ground and they were enjoying ice cream cones, Marcella introduced Symphony to the owner of Big Walker Lookout.

"Symphony joined our Museum staff in January. She is in charge of curating and any other project Allison sends her way." Marcella took a big bite of lemon crunch ice cream. "This is so good. I have dreams about it. Symphony, this is Mr. Abbey and one of his employees, Grae White."

"That's wonderful and marvelous," Mr. Abbey said with a slight resemblance to Santa Claus. The older gentleman handed Symphony a big cone of chocolate pecan. "Always happy to hear of new people on Allison's team. History preservation is so important."

"I understand that you have quite a history here, sir. Marcella told me that your family has owned this business for over seventy years."

"That would be correct, young lady. My parents started this business when I was just a little one. It's grown and changed a lot through the years, and we've had our share of tragedy. But we keep on plugging and looking for new ways to encourage people to drive up to see us."

"Goodness, I would think the view alone would be enticement enough. That and this luscious ice cream." Symphony's eyes rolled with her next bite.

"I told you it was worth the drive." Marcella walked away and began looking around the general store.

"Where are you from, Symphony?" Grae asked. She was behind the counter busily grinding coffee beans.

"I grew up in West Virginia, near Charleston." Symphony chose her words carefully.

"Cool. I have a friend in college there. I grew up in Charlotte, North Carolina. My mother, my brother, and I moved here a couple of years ago to live with my grandfather. It was a big change moving to a small town."

"Grae's grandfather is the caretaker of Graham Mansion."

"The historic Graham Mansion?" Symphony finished her ice cream.

"Yes. It's been a real trip living in that big old house." Grae handed Symphony a cup of coffee. "Hope you like coffee. This is one of my special brews."

"Grae roasts the beans herself and comes up with the most interesting flavors." Mr. Abbey took a big sip from the cup Grae handed him. "What's this one called?"

"Christmas in July." Grae giggled and winked at Symphony. "It's like visiting another world."

The unusual comment made Symphony wonder what Grae meant. Several customers approached the counter, which caused Symphony to walk away so Grae could help them.

After exploring the store for a few minutes, Symphony wandered outside and found Marcella sitting in a chair on the store's front porch. Several people were lined up in front of a nearby table where a local author signed books while a pretty young lady sang nearby.

"All of these different things going on, is this a special weekend?" Symphony sat down next to Marcella.

"No. They have activities like this every weekend through the summer and fall. The woman singing is Emily and that's her husband, Zach, who is signing his books. The little girl dancing is their daughter, Bella."

"Wow. It's a family affair." Symphony watched people move about. "There's something very real about this place."

"Maybe authentic is the word you are looking for. I think that's one of the reasons this attraction has survived. In the early years, when Mr. Abbey was growing up, the road we travelled up on was the main drag north and south through this part of the country. The original building had a big dining room and a thriving restaurant. Then, the interstate came along and took all the traffic away."

"What happened to the building?"

"It burned down one winter."

"You were serious when you said that they had dealt with tragedy. What made them rebuild and open this store?"

"The observation tower that you made me climb up," Marcella rolled her eyes, "was always the focal point. It gives a bird's eye view of these beautiful views." Marcella paused a moment. "I really think though that there has always been a fire in Mr. Abbey to keep it going. It's his family's heritage. That and the fact that spit and vinegar runs through his veins."

"Spit and vinegar?"

"It's a southern saying. He's got the strength and tenacity to not give up."

"Yes. I'm familiar with the saying. It was how we described my Grammie."

"That snack was good, but I'm hungry." Marcella rose from her chair. "Let's go back down the mountain and have some dinner."

Symphony followed Marcella to the parking lot, looking back at the store and the people around it. She wondered if Amburgey ever spent a Saturday afternoon there. Symphony smiled realizing that her biological mother obviously had some of that 'spit and vinegar' persona. Which meant she did, too!

"You sure did sleep late this morning." Symphony found Nadia sitting on the patio drinking coffee when she stumbled downstairs on Sunday morning. "I hope that means you didn't have that dream last night."

"I had another dream. It was sort of the same. Only this time, I was at the bottom of the tower at Big Walker and someone was throwing something down at me." Symphony stretched out on the lounge chair next to Nadia with her own cup of caffeine. "When I looked over my shoulder, there was a building on fire behind me. I guess my brain jumbled all of that together after Marcella told me about the history of the business."

"That fire was quite a tragic event. It happened during the winter while Mr. Abbey was out of town. The building that originally housed the restaurant had beautiful chestnut wood in it. Big picture windows showed the most breathtaking views of the mountain range in the summer and fall seasons. Actually, it was equally beautiful in snow cover."

"I guess I'm reading and thinking too much about fire. It's

smoldering in my subconscious." Symphony gave Nadia a weak smile as her grandmother shook her head. "I'm not functioning on all cylinders this morning."

"I still want to hear about your meeting with Cybelee. I believe that you mentioned it had something to do with her website."

"Have you ever met her?" Symphony reached over to refill her mug from the carafe of coffee that was on the table between them.

"No, I have not. I almost did once at a historical society fundraiser. The event was 'all a hum' with anticipation of the mysterious Cybelee being in attendance. She didn't show up. She sent a lovely donation but did not make an appearance."

"She's reclusive. There's no doubt about that. It's almost like in an old Hollywood kind of way."

"Old Hollywood! You've been spending too much time with Garon."

"Perhaps. I think I got more of an idea of what old Hollywood was like though from all of the movies I used to watch with my Grammie."

"I bet she was a wonderful woman."

"She was. The two of you would have gotten along splendidly. Enough alike to get along, yet different enough to be interesting to each other."

"And we both love you. That's the clincher."

"Indeed." Symphony took a deep breath and looked into the forest area that surrounded the back of Nadia's property. "In some ways, your home reminds me a lot of hers. Her house was a totally different style—more old farmhouse-like. The grounds are quite similar in character and the relaxing feeling they convey."

"Despite the way I received this property, I do love it here."

"My meeting with Cybelee was more complicated than I

expected. It seems that she knew Amburgey." Symphony searched Nadia's face for some sort of reaction. "You don't seem surprised."

"It's not something that Amburgey and I talked about. She knew that I did not want her to have any part of that time travel business. I knew that she was visiting a mountain woman who some called a witch. Honestly, I thought it was a phase she was going through and, as I told you, I was preoccupied with Nathan's health. Before his fatal heart attack, he had a couple of less severe ones. Amburgey never really developed much of a relationship with Nathan. They were cordial. It never progressed to the point where she really thought of him as her stepfather. Her own father obviously still loomed large in her life."

"I can see how that was the case."

"It did bother me that Amburgey was spending so much time over there. I had not heard anything negative about the woman, but many strange stories were associated with people who visited her. I hired a local police officer to do a little private detective work for me."

"Was this the same one who helped you look for Amburgey and me later? Because he didn't do so well."

"I learned that you couldn't find someone who does not want to be found. She did not want me to find you." Nadia sighed and shook her head. "Anyway, the detective found the location where Amburgey was going and some basic information about the woman who lived there and the woman's daughter. I'm fairly certain that Cybelee is the mountain woman's daughter."

"Really? That's interesting. That would explain some of what she told me about her interaction with Amburgey."

"Does she know where Amburgey might have gone?"

"No. At least, she didn't reveal that she knew. Talking with her was sort of like listening to riddles."

"Considering the woman's reputation, it does not surprise me. You do not become that elusive and not have some of the personality traits."

"She knew enough about Amburgey to suggest that I should look for a diary that belonged to Tyler. Do you know if such a thing exists?"

"Yes, it existed. I would wager that Amburgey took it with her when she left. I've never found it in the years since. The bulk of the important stuff that Amburgey cherished is in that suitcase I gave you."

"Cybelee said that I might find it in your cabin."

"It's Amburgey's cabin, not mine." Nadia stood up and walked to the edge of the patio, in the same direction that would lead to the cabin. Symphony was quiet. Nadia seemed to be lost in thought. "You can certainly look there. I cannot imagine where it might be. I combed that cabin looking for clues to where Amburgey might have gone after she left."

"Could I borrow the key later and do a little snooping?"

"You don't need a key." Nadia turned around. "It's never locked."

"Why is that?"

"I didn't want anything to hinder Amburgey from coming back—least of all, a lock on a door."

A CLUSTER OF TALL locust trees stood nearby. The swift flight of a bird caught her eye. Following its movement as it landed, she saw the red head of a woodpecker ready to leave its mark.

The cabin was as she remembered. It looked out of place in comparison to the grand house that Nadia called home. Its age could not be estimated by the naked eye, but Symphony surmised that at least one hundred years had passed since the first log was laid in the building of it.

The small door in the middle of the two large windows gave the structure an almost whimsical look. She imagined the cabin being part of a fairytale; no doubt with some twists and turns in the story.

From her previous visit, Symphony remembered Nadia telling her that the windows had once been in a grand hotel that stood on Main Street over a hundred years previously. Apparently, Amburgey learned that they were being sold in an estate sale and begged her mother to buy them for inclusion in the old cabin.

"I bet it cost a fortune to add electricity and plumbing to this tiny cabin." Symphony's voice pierced the quiet while she walked in front of one of the beautiful windows. "It seems like an awful lot of trouble. I wonder why it was so important to Amburgey."

Symphony counted fifteen panes in each window; the seams were so thin that it created the illusion of one large piece of glass. Peering through the glass into the inside, she knew her mind was playing tricks on her. For an instant, it appeared the rocking chair—the one she was first rocked in—was moving. Symphony closed her eyes and shook her head before moving away from the window toward the door.

Just like during her first visit, when Symphony walked across the doorstep, a familiar feeling came over her. She discounted the feeling the first time; now she knew that it was a surge of remembrance that she could not ignore. She stopped and drank in her surroundings. In her mind, she remembered Nadia's words on the day they were in the cabin together. 'Look around, Symphony. If you are indeed the daughter of Amburgey Gibboney, then this is the room in which you were born.'

There was no mistaking it now. Symphony was her mother's daughter—a time traveler. If Cybelee was correct, there was a secret in the cabin. It was a secret left from mother to daughter. It might help her unravel the mystery of how it all began.

Words of the Granny Witch

"Everyone's secrets are one layer from the surface. We think some are deep and dark, buried forever for no one to know. Someone always finds out. People live and die. Secrets are eternal. Sooner or later, some snippet of it springs out like a dam breaking. No one is safe from the knowledge then.

"Sometimes, a secret will drive a person mad. How sad to lose your sanity holding something inside. Losing your last shred of dignity hanging on the weight of something you felt shamed by. It's a greater shame to lose what little sanity any of us have, than the stink of some sin when we are all sinners.

"Far better to share your secrets with the next generation and the one before you. Make them all accomplices and wake up happy each morning with the knowledge that you are sharing the weight. It makes each load lighter. Maybe one day then someone will share a secret with you. You can help them tell the story. And, then, well, the secret is free. It's not even a secret at all."

Chapter Six

"I LOOKED IN ALL OF THE OBVIOUS places. That was a waste of time. Why in the world would Amburgey hide anything somewhere obvious? Nadia would have found it."

Symphony sat across the table from Jason. He had arrived home late Sunday evening as Symphony was busy having a late and fast dinner with her parents and Nadia when they stopped by while less than two hours away on their way home from a reunion. The dinner was full of polite conversation with the two 'sides' of Symphony's family becoming more acquainted.

She rushed through her work on Monday with the anticipation that she and Jason would have the entire evening together. She planned to cook dinner for him at his apartment. Those plans quickly went by the wayside when the sprinkler system in the Rock House sprang a leak. Symphony was asked to stay until a repair crew could arrive. That led to them having takeout instead.

"So, you really think that Cybelee knows what she is talking about? You think that she would know that Amburgey hid her father's time travel journal in that cabin?"

"What can I say? The woman sounds convincing. I think she had a personal connection to Amburgey when I was born. It's like she knew her at a time when no one else did."

"That's an interesting way of putting it. I get what you mean though. At some points in anyone's life, you kind of close ranks and only let a few people know the real you. I think those are the times when we are really changing."

"You are more than just a pretty face. You know that?" Symphony reached over and took hold of Jason's hand.

"This pretty face hasn't seen your pretty face near enough these days. What do you say we make a daring relationship step and go away for a weekend?"

A small jolt of excitement ran through Symphony. Since she returned from 1950, she noticed that he seemed more serious about where their relationship was going.

"A weekend away would be great. Did you have a place in mind?"

"I thought we might spend a few days on the Blue Ridge Parkway. There are several nice places to stay. A buddy of mine recently took his wife to a resort called Primland for an anniversary weekend. He said it was very luxurious."

"Luxurious sounds wonderful. You don't have to break the bank though."

"I think it would do both of us good if we went to a place where we could relax. I feel like I am always working."

"You *are* always working." Symphony picked up their plates and set them on the counter that separated the small dining area from the kitchen. "It is how people make their dreams come true."

"Yes. I've been wanting to talk to you about something. I've been approached by someone who would like to financially back my brewery."

"That's wonderful." Symphony sat back down across from Jason. "May I ask who it is?"

"You've answered my next question. I guess you don't know."

"No. Is it someone I know?"

"It's Nadia."

"Nadia?"

"Nadia and Millie Monroe, actually. Your grandmother and her friend offered to provide the financing to get my brewery off the ground."

"That's wonderful, I guess. What do you think?"

"Honestly, it concerns me a little that it is your grandmother. But she did make a subtle offer when I first started learning the business. That was long before either one of us knew you." Jason took a drink of his beverage. "That sounds weird—before your grandmother knew you."

"Yes. It's almost like I married into my own family."

"Well, you did grow up in West Virginia." Jason snickered and winked.

"Watch it. I almost became your aunt."

"That is a mental image I do not want to ever have again. By the way, Uncle Belcher called my mother and told her about meeting you."

"You better go ahead and tell me because my heart stopped beating when you started that sentence." Elbows on the table, Symphony rested her face in her hands.

"He told Mom that he now believed that everyone has a twin. That it sure was a grand coincidence that the girl he knew also had an unusual name like Symphony." Peeking through her fingers, Symphony waited for Jason to continue. "Mom told me that now she remembered Belcher telling a story when she was a child about a girl he met in the 1950s who worked at the polio clinic. She said that Belcher was quite smitten. The girl just disappeared one day."

"Garon says that he doesn't think he had any memory of meeting me back in 1950 until after I came back from the trip. It's like in the time sequence, it doesn't happen until it happens."

"Now you are making my head hurt. I'm going to need something stronger than this iced tea if we continue talking about time travel." Jason rose from his side of the table and pulled Symphony up from where she was sitting. "The encounter with Uncle Belcher did do one thing for certain."

"What's that?"

"It made my mother even more curious about you and determined that it is time for you two to meet." Symphony started to speak, but Jason put his finger to her lips. "My suggestion is that if you want to do it on your own terms, you better let me arrange a dinner with my parents. Otherwise, she will show up at your office one day when you are covered in dust, or worse."

"I still cannot believe that no one told me she was at the symposium. I feel like I earned rude points that night."

"Don't worry about that. She knew what she was doing. Alice Newberry is sly like a fox."

"You know, I just remembered something. Belcher told me that his mother was a Newberry. What have you got going on in your family tree?"

"It's complicated. Let's say that Jones and Newberry are fairly common names around here as layers of big families married other big families. There are lots of stories about brothers in one family marrying sisters in another family and their children being double first cousins. It makes genealogy research like a board game. Roll the dice and find out how you are related."

"So, if I was your aunt, it wouldn't be so bad?"

"It would be horrendous. We do have our principles. I would not be able to do this."

Jason drew Symphony into his arms. What began as a playful kiss gradually turned into what was certainly the best one of her life.

"You've got some kind of magic, Symphony Wallace." Jason looked into her eyes after their kiss ended. "You've made me rethink this whole bachelor thing. I didn't see this coming."

Symphony understood that an admission like that was not easy for any man to make. It was not the time to make light of it.

"You bring out the magic in me. I'm so glad you knocked me down that day."

"A great story to tell our children." Jason rolled his eyes and shook his head. "See. That was not a sentence I have ever said before."

"You need to keep trying new things."

"Darling, remember that when we have that weekend on the Parkway." Symphony could feel herself blushing. Jason smiled and touched her hot cheek. "It's okay. I'm blushing on the inside, too."

"I left you a spinach salad with grilled chicken in the fridge." Nadia was gathering her purse and keys when Symphony came through the door the following evening. "It's knitting night at the yarn shop. I don't want to be late."

"Is all the good yarn taken if you get there late?" Symphony could not resist kidding her grandmother about her weekly event. "Do you have to use the scratchy stuff then?"

"I would tell you how much you sounded like Amburgey, but I have to use my time to travel. Pun intended." Nadia winked at her granddaughter. "If you get there late, you miss the beginning of Susan's story."

"Dr. Griffin, the woman who owns the shop? She tells stories?"

"Mercy, yes. She's got some great ones. If they are not about growing up in the Deep South, they are about her time as a trauma doctor. She's a hoot. But, if you miss the beginning, the rest of the story does not make sense. Susan will not go back and retell it."

"You don't need to be late then." Symphony gave Nadia a hug. "Thanks for the salad."

"What are you planning to do this evening? I hope the answer is not work." Nadia picked up a multi-colored tote bag with the words 'May the Yarn Be with You' emblazed on it.

"No. I've worked so much on the fire exhibit, I must reek of smoke." Symphony smiled as Nadia sniffed the air around them. "I was kidding. People who carry bags like that should catch on to my jokes quicker."

"I was playing along. I'm opening the door now. Please tell me what you and Psycho are going to do while I'm gone." As if on cue, the big Golden Retriever appeared in the foyer. "There's extra c-h-i-c-k-e-n for him." Nadia pointed at her furry friend.

"I'm going to go back to the cabin and see if I can find Tyler's diary."

"Well, good luck to you. Maybe Psycho can sniff it out." Nadia glanced at the clock. "I'm going to have to go faster than the law allows."

"Having ridden with you, I don't think that will be a problem. Happy knitting!" Symphony yelled while her grandmother hastily ran down the sidewalk to her vehicle. Closing the door, Symphony looked down at her waiting friend. "Okay, buddy. I'm going to change into some shorts, and then we will eat some dinner. I think that nice lady just gave me a great idea and you get to help."

Thirty minutes later, after they had each eaten, Symphony and Psycho got into Nadia's pink and black golf cart, and headed to the cabin. In the box of Amburgey's special things that Nadia had first given her, Symphony knew that there was a brown tie. Nadia told her that it had been Amburgey's gift to Tyler on Father's Day when Amburgey was five. Symphony was hoping that there might be enough scent left on the personal item that a special dog like Psycho might be able to sniff out anything else that belonged to Tyler.

Once inside the cabin, Symphony pulled the tie out of a plastic bag she had in her pocket and kneeled down in front of Psycho.

"I need you to take a really good sniff of this tie, Psycho. Then, help me find that scent again. Can you do it?"

As if Psycho understood every word Symphony said, the dog took a big sniff of the tie, and then began sniffing all around the cabin. Only a few minutes and lots of sniffs passed before Psycho walked back out of the front door. Turning toward the left side of the porch, he jumped up on a small table that held a variety of country-style decorations. One of them was a heavy looking sign that said 'Open.' Upon reaching the sign, Psycho's tail wagged in rapid motions; he looked up at Symphony.

"It's just a sign, Psycho." The dog took another sniff and his tail started wagging again. "Okay. I'll humor you."

Symphony picked up the sign. It was heavier than she expected. Turning it over, she saw that there was a box on the back of it—a box with a latch. Slowly, she sat down in the chair next to the table.

"Oh my." Symphony gave Psycho a big-eyed look before she moved the latch. The little door sprang open revealing a handkerchief wrapped around something. "I bet this is Tyler's handkerchief, too." Psycho sniffed and wagged his tail again.

Symphony set the box portion down and began to unwrap the cloth from around the object. She held her breath as the object began to be revealed. It was a small notebook with a worn leather binding. It looked old. It looked mysterious. Opening the cover, revealed the words she was longing to see—The Chronicles of Tyler Gibboney.

"Cybelee was right. I can't believe it." Psycho laid his head on Symphony's knee. "Did you know Tyler, too? Was he your friend?"

Psycho sniffed the diary and gave it a little lick. Symphony searched her mind for what Nadia told her about Psycho's origin. She said that he was Amburgey's dog and returned with her from a trip. With Psycho's reaction to Tyler's belongings, Symphony couldn't help but wonder if he had, perhaps, originally belonged to Amburgey's father. Maybe, Amburgey found Tyler during one of her trips and he sent his companion to take care of her.

Still clutching the handkerchief with one hand and holding the journal with the other, Symphony walked back into the cabin. She immediately sat down in the rocking chair in the center of the room, remembering it was the chair that she was first rocked in. Symphony seemed to gravitate to it—the best location to read the words of her grandfather.

Remembering Psycho, Symphony rose from the chair and went to the kitchen. Filling a bowl with cool water, Symphony also filled a glass for herself. She set her water down on a small table beside the rocker and picked up the journal again. As she did so, something fell out. Symphony gasped.

"It's the same photo I have! The photo that was left with me. Psycho, it's the exact same photo!" Symphony turned the photograph over. "I was hoping there might be something written on it. There's no doubt now that this man was someone important to Amburgey. Having seen photos of Tyler Gibboney, I know that it is not him. Psycho, do you know this man?"

Symphony held the photo out to Psycho. The dog sniffed it but showed no reaction.

"I'm delusional. Asking a dog if it recognizes a photo." Symphony took a deep breath as she watched Psycho go to the water bowl and sloppily lap up some refreshment. "I don't know if I dare say what I am thinking. If this photo is not Amburgey's father, I wonder if he could be mine. I can't say that it isn't the first time that idea crossed my mind. I never allowed myself to think about it for very long. It was hard enough imagining my mother."

Symphony set the photo down on the table beside her. Picking up the journal again, she turned past the title page to where the first entry was recorded and began to read out loud.

"March 10, 1924. If you want to know the truth of a matter, you must witness it for yourself. I find that I developed a yearning to see things beyond the imagination. I must know what lies ahead in this brilliant century that we are only a quarter of the way into.

"I thought that I was under a grand misfortune when, on my journey to the tropical state of Florida, my train stopped in a small Virginia town. It was supposed to be just an overnight stop for me, as I awaited another train that would, on the following morning, take me on to my destination. That one night in the tiny town of Wytheville proved to have life-changing consequences.

"You see, when I arrived, it was a few hours since the Main Street area was engulfed in fire."

With her mouth gaping open, Symphony laid the book down on her lap and looked at Psycho.

"I don't believe it. My grandfather was in Wytheville during the time frame of the Great Town Fire. I felt a chill. Did you feel it?" Psycho opened his eyes, but did not raise his head from where he lay on the porch. "This cannot be happening. I can't believe that I am finding his journal right at the time that I am doing research about 1924. Listen, Psycho."

"The fire began early on a cold Saturday morning. I am told that by the time it was over, more than thirty businesses were consumed by the blaze. I walked the smoke-filled streets and almost two town blocks on both sides of Main Street were destroyed. I was happy to learn that no lives were lost. There is a story though that tells a tale that could easily have been a tragic one had it not been for the delightful woman I met yesterday. She is the reason I am now keen on travelling to the future."

Symphony set the book on her lap again. She gazed at the photo and took a sip of her water. Following her lead, Psycho rose and went to his water bowl where he took another long drink.

"I'm almost afraid to keep reading, Psycho. I sure hope that it isn't me that he meets." Symphony let out a nervous giggle. "I guess I shouldn't kid around about such. Truth is stranger than fiction these days. Enough stalling, I must continue."

"The blaze began in a business building almost in the center of the town. The owner of the business and his family lived above the store. A member of the household discovered the fire and awakened his family. The fire was already so far out of control that they were forced to try to escape from a second-story window. There were four of them—three adults, two men and one woman, and a small child. Two of the adults jumped to the ground first. They landed safely, but not without peril. The third adult then threw the child to the waiting arms of the father on the ground below, before jumping himself.

"It was during those final quick moments before the child was thrown that the story takes a truly miraculous turn. It was still the dead of night with great darkness as well as much smoke billowing from the blaze into the street. It was difficult for the man above to see where he was throwing the baby. As it would turn out, it was a couple of feet from where the now-injured parents were standing. It just so happened that a young woman was walking down the street. She was working the night shift at a business up the street and was walking to the boarding house where she lived. Hearing the commotion and smelling the smoke, she quickened her pace down the sidewalk toward where the parents were on the ground. Looking back up, as she continued to walk, she saw what she described as a bundle being thrown from the upstairs.

"Instinct kicked in and she began to run down the street and was able to catch the bundle before it hit the ground. It was a little boy—a young man who shall forever be in the debt of this young woman.

"My hand is shaking while I write this next line. I know whoever shall read this in the future shall think that I am a man who indulges excessively in the spirits or who has certainly lost his mind. If I did not know that it was possible, I would think the same. I cannot hide from what I know just because it sounds too extraordinary to believe. The young woman is named Amburgey Gibboney and she is my daughter."

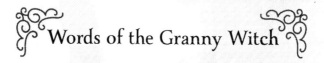

Words of the Granny Witch

"People love the products of imagination—grandiose tales of wonder that fill the pages of books and the screens of movie theaters. Unfortunately, people are less inclined to do the imagining themselves.

"You can look up into the heavens and believe that there is a supreme God above who created your world. With the same brain cells, you refuse to believe that any other life forms, like you are superior, might exist in another world like yours.

"You will not challenge that you can travel to the other end of the Earth in some form of transportation, fast or slow. But, to think that you could travel there in another time is folly and foolishness.

"For all the knowledge we have gained since humans have existed, for all the wonders of nature and invention that we have seen, we refuse to believe in things we have not personally experienced even when the fundamental principles on which we believe are just as magnificent and unimaginable.

"It is a good thing that the Granny Witches, the Queens of Appalachia, have carried the torch to shine a light on that which people shroud in darkness. Their eyes are open and their ears alert—ready to turn those who doubt into believers, ready to help guide them into adventures beyond their wildest dreams."

Chapter Seven

"MY GOODNESS! YOU FOUND YOUR grandfather's journal?"
After locating the diary, Symphony texted Marcella and
asked her if she would mind coming in to work a little early the
following morning. Symphony needed to talk about what she found
and learned. She was not ready to have the conversation with her
grandmother.

"Yes. Cybelee told me to look at the small cabin on Nadia's
property. It was Amburgey's favorite place. Nadia told me that she
did not believe I would find anything like that there. She said that
she searched through the cabin after Amburgey left to try and find
any clues about where her daughter had gone."

"You told me before that Cybelee seemed to know Amburgey for
a time. Did she know where the journal was hidden?"

"No, not exactly. I had to enlist the help of someone who could sniff it out." Symphony smiled. A confused look crossed Marcella's face. "I had to use some canine ingenuity. I remembered that there was one of Tyler's neckties in Amburgey's treasures. Like most little girls, she gave her father a tie as a gift. I let Psycho sniff it and he went searching around the cabin."

"He sniffed out the journal?"

Symphony nodded.

"Where did he find it?"

"It was hiding in plain sight. It was actually on a table on the porch. There was a small box behind a sign on the table. Guess what the sign said?"

"I cannot even imagine."

"Open."

"You are kidding me?" Marcella's eyes were big with amazement.

"Not even slightly. Whenever I tell Nadia about it, she is going to flip out. The interior of the cabin is kept spotless. I guess since the sign was on a table outside, it hadn't been moved. Who cleans an old wooden table on the porch of an abandoned cabin?"

"True. It's incredible to think how long it sat there waiting." Marcella moved things around on her desk to begin her day. "I guess there is something to be said for a secret not to be found until the right person comes along to find it."

"That's an interesting way to put it." Symphony took a deep breath. "I've got to tell you something else. I have a funny feeling that all of this research I am doing about 1924 is not only for the exhibit."

"Why do you say that?" Marcella picked up her beverage to take a drink.

"I read the beginning of Tyler's journal. After I got to a certain point, I was afraid to read any further." Symphony paused until Marcella stopped what she was doing and looked at her. "The first entry in his journal was from March 1924 and he was in Wytheville at that time."

"What?" Marcella set the container down without drinking.

"Apparently, Tyler arrived in Wytheville a few hours after the Great Town Fire occurred. He wrote that he was on a train trip to Florida and he changed trains in Wytheville. You remember hearing the story about the family who jumped from the second story of the building where the fire began?"

"Yes. I remember that they threw a child down to safety. It seems like there was something questionable about who caught the child."

"Tyler told that story in his journal. He said that a woman named Amburgey Gibboney caught the child."

"That's incredible."

"That's not the most incredible part." A sudden surge of emotion passed through Symphony. She took a deep breath. "He wrote in the journal that to most people it would sound crazy but that Amburgey Gibboney was his daughter."

"No."

"Yes. It was right there in his handwriting."

"He had to have travelled into the future by that point."

"I suppose. Or else the trip in March 1924 was a journey backward in time for him." Symphony stood up, began to pace, and shook her head. "I'm not sure I believe what I said. It seems that both Tyler and Amburgey did a lot of hopping through time. It appears that they met each other, too. From what Nadia told me, and Amburgey confirmed it in 1950, she was looking for her father. From the entry in Tyler's journal, she may have found him."

"Since he was her father, it wouldn't be a situation where Amburgey did not recognize him. She knew what her father looked like as an adult. But I wonder how he recognized her."

"I haven't got to that part of the journal yet."

"Well, hurry up and get there, I want to know. Better yet, give it to me, I'm a fast reader." Marcella raised her eyebrows and gave Symphony a big smile. "I would be glad to give you a synopsis later."

"That's your 'I'm-not-up-to-something' voice. I've learned to recognize it." Symphony cleared her throat and pointed to the foyer area. Allison was approaching. "I think I will read it myself."

"Good morning, ladies. I hope everyone had a great weekend. Did you do anything fun?"

"Symphony was just telling me about her interesting weekend. She's been doing research."

"Now, Symphony, I do not want you to spend every weekend working. I know that I said we needed to get this fire exhibit going, but that doesn't mean you have to work on it night and day." Allison walked past Symphony and Marcella and into her office.

"I accidentally came across some information about it when I was researching some Gibboney family history." Symphony watched Marcella roll her eyes at the comment.

"The Gibboneys who lived in the Rock House?" Allison returned to Marcella's desk.

"No. The Gibboneys who are my ancestors." Symphony smiled. She picked up her belongings.

"Oh, silly me. I forgot that your biological mother was a Gibboney." Allison gestured like she was having an idea by pretending to hit her hand on her head. "It seems like a minor detail considering the rest of her history."

"Indeed. I can see that."

"So, you've been researching her father's family."

"Sort of. I've been reading a journal of my grandfather's that I found."

"To be as adventurous as Amburgey was, her father must be some man. I don't see Nadia as the adventurous type."

"No. I think the most daring thing Nadia did is enter the Miss America pageant. She seems to enjoy the normal life more. No time travelling for her."

"It sounds like an interesting read. I hope it sheds some light on what you are trying to discover. I've got to get to my grant writing. These projects won't fund themselves." Allison laughed. She left Symphony and returned to her office, talking over her shoulder. "Marcella, I don't want to be disturbed this morning. I've got to finish this grant. I'm going to forward my phone to you."

"Oh, lovely." Marcella shook her head. "That is a sure sign that she will get a dozen calls before ten o'clock. It will be delightful."

"Well, I guess I better get out of your way. We can talk later."

"Yes. We must continue this conversation." Before Marcella could finish the phone began to ring. "See. What did I tell you? It will be like this all morning."

Symphony waved goodbye and Marcella answered the phone. Making her way out of the building, Symphony spoke to the volunteer who was working in the research library. A middle-aged woman was seated next to the volunteer and they were poring over, what from a distance, looked like an old deed book. Many people, from all over the United States, traced their heritage back to Virginia. It was interesting to hear the excitement in their voices when they learned about their ancestors.

Walking in the parking lot, Symphony saw a familiar car parked close to the door, with an even more familiar occupant getting out. What did a retired movie actor drive in his later years? A Porsche? A BMW? Not Garon Fitzgerald.

"Your mode of transportation doesn't fit your place in society,

Garon." Symphony laughed. Her new friend got out of his old silver Ford Taurus. "Your car doesn't match your clothes."

"I like to go incognito. Sneak up on people. It's a grand entrance." Garon lowered his sunglasses, and then gave Symphony a wink. "I've been looking for you, young lady. We have more research to do. I understand you have much to tell me."

"About?" Symphony narrowed her eyes while giving him a side-glance.

"Your second visit with our friend, Cybelee."

"How did you learn about that?"

"I have informants in many places. They tell me who comes and goes."

"You talked to that woman at the guard house at the BloomSpoons compound."

"As I said, I have informants."

"Yes, women in their golden years who remember you in your golden days." Symphony walked toward the sidewalk to go back to her office at the Rock House. "I'm going to have to start wearing disguises."

"Where do you think you are going? You must fill me in."

"I must?" With her back to Garon, Symphony smiled and rolled her eyes. "Why must I?" She said turning back toward him.

"Because you need my help. I can help you with all of your research. I can help you understand the secrets you don't want to know. Because I'm your friend."

She knew it was true. Garon was her friend. In her heart, Symphony understood how fortunate she was to be with the people who were now in her life. The haunting feeling that she seemed to carry with her everywhere she went could only be lifted by the strength of friendship. Grammie would say that Garon's words were a sign she should cultivate.

"Okay, Garon. You got me there. Follow me to the Rock House. I have something to show you."

Symphony presumed that Garon was going to drive his car to the parking lot across from the Rock House, where her office was located. Instead, she heard him walking behind her.

"Aren't you going to drive? It's a fairly hot day."

"Hot? You haven't lived in Southern California. This feels like the winter in comparison. I'm not taking any chances that you are going to change your mind. I walk several miles a day in my neighborhood; I can walk two blocks to your office. I'm intrigued about what you have to show me. I hope it is another piece of jewelry that likes to travel."

"Guess again. It's not jewelry, but it most certainly has travelled." Symphony and Garon rounded the corner onto Tazewell Street. "Does the lady who works for Cybelee have you on speed dial?"

"She's a fan—a devoted fan. I called after our last visit and offered her my email address. I said I was concerned about why you were visiting Cybelee. I told her that I wasn't sure what your intentions were, and that I was going to monitor your visits. Brenda Sue was more than willing to let me know about your comings and goings."

"Really, Garon? Is that any way to treat a friend?"

"Symphony, you are an impressionable young woman with a heavy load on your mind and heart. I was more concerned about what you might find out from one of your visits. My intentions are good."

"What did you have to promise Brenda Sue in return? An autographed photo? Dinner for two?"

"Actually, I promised her something more valuable than either one of those things. Although, dinner with me is delightful." Garon chuckled. "I am going to give her a pair of sunglasses that once belonged to Elvis. Not those big ones he wore toward the end. These are a pair he owned while he and I were making movies on that same Hollywood lot for several years. We went for a drive one afternoon between shooting scenes and he left them in my car."

"That lovely Taurus you are driving?" Walking side by side, Symphony turned and gave Garon a smile.

"No, smarty pants. I was driving a convertible in those days. If I recall correctly, I believe it was my baby blue Cadillac Eldorado. Elvis liked cars, you know. We had a nice chat about acting. He wanted to do more serious roles. I wanted to do less serious roles. Anyway, the sky turned dark and we headed back to the studio. At some point, he took off his sunglasses and laid them in the seat. I slipped them into the glove box later and didn't think about the glasses again for a year or more. I never remembered to return them to him."

"So you are parting with them to keep tabs on me? That doesn't seem like a fair trade."

"They're only something that an old friend of mine wore for a short while. You are a new friend of mine that I hope to keep for a long while. Brenda Sue will cherish them. It is a very fair trade."

"It is an interesting tale, nonetheless." Symphony and Garon reached the side door of the Rock House Museum. "It earned you the revealing of a secret."

"Then, it worked." Garon walked ahead of Symphony into the foyer area near the medical exhibits. Garon glanced into one of the glass cases. "As I have worked in this house with Allison and her staff over the past few years, I have often wondered what old Dr. Haller would think of today's medical breakthroughs."

"I imagine he would be quite surprised by some of them. Ways to diagnose illnesses have certainly changed dramatically since his time of practicing medicine."

Symphony put her belongings down on a chair near the doorway.

"Yes, being one of the first doctors in the area made him cutting edge for his time, in some ways. I'm sure he must have felt quite helpless not to be near other physicians or hospitals." Garon stopped looking at the display case and returned his attention to Symphony. "I've made enough polite chit-chat. What's the secret?" There was a gleam in Garon's eyes. He rubbed his hands together and walked over to where Symphony stood.

"I had a feeling that your interest in chatting about Dr. Haller wasn't completely historical in nature."

Symphony pulled Tyler's diary out of her bag. Something fell from between the pages and onto the floor. Kneeling down, she saw that it was a dried pressed flower. From its appearance, it seemed quite old. She could still make out that it was a pansy.

"That looks like an old book you have there."

"Yes." Symphony picked up the flower and slipped it back inside the book. Rising to respond to Garon, she thought she heard a noise in another room. "Did you hear that?"

"Hear what?" Garon looked around.

"It sounded like footsteps."

"Perhaps we interrupted Dr. Haller's afternoon nap."

"Funny, Garon. Do you believe that the doctor still resides here?" Symphony walked from the foyer toward the staircase and stopped to listen.

"Living or dead, I think everyone leaves some of their aura behind. Can I see the book?"

From the corner of her eye, Symphony could see Garon's hand reaching toward her as she continued to listen. Knowing that it was useless to try and stop him from looking at it now, she let go of her grasp when she felt him take hold. Still listening for further sounds, she took a few more steps alongside the staircase.

"There it is again. Didn't you hear that?"

"No. Sorry. I only hear what I want to. It was a skill I picked up in Hollywood. I rarely heard any of the questions that were thrown at me from reporters on the red carpet. I could always hear fans when they asked for autographs though. I loved those people."

The noise grew louder. Symphony moved closer to the front door she thought it sounded like something hitting the door from the outside.

"Symphony!" Garon walked up behind her. "This can't be what I think it is."

"Shhh, Garon. I'm trying to listen. It almost sounds like there is an animal or something trying to claw through the door."

Symphony did not turn around but instead leaned closer to the front door. It was all wood without any windowpanes that she could look out. She imagined it was once the main entrance into the structure when a dirt path was in front of it. Now, the traffic of busy Monroe Street zoomed by a few feet from the threshold. She was shown how to open it, in the event of an emergency. That was the only reason it was currently used.

"Have you read any of this? Tyler was in Wytheville during the 1924 fire. What are the chances of that? Oh, my stars. Where in the world did you find it?"

"It was in the cabin behind Nadia's house." Her voice was monotone. She focused on the sound she kept hearing. "I've read the first few pages. I found it last night."

"Symphony! Look at this! Tyler is describing a pendant."

The sudden change in the tone of Garon's voice coupled with what he said caught Symphony off guard. She quickly turned to find him right behind her, holding the book out toward her, and pointing to a page within. Instinctively, her hand went to the pendant that hung around her neck and she focused her eyes on the words Garon was pointing toward. The quick movement caused her to lose her footing. She grasped the book that Garon held out. In a split second, Symphony began to fall backward. Before she realized what was happening, she could feel her right shoulder making impact with something hard behind her.

It was at that moment that the chiming began---one, two, three—a feeling of fear passed over Symphony. The clock that did not chime was making its presence known—four, five. With her right hand clutching the pendant and her left hand holding the book, she looked up to see a blur of Garon over her—six, seven, eight.

"Garon! Help me!" She could see his hand reaching for her. When the ninth chime rang out, smoke engulfed her. All Symphony could do was scream. She felt herself being pulled away.

Words of the Granny Witch

"There are four pillars to the work of magic—air, water, fire and earth. All four must exist for a spell to be conjured, but it is the fire—the will—that makes everything work.

"Nothing ever happens until someone believes. I've given plenty of scared folks the power to believe. They walked away from my cabin with a trinket that each one thought gave them the power to do whatever was in their heart. It was just a token—a little bag of herbs with butterfly wings, a pebble from a creek bed smudged with elderberries, a bird's feather dipped in perfumed oil. Each one came from nature and gave off the power it naturally owned. Just like the one who carried it, the one who had the power all along.

"Travelling through time is dangerous business. There are rules that should be followed. Some think they know better and suffer the consequences. The one who wrote down his travels weaved a spell of magic that no granny witch could undo. Some secrets are not for telling.

"Fire came down one night. It took the man somewhere he should not have been. It set in motion a series of circumstances that would forever haunt those who loved him, even before they knew his love. You don't have to feel the fire to be burned."

Chapter Eight

SYMPHONY SLOWLY OPENED HER eyes. The pounding of her head made her reach for her temple. Trying to focus, she realized she was in darkness. Moving her right hand by her side, Symphony felt below her. She was lying on a bed.

The last thing she remembered was seeing Garon's face blur when she saw his hand reach toward her. Symphony took a deep breath. The last moments became clearer. The clock chiming. The pendant. Tyler's diary. Falling backward into the clock—the clock that transported her to another time.

Symphony did not know where she was. She had a good idea of when it was, though.

"1924." Symphony sat up in the bed.

"That's right."

The voice was coming from the corner of the room. A feeling of fear passed over Symphony combined with a strange sense of calm. The voice sounded familiar.

"You are going to have to tell me why you keep following me. How can you possibly know when and where I am travelling to? Are you a witch?"

Symphony's suspicions were confirmed. A laugh rose inside her making her think of the stereotypical witch in her time.

"I'm not referring to the kind that Dorothy dropped a house on either. You've got to have some level of power to be a time traveler."

"So do you."

Symphony swung her feet over the edge of the bed. The quickness of the movement made her dizzy. She realized her feet were bare when the soles touched the floor. She wondered where her shoes were. It was still too dark in the room to determine what the situation was.

Hearing footsteps, she turned in the direction of the sound. The curtains were drawn back and the rustle of fabric moving preceded slivers of light entering the room. Symphony could see the outline of a person by the moonlight. Turning to face her, Symphony's eyes began to focus on the face—Amburgey Gibboney.

"It's time for you to tell me who you are and why you are following me."

Symphony's mind raced. Her gut said it would not be a wise decision to reveal her connection to Amburgey. She risked enough during their previous encounter by telling Amburgey who gave her the pendant. She hoped that tidbit would not be remembered.

"I checked you when you arrived. You still have that pendant. I don't understand why you think I gave it to you. You were a stranger to me before I met you in 1950."

Symphony closed her eyes and tried to conceal her emotions.

The irony of Amburgey's words hit full force. Her biological mother was indeed a stranger.

"What do you mean when I arrived? Where am I?"

"You are in a boarding house in Wytheville, Virginia. You are correct that it is 1924. Why did you follow me here?"

"A boarding house? How did I get to a boarding house?" Symphony's eyes began to adjust to the light in the room. She rose, walked around the bed, past Amburgey, to the window, and looked out onto the dark street.

"You appeared here, in this room. Don't you know anything about time travel?" Amburgey made a huffing sound. She moved to the bed that Symphony vacated and sat down.

"Actually, I don't. It's not like you buy a ticket to your destination."

"You are right about that." Amburgey snickered under her breath. "I was beginning to think that you died in the transition."

"Died? Why do you say that?" Symphony turned to face Amburgey.

"Because you've been sleeping for over eight hours. You arrived before I left for my shift at the hotel, and I just returned when you woke up. I couldn't wake you. It scared me."

"So, you left me here? You didn't go get help?" Symphony crossed her arms over her chest and narrowed her eyes. "What kind of a moth—" Symphony stopped herself.

"What did you say? Don't get huffy with me. I didn't invite you here."

"Actually, you did." Symphony's anger was taking over her restraint. "That's a whole other story though. Why did you leave me?" Symphony paused, thinking about the double meaning of her statement. She could not let her anger and frustration, old and new, put her in jeopardy.

"What am I supposed to do? Go and get a doctor and tell him that someone suddenly appeared in my room, and I think she might be dead. That's not a plausible statement in our time, much less this one."

"Our time."

"Yes, you are from the 1980s, too, aren't you?"

"Sure." Symphony turned her back on Amburgey and rolled her eyes. She was born in 1989. At least, it was not a complete untruth. Symphony faced Amburgey again. "Okay. I understand. You were in a difficult situation. I'm not as experienced in this time travel stuff as you are."

"How do you know what my experience is? You keep being evasive about why you are here. Who are you?"

"You know me, I'm Symphony. We met a while ago." Symphony could not think of an alibi that would make a shred of sense without jeopardizing both of their situations. "We were together in 1950."

"Yes. You left suddenly, and you took me with you. Only when I awakened, you were nowhere to be found. This is the first time I've seen you since. Explain that."

"Like you could not explain my entrance to this time to a doctor, I cannot explain to you where I went. It's complicated. I honestly don't understand myself. You are going to have to trust me."

Symphony sat down next to Amburgey on the bed. Out of the corner of her eye, she could see that sunlight was beginning to peep through the window. Glancing over her shoulder, Symphony looked around the room. It was small and plain. There were two twin size beds with a small table between them. A chest of drawers sat near the wall opposite the beds beside the door. A washbasin was on top of it.

"Why should I trust you?"

"Because for better or worse, we are thrown together again. We are in similar situations. We are stranded in another time. If, for no other reason, we need to stick together to try and get back to the time we came from."

"Back to the time we came from. That's funny. Sometimes, I think I started off in the wrong time. Maybe that's half the reason I've gone on these trips—I'm searching for my real time."

Symphony pondered what Amburgey said. Perhaps, that was the root of her mother's issues.

"You were helpful to me when we met in 1950. You found me a job and a place to live. I sure hope you will help me again. I don't have a clue what I will do in 1924. I don't think I am dressed for it either." The sunlight was shining brighter; Symphony realized she arrived in 1924 in twenty-first century clothing.

"You look rather modern. This is not a modern time. I am working as a nurse. There is a small clinic up the street. It's nothing like the one we worked in during our time in 1950. It does operate around the clock though. I'm the night nurse. An orderly works with me. He's studying to be a doctor. Thankfully, I picked up a lot of nursing skills when we worked at Chitwood Clinic. Later, I might pursue medicine as a career."

"I didn't pick up any nursing skills then. I mostly handled getting the patients' paperwork ready."

"Yes. You have a nice voice though. Yesterday, I heard someone mention that the telephone company is looking for switchboard operators. You could do that."

Within Symphony's mind flashed an image of one of the exhibits at the Boyd Museum. It was a big board with holes in it. Long cords were plugged in to connect one circuit to another. Her brief perusal of the contraption did not produce any feelings that she longed to know how to use it.

"I guess so. How hard can it be?"

"Harder than you think." Amburgey rose from where she was sitting and walked toward the window. "That's one thing I have discovered during these trips into the past. Things that look easy in retrospect are really quite difficult. Our modern lives are fast paced. Our ancestors worked much harder."

"I'm going to need some clothes." Symphony looked down at her outfit. She did not imagine that women wearing slacks in the workplace was acceptable in 1924.

"You will. Switchboard operators are expected to be prim, proper, and single."

"Single?"

"Yes, apparently married women are not suitable for this work. I have no idea why." She turned back around to face Symphony and rolled her eyes. "I normally wear a uniform, so I only have a couple of dresses. I'm sure they will fit you and we can go shopping tomorrow, if you get the job."

"I'll get the job."

"What makes you so sure?" Amburgey gave Symphony a raised eyebrow look.

"I love to talk. That will surely be in my favor."

"A pleasant voice will be in your favor. Remember, you were given two ears and one mouth for a reason. Being a switchboard operator will require that you listen more than speak. Make sure you do that in your interview and don't cross your legs."

"What?" Symphony looked down at her legs. She had sat down on the bed a few minutes earlier and automatically crossed her legs. She quickly uncrossed them.

"I saw a flyer about switchboard operators. Besides being prim, proper, and single, it said something about not crossing your legs or chewing gum. I don't make up the rules. Remember, we are in a different time. What's acceptable in our modern world might be the opposite in this one."

"Okay. I'll remember." Symphony watched Amburgey walk to a tall wardrobe in the corner. "I didn't even notice that piece of furniture until now. It's beautiful."

"It was rather dark when you arrived."

Amburgey smiled at Symphony. The simple action touched Symphony's heart in a way that surprised her. Tears welled up in her eyes.

"Hey, what's the matter? You are okay." Amburgey walked toward the bed and sat next to Symphony. "I didn't mean to be so hard on you. It really scared me when you arrived. People don't just appear out of nowhere, you know. My bark is worse than my bite."

Symphony tried to compose herself. Amburgey went back to the wardrobe and opened the doors. Rarely seen as a modern piece of furniture, the wardrobe had two drawers on the bottom with the top two doors opening up to reveal a little closet-like area. Despite what Amburgey had said, she seemed to have several dresses.

"I think a couple of these dresses might be nice enough for an interview. There's a nice little dress shop down the street." Amburgey pulled out a dark green dress with stripes.

"I was thinking there would be something more like the flapper dresses you see for this era."

"That's what you wear to go to out for a night on the town." Amburgey winked. "I have one of those, too. It's not what you wear for a job interview. This is what I wore when I applied for the nursing job. It was demur enough."

Symphony stood up and took the dress from Amburgey. Going over to a long mirror on the adjacent wall, she held it up in front of her. It was a below knee length drop waist dress with a loose, straight fit.

"At least there isn't a corset involved."

"Thankfully, fashion has now moved to more comfortable clothing for women. I've got one pair of dress shoes. The rest of mine are for work. You can wear my coat. I have one that goes with my uniforms."

"I really appreciate this, Amburgey. I'm sure it is getting tiresome having to look after me."

"It's okay. It's like having a little sister that you didn't know about who shows up once in a while." Amburgey laughed, then stopped, and got a faraway look in her eyes. Suddenly, she looked at her watch. "It's almost eight o'clock. You need to get ready and go to the telephone company. I will get you some underclothes and towels. There's a bathroom down the hallway. This boarding house is owned by Mrs. Bailey. There's a floor for women and a floor for men. There's one bathroom per floor. Don't wash your hair. There aren't any blow dryers in this part of the century yet. We will put your hair up in a bun. Come on, I'll show you the way."

Amburgey gathered the other clothing items and Symphony carried the dress. Like her previous experience with time travel, everything happened quickly. It made the events blur in her head. Following Amburgey down the hallway, she counted two more doors before reaching the bathroom. The small room was open. Symphony was surprised at how much it resembled older homes she visited in her own time. While Symphony paused to take in her new surroundings, Amburgey placed the clothes on the seat of the toilet. Symphony noticed that counter space was non-existent. The tub, sink, and toilet were made of white porcelain. Small black and white tiles adorned the floor. A simple white shower curtain stood ready to encircle the occupant. The only color in the room was the yellow of the window curtains and matching bath mat.

"There's a hook on the back of the door where you can hang the dress. Let the water run for a couple of minutes before you get in, but don't take too long of a shower. Mrs. Bailey will complain. I'm not sure how I am going to explain you to her, but I'm sure that it is nothing that a few more dollars a week can't cure. I will have to vouch for your chaste behavior. I've got to try and remember the name of the fellow who was so sweet on you in 1950." Amburgey turned to walk out the door. Symphony was ready to close it when Amburgey burst back through. "I know, I will say that you are a relative from…"

"West Virginia. I grew up in West Virginia. You would be telling her the truth."

"About where you are from, at least. A little white lie about you being a relative won't hurt anything. Don't take too long. Miss Bailey is already serving breakfast. I will go downstairs and talk to her about you." Amburgey pulled the door closed.

"A little white lie." Symphony laughed quietly. "Not even close."

"Yes, Mrs. Bailey. Symphony is my cousin from West Virginia. What's the name of that little town you grew up in? I can never remember it."

"Charleston." Mrs. Bailey handed Symphony a platter of fried eggs. Besides she and Amburgey, there were four other people at the breakfast table—three men and one woman. "I grew up in one of the little suburbs to the north of Charleston, Hillsdale."

"I dated a girl from Hurricane once." A middle-aged man with small round wireframe glasses and slicked back black hair spoke as

Amburgey passed the plate of eggs to him. "I met her at the West Virginia State Fair."

The other two men continued to eat without seeming to notice the man. The woman at the opposite end of the table was drinking her cup of coffee. She was dressed in a white uniform.

"Amburgey tells me that you are planning to apply for a position as a switchboard operator at the telephone company. Do you have experience in that field?"

"No. I do not. I've talked on the telephone a lot though." Symphony let out a nervous giggle. Out of the corner of her eye, she could see Amburgey shaking her head. "I've worked in offices before and had to answer the telephone and direct calls." Even to her ears, the second answer did not sound any better. Symphony decided to fill her mouth with food and let others talk.

"Kathleen is a nurse like Amburgey." Mrs. Bailey smiled and nodded in the woman's direction. The woman continued to drink her coffee.

"I've been working lots of long shifts lately." Kathleen made eye contact with Symphony. "I was hoping that Amburgey was going to say that her guest was a nurse, too. We sure could use another one."

"Is there some sort of sickness?" Symphony briefly made eye contact with Amburgey.

"No. The town and surrounding area has grown." Kathleen finally put down her coffee cup. "More people equal more illness. Lots of children with an assortment of different ailments. When one child gets the measles, the whole community of children has them."

"I hope that growth also means that the telephone company will be anxious to hire more workers." Symphony paused and took a bite of her biscuit. It amazed her how different the food tasted. Every bite she took was more delicious than the previous one. "I need to be able to earn my way here."

"We can certainly extend you a little courtesy until you get on your feet." Mrs. Bailey handed Symphony a steaming bowl of oatmeal. "Now, eat up, young lady. It would be quite unladylike for your stomach to be growling while you are being interviewed."

"That's very kind of you, Mrs. Bailey. But I have no assurance that I will even get an interview."

"Oh, yes, you do." Mrs. Bailey winked and nodded. "My nephew is the manager. I've already called him and arranged it."

"Your application says that you are single. Is that correct?"

The tall, lanky man paced in his office while reading Symphony's application. Symphony was careful not to cross her legs and to maintain perfect posture sitting in the hard chair in front of his desk. 'Lancaster Smothe' stared at her from the brass nameplate on his desk.

"Yes, sir. That is correct. I am not married."

"Do you have a beau?"

Symphony was not accustomed to such a question in her own time. She knew, however, in 1924 that type of personal inquiry was acceptable. She searched her mind for a way to honestly answer it.

"Not at this time, sir."

"Excellent. I'm sure that a lovely young woman, such as you, can have her pick of suitors." Lancaster Smothe allowed his gaze to rest on her longer than Symphony liked. "But, we have strict rules here at the telephone company. We do not employ women who have the distractions of marriage and family or those events leading up to them. Have I made myself clear?"

"Yes, sir."

"I will be periodically checking with my aunt regarding this. She keeps a close eye on the girls who board with her."

Symphony nodded with a tight smile. She said a silent prayer of thanks that she was born into a time that did not condone such an invasion of privacy. She wondered how many other employers of the era kept such close tabs on their employees.

"Mr. Smothe, may I ask you a question?"

"Certainly, Miss Wallace." The man stopped pacing and sat down in the chair behind his desk.

"I understand that there are some male telephone operators."

"Yes, we do still have a couple. We are trying to scale that back and fill these positions with women. You ladies have a gentler voice and manner with our customers." Mr. Smothe paused. "Why do you ask?"

"I was wondering if they also had to be unattached."

"No, we have employed married men in the jobs. It is usually a stepping stone to another position within in the company. Unlike married women, we know that married men are not as distracted with things going on at home. They can focus their attention on their jobs."

There were many things Symphony wished to say in response, but she did not say them. She needed the job in order to be able to support herself as long as she had to stay in 1924.

"Thank you, Mr. Smothe, for clarifying that for me. I hope you will consider me for the open position."

"What brings you to Wytheville? Do you have family here?"

"Well, my mother was from here. She lives somewhere else now."

"I see. What is the family name?"

"Gibboney." Symphony's heart missed a beat as she realized what she said. Her mind raced wondering if there were any Gibboneys in the area during 1924. She could not remember.

"I've heard that name mentioned historically. I can't say that I know any Gibboneys who currently live here, except for your cousin."

"My cousin?" Symphony tried to not look puzzled despite the fact that her eyes were darting back and forth. Her mind raced to understand whom he was talking about.

"Your cousin who you are visiting here. Her last name is Gibboney."

"Oh, yes. Amburgey Gibboney. Silly me." Symphony fluttered her eyelashes to exaggerate her forgetfulness. Apparently, the slight flirting worked with Mr. Smothe. He smiled and continued to look at her application.

"I've tried to get my aunt to invite me to dinner so that I can get to know Amburgey better. She has not found a suitable evening to do that as yet. Perhaps, you can encourage her to do so. I would be *very* grateful."

The way that he said *very* made Symphony's skin crawl. Nevertheless, she nodded and used the opportunity to make her own point.

"I suppose that could be arranged if I am able to stay in Wytheville. I will need to be employed to be able to afford my board at Mrs. Bailey's house."

"You're a sly one. I like that in a lady. I imagine that Amburgey shares the same characteristic." Lancaster Smothe wrote something on Symphony's application. "You can start to work this evening at three o'clock sharp. We will eventually move you to the overnight shift, but you must train on the evening and the day shift before you can be left alone at night. You will be training with Joy Kiracofe. She's one of our best operators. Sadly, she will be leaving us soon."

"Oh, is she moving away?"

"No. She is getting married. I said that we do not employ married women." Mr. Smothe rose from his desk and handed Symphony a sheet of paper. "It's a shame. She is an outstanding operator. Being a young couple starting out, they could probably use the money. I'm sure she will find something else to occupy her until she has children."

Symphony might end up biting her tongue in two if she had to have too many such conversations with her new employer. She could only imagine how a date with Amburgey would go. He might find himself knocked into another time. The thought made her smile.

"Is something funny?"

"No." Symphony instantly became interested in the paper that she was handed.

"You were smiling."

"I am happy to be chosen for the position, Mr. Smothe." He walked around his desk. Symphony rose from her chair. "It was a smile of happiness. I'm sure that your aunt will be pleased. Amburgey, too."

"Indeed." The expression on his face did not reveal that he was satisfied with Symphony's explanation. "Be back here this afternoon to begin training. I suggest you are early. Miss Kiracofe is quite prompt and begins her shift early. We will expect nothing less from you."

"Yes, sir." Symphony turned and began walking to the door.

"And, Miss Wallace."

"Yes." Symphony looked back over her shoulder.

"Don't forget to tell Amburgey that I am the one who is helping you stay in Wytheville." Mr. Smothe's gaze passed from her face down to her shoes. "And get some better shoes. We like our ladies to be dressed in well-kept business attire. Those shoes need polishing, at the least."

Symphony nodded. Once out of his vision, she stopped in the middle of the outer office and rolled her eyes. She did not notice that she was in view of another desk.

"You don't know the half of it. Wait till you come to work here." The woman who was speaking had beautiful red hair that was styled in a loose bun. There was something about the tone of her voice that was familiar to Symphony.

"What makes you think I have been hired?"

"Your looks, honey. Our customers don't see us through the telephone lines, but he sure does like us to look pretty." The woman lowered her voice. "You're going to have to learn not to roll your eyes before you come to work. It's not in the handbook, but Mr. Smothe doesn't like eye rolling in his girls any better than he likes wedding rings on their fingers."

"May I ask what your name is?" Symphony did not see a nameplate on the woman's desk. She could not shake the nagging feeling that she knew the woman. "I am Symphony Wallace. You are right. I start to work this afternoon."

"I can pick 'em every time." The woman smiled. "My name is Marcella White. Nice to meet you. You remember what I said. You better clean up those shoes, too."

"I WILL NEVER EVEN see a client in person." Symphony's voice was bordering on exasperation while recounting her experience with Lancaster Smothe to Amburgey when she returned to the boarding house. "What difference does it make what my shoes look like? Or even if I have any on?"

"You got the job. Great." Amburgey's sleepy voice was barely above a mumble from her position in the bed closest to the door. "Can we talk about this later? I need to sleep." Amburgey rolled over and pulled the bed sheet over her head.

"Sorry." Symphony lowered her voice. "I'll go downstairs and let you rest."

Symphony tiptoed around the room and wondered what she was going to wear that afternoon. All of a sudden, Amburgey sat up in the bed like a zombie with her eyes closed and spoke.

"I've got twenty dollars in a change purse in the bottom of my underwear drawer. Take it and go buy yourself some clothes and shoes. You can pay me back later."

Without opening her eyes or any emotion showing on her face, Amburgey fell back on the bed and immediately began snoring. Symphony was afraid to giggle despite the fact that she had witnessed a scene from a bad horror movie. Quickly and quietly, she went to the drawer and found the purse. A ten dollar bill and two fives were carefully folded within it. Symphony took the money, slid it in her pocket, and immediately headed downstairs.

Symphony saw Mrs. Bailey walking toward the kitchen when she reached the foyer near the front door.

"Symphony, I did not hear you return. How did things go with Lancaster?"

"My interview was fine, Mrs. Bailey. Mr. Smothe offered me a job." Symphony chose her words carefully.

"Wonderful. I knew he would make the right decision. Where are you hurrying off to?"

"Amburgey is sleeping, so I thought it would be a good time for me to go find a new outfit to wear this afternoon. I only brought a few clothes with me." Symphony immediately regretted offering the last detail. She hoped that Mrs. Bailey would not use it as an opportunity to question her further. "I thought I would try to find a dress shop downtown."

"We have many nice shops to choose from. I would suggest that you start with Eileen's. It's on the corner of Main and First Street. I will call ahead and tell them that you are boarding with me and getting ready to start a new job. I'm sure on my recommendation they will offer you store credit and allow you to buy some items on time."

"I appreciate that, Mrs. Bailey. But I have some money."

"Nevertheless, you might find more pretty things than your purse can handle." Mrs. Bailey laughed softly and looked at Symphony's hands. "Where is your purse?"

"Well, the handle broke while I was travelling here, so I've just slipped my money in my pocket. That's one thing I intend to purchase today. A lady must have a nice purse."

"Indeed. Lancaster likes his girls to look like ladies. You must get some nice stockings as well and some better shoes." Mrs. Bailey made a sucking sound with her teeth when she looked at Amburgey's shoes that Symphony was wearing.

"Yes. Mr. Smothe mentioned that. I better get going so that I can have some time to rest this afternoon before I go in for my first shift." Mrs. Bailey opened the door and Symphony slipped out. "Walk two blocks north and you will be on Main Street, another block to the left and you will find Eileen's. I will call ahead for you. Find some pretty things. When you return, I will have a nice lunch ready."

After walking toward the wrought iron gate that separated the yard from the street, Symphony turned to find Mrs. Bailey watching her. Symphony waved and the woman closed the door. While the woman was friendly enough, she suspected that there was a level of distrust on her part regarding Symphony's sudden arrival. She could not say that she blamed her. There would be no calls of recommendation for Symphony had Mrs. Bailey known that Symphony's true means of transportation was not by means of a railroad track but on a mystery train of time travel.

Turning in the direction that Mrs. Bailey told her to go, the majestic structures that soon came into view made Symphony realize that she was on Church Street. Despite almost a century difference in time, there was something familiar and comforting with the recognition of her whereabouts. This was the Wytheville she had come to love. The town of her birth that was quickly becoming the place she saw as her home. Lost in her thoughts, Symphony did not see that someone was walking toward her until he spoke.

"Good morning, ma'am." The man tipped his hat. "It's a lovely day to be strolling."

For the second time in less than three hours, Symphony felt like she recognized someone in 1924. As impossible as it seemed, this man was familiar to her. She decided to stop a moment and speak to him in order to stall for time and let her memory catch up.

"Good morning. It certainly is a beautiful day."

Tall and lanky, the man looked like he might have walked right out one of the old black and white movies that her Grammie loved so much. The image of Gene Kelly dancing in the rain around a light pole flashed in her mind. She bit her lip to keep from laughing.

"Makes you want to dance down the street." The man's smile was broad.

Symphony could not hold her emotions in any longer. A large laugh escaped, causing her whole body to move with continuous giggles. She suspected that the outburst was partially due to the anxiety she was feeling about travelling through time. She imagined that the man would not be so friendly if he knew where she was on the previous day.

"I promise you that my dancing ability would not be that funny."

The words were on the tip of her tongue. Symphony was a breath away from verbalizing the image that had crossed her mind. She briefly closed her eyes and held her breath. The tiredness of time travel was starting to affect her. She would need to keep her guard up to prevent herself from making references to things that occurred since 1924. This trip was going to be harder than the previous one.

"I'm sure you are a lovely dancer, sir. I was merely laughing at the wonder of it all. Here I am, a brand new resident to this fine town, and so many people are greeting me with welcome."

"My manners have fled me. I should be more of a gentleman than to so boldly speak to a young lady I have not met. Allow me to correct my error by introducing myself. The name is Tyler Gibboney. I am a relative stranger to the area myself."

Symphony thought that she once read that a sudden shock could make your heart stop. She hoped the constricted feeling she was experiencing in her chest was only the anxiety of realizing that she was face-to-face with her grandfather. Her mind went to the conversation she recently had with Nadia in which she revealed the research that indicated that this same man put the home where she and her grandmother now lived in his daughter's name in 1924.

"It's a pleasure to meet you, sir." Symphony regained her composure. She needed to use this opportunity to gain further information. "My name is Symphony Wallace."

"Miss Wallace, do you need any help finding your way around town? I've managed to walk the bulk of it over the past few days. I am an explorer by nature, even if it's only the streets in a small town."

"I am heading to a dress shop called Eileen's. The lady who I board with gave me adequate directions, I believe. I recently secured a position with the telephone company. I must find some clothing that is suitable for my new position."

"Connecting one person to another for thoughtful discourse. It seems like a simple task, yet I'm sure it requires the utmost training and concentration to master this tool of communication. My wandering mind can't help but wonder how we shall talk to one another a hundred years from now."

"You have a mind that likes to vision, Mr. Gibboney?"

"I'm afraid, it's true. It shall probably be the death of me." Tyler Gibboney pulled out a watch from a pocket in his vest. "I believe the noon chimes will soon be ringing out. It's a glorious sound. May I be so bold as to invite you to dine with me? I was planning to get a bite to eat at a small restaurant that would be on your way to the dress shop you are seeking."

Symphony's thoughts scattered through her head. She could not go on a date with her grandfather. At the same time, she could not let this opportunity to get to know him pass her by.

"I've been too forward in my invitation. Please accept my apologies, Miss Wallace. I will leave you to your plans." Tyler tipped his hat and started to walk away.

"No. Don't go. I am the one who is rude. I was trying to calculate in my mind whether I had enough time to accept your offer and also do my shopping. I have to be at the telephone company no later than three this afternoon. I must be early on my first day."

"Indeed. Punctuality is a trait most prized by an employer." Tyler paused for a moment. Symphony watched his eyes shift back and forth. "How about I walk you to the dress shop? While you are making your selections there, I will go to the diner and get us a sandwich. I would be happy to help you carry your packages back to your boarding house."

"Again, I do not mean to be forward. I really should explain myself. I am not trying to court you or be fresh. You remind me so much of my younger sister. The resemblance is uncanny. Please do not be startled."

Symphony felt sorry for the man—if he only knew how possible it was for her to have such a resemblance.

"What is your sister's name?"

"Cecelia. She is just past twenty years of age and already married. I would like to say that I liked the chap, but I was taught not to lie. He is not a total scoundrel. I fear though that he shall stifle her creativity and make her the mother of too many of his children. I have plans to whisk her off on a grand trip at even the slightest of evidence that he is not worshipping her with devotion."

"My goodness! That was quite a speech. Your sister is fortunate to have a brother who is so attentive to her happiness. I am honored to remind you of her. I believe we need to hurry on to my destination. I may need to go to more than one shop to find what I need."

"Of course. I am holding you up with my chatter. Please, walk ahead of me. I will not distract you, nor will I give the appearance that we are walking together. I understand that the telephone company has strict rules regarding their operators not being married or having suitors. We shall not start any idle gossip. After I see that you have safely reached the store, I will secure our lunch and wait for you nearby. I will make myself visible as someone who is merely assisting you with your packages—a delivery boy. It shall all be done with the utmost discretion."

While his explanation sounded complicated, Symphony knew that the era in which they found themselves had strict rules of chivalry and decorum. He was being a gentleman as she had suspected Tyler Gibboney most surely was.

Following several feet behind her, Symphony could not help but feel a surge of excitement. What a stroke of luck it was to come upon the man who would later become her grandfather. The depths of her imagination entertained the idea that perhaps it was not luck at all. Maybe Tyler Gibboney knew who she was and had orchestrated the timing of their meeting. It seemed quite an outlandish idea. Yet, the whole of her experience in Wytheville and with time travel seemed to be pulled straight from a work of fiction.

"FORD, COME TO Mama. You have got to stop running through the racks of clothing. You are going to knock that poor young lady down."

Symphony smiled as the raven-haired woman pulled her little boy out from under the dress rack where Symphony was looking. The boy could not have been much more than two years old. He appeared to be full of energy. He slipped through his mother's fingers and ran toward the small stroller that sat nearby.

"Baby." The boy smiled. He pulled on the side of the stroller to see inside. "Sista."

"He refuses to say 'Mama,' but will say 'baby' all day long." The woman shook her head. "I used to think I wanted a houseful. I'm not sure if I have the strength for it. Do you have children?"

"No. Not yet."

"I'm sorry. We seem to be about the same age. You must be a single lady looking for something to wear to work. I bet you are a secretary or a teacher or something."

The woman was tall and slender. She had a pretty face, but her eyes looked sad and tired—like they had seen too much of life already.

"It's all right. Yes, I am shopping for a dress for work. I'm starting a job at the telephone company this afternoon. I do hope to have a family one day. Your children are beautiful." Symphony peeked into the stroller to see a baby wrapped in a pale pink blanket, cooing and moving her arms and legs.

"That's what they tell us, isn't it? Find you a man. Have a baby. Make a home." She fingered the dress that was on the rack in front of her. The woman took a deep breath. She had a faraway look in her eyes. "My mama died when I was five years old. That was mighty young to learn about death. I didn't expect to be on the receiving end of it with one of my own."

Symphony remained silent after the woman paused. She glanced behind her to see the little boy playing in the floor with a box he had found. She wondered who the woman was and if she had any connection to people Symphony knew in her own time.

"My first baby died in my arms. That influenza took a hold of my Margie so fast, she was gone before we knew what was happening." Tears formed in the woman's eyes. "They don't tell you about that. Those old women who say, 'get married, have babies.' They don't tell you they can die. They don't tell you. I'd like to think that my mama's rocking my baby to sleep at night. It's a comfort. You've got to have some comfort to get you through the sadness." The woman looked straight at Symphony. Her eyes grew wide like it was the first time she saw her. "Listen to me, rambling on to a stranger. You only came in here to find a pretty dress and instead you're hearing my sad story. I'm sorry to bother you."

The woman took hold of her baby stroller and moved toward where her son was still playing. The shop clerk came out from the back while the woman was heading to the door.

"I found a pair of those shoes in your size. Let's see how they fit."

After trying on the shoes, the clerk tallied up Symphony's order. She found a dress, a skirt, two blouses, some stockings and other undergarments, the shoes, and a purse.

"Your total comes to $34.67. Mrs. Bailey called and asked us to start an account for you."

"I can't believe that's the total." Symphony shook her head. She reached into her pocket. "I would like to go ahead and pay part of it. A down payment on the credit." Symphony handed the clerk one of the five-dollar bills that Amburgey gave her.

"Well, if you think that sounds too expensive, I could ask Miss Eileen if we could discount the shoes. The other items were already marked down." The female clerk appeared to be in her late teens and furrowed her brow when she took the money from Symphony.

"Oh, no. You misunderstood me. I'm very happy with the cost. I'm amazed that I got so many things under forty dollars. Why, I expected to pay almost that much for the shoes alone!"

"My gracious. Where are you from? You must live in some really big city like New York for things to cost so much. Forty dollars for a pair of shoes!"

Symphony thanked the young woman and left. Walking out of the store, she could see Tyler leaning against the front of a building about ten feet away. Carrying her packages with both hands, she began to walk toward him, almost reaching his location before he looked up and saw her.

"It looks like your visit was successful." Tyler began taking the packages from Symphony's right arm. He handed her a brown paper bag.

"It was. I'm amazed how much I was able to purchase for so little money."

Symphony stopped herself before she said anything further about the prices. About a half block ahead on the sidewalk, she thought she saw the woman who had talked with her in the store. Looking in the window of a store they were passing, Symphony got an idea.

"Can we stop here a minute? I would like to purchase something."

"Certainly, I'll wait right here."

Within a few minutes, Symphony came out carrying a small bag.

"Do you have a sweet tooth?" Tyler commented to Symphony exiting the candy store.

"No. I think I know a young fellow who does though. We're going to have to speed up a little if we are going to catch him."

By the time Symphony and Tyler reached the woman, she had sat down to rest a minute on a bench. The little boy seemed fussy and the baby was crying.

Before Symphony realized what he was doing, Tyler set the packages down under a nearby tree and approached the woman.

"May I?" Tyler pointed to the crying baby. "I'm the oldest of seven. I've rocked a lot of babies."

The woman looked even more tired than when Symphony saw her earlier. She nodded in Tyler's direction, and he immediately leaned over the stroller and gently picked up the crying child. Symphony and the woman watched in amazement as within a few rocks and a soft humming song, Tyler had not only gotten the infant to stop crying, but she was cooing in amusement and falling asleep.

"Would you like to come home with me?" The bewildered woman blurted out. "That's not exactly what I meant to say." She bowed her head in embarrassment before surrendering to laughter. "Lemie would kill me for saying such to a stranger. I know that he would like to get some sleep, too. This little girl stays up all night like she's having a party."

"That's a mighty kind offer, ma'am. But I think I will decline. I will tell you to ask your husband to hum or sing to her. She seems to like it. I never met a girl who doesn't like for a man to sing to her. Is your husband musically inclined at all?"

"Oh, my, yes. Lemie can make a banjo come to life. He's not much on singing, but he always hums along to the tunes he plays. I will tell him that. It's a miracle."

"I was trying to catch up with you to share a little treat with this young fellow." Symphony kneeled down in front of the little boy who suddenly became shy and hid behind his mother's skirt. "I believe that I heard your mother call you Ford." The woman shook her head and smiled. "Ford, if you will come out from behind there, I have some candy for you."

Despite his young age, the boy knew the word 'candy.' He quickly came out from behind his mother smiling from ear-to-ear. Symphony looked up at his mother. She nodded her permission. Slowly and carefully, Symphony opened the bag and Ford peeked inside. He looked back at Symphony before quickly letting his little chubby hand pick a piece. Before Symphony could see what he chose, the child popped the candy in his mouth and was munching happily.

"Maybe this will make your day better. There's enough in there for Mom to have one, too." Symphony stood back up and handed the bag to the boy's mother.

"You certainly have made it better. Both of you." The woman nodded to Tyler. "I couldn't imagine why you would want to see me again. I made such a fool of myself talking to you in that store."

"You did no such thing. It was an important story for you to tell. I'm glad I was there to listen." Symphony reached out to shake the woman's hand. "My name is Symphony."

"That's a beautiful name." The woman refused Symphony's hand, opting to pull her into an embrace. "My name is Rosa. I sure do hope our paths cross again."

"I hope so, too."

"I think I better give you this little one back now." Tyler put the sleeping baby back into the stroller. "It's one o'clock."

"Oh, my goodness. I've got to go. I'm starting a new job today." Symphony turned around to see Tyler hurriedly picking up all of the packages. "It was nice to meet you, Rosa. You take care of yourself. I know there's a lot of happiness ahead for you. Let the sadness be a reminder of all the wonder that lies ahead."

The woman smiled and waved. Symphony and Tyler crossed the street and headed back down Church Street toward the boarding house. Before they were out of sight, Symphony turned and saw that the woman was still watching her. For the first time, Symphony saw a real smile cross her face and years of sadness seemed to fall away.

"SLOW DOWN. You met a man and he carried all these packages back for you from Main Street. Do men just come out of the woodwork everywhere to help you? Belcher went out of his way to even find that stupid clock. Belcher! That's his name! I was dreaming about what his name was. Oh, I'm so glad to remember that." Amburgey collapsed back on the bed.

Belcher. Symphony did not have any trouble remembering the name. Especially since she became reacquainted with him in her own time. Belcher Jones knew something about Symphony that few others did. She hoped he would not figure that out.

"At least you didn't meet your own father. I could not believe it when mine walked into the clinic the other night."

Symphony turned around from the mirror where she was trying to unsuccessfully put her hair back up into a bun. She was amazed to see how calm Amburgey seemed.

"Your father? You met him?"

"Yes. He fell and had a gash in his leg. The doctor put a few stitches in it." Amburgey rubbed her eyes. "I wonder if Mrs. Bailey has any coffee made at this time of day. What time of day is it?"

"It's almost two. I've got to get going soon. Did your father recognize you?"

"No. I believe he has not travelled to our time yet. In his journal, he wrote that he took his first trip in time to 1924. He didn't say when. I don't think I existed yet in his world."

"Do you have any idea how scary that sounds?" Symphony sat down on the edge of Amburgey's bed. "What if something happened and he decided not to take the trip to the future?"

"I guess I wouldn't exist then."

"You're not the only one." Symphony mumbled. She walked back to the mirror to finish dressing.

"What?"

"I guess you won't be too shocked then when I tell you that it was Tyler Gibboney who helped me with my packages."

"No! I cannot have my father be sweet on you. He cannot fall in love with you. He has to go to the future and meet my mother." Amburgey rose from the bed and walked toward Symphony. "You cannot see him again. Understand?"

"He's not sweet on me. He says I remind him of his sister. He was being a gentleman, chivalrous."

"His sister? Cecelia?"

"Yes. I believe that is the name he said. Did you know her?" Symphony said the words and wondered if it was even possible.

"No. I've never met her. She is somewhere in our time though. I've never been able to find her."

"In our time? How did she get there?"

"My father took her there. She was escaping from her husband. He was abusive. Only problem was that she liked the future and she disappeared. It broke my father's heart." Amburgey lay back down on the bed and then pulled the covers up around her. "Time travel has caused a lot of heartache in my family."

Symphony took a deep breath and looked at herself in the mirror. For the first time since she arrived in 1924, she pulled the pendant out from under her blouse and held it in her hand. She knew there were secrets still left for her to learn. She wondered what scars she would carry with her, once she knew them all.

Chapter Nine

"**T**HIS IS VERY IMPORTANT WORK. I hope that you will be serious about it."

For the previous hour, Symphony had listened intently as Joy Kiracofe explained how to work the complicated board that connected a telephone call from one part of the world to another.

"You must be quick, efficient, and patient with all of your customers. You must learn to understand a variety of accents and dialects as well as when a person speaks with something in their mouth."

"I'm sorry." Symphony interrupted. "Something in their mouth? What do you mean?"

"It is an unfortunate aspect of our jobs, Miss Wallace. You will find that many of the gentlemen who place calls will not show the courtesy to remove the cigars from their mouths before they ask for their number. Many people also seem to be eating while making their calls. Some who are enthusiastically chewing large wads of gum also are difficult to understand."

"Oh, I see. May we ask them to remove the impeding items?"

"No, we may not. If you have no idea what they have said, it is permissible to kindly ask them to repeat the number. You must under no circumstances ask them again."

"But, what if—"

"I said under no circumstances, Miss Wallace."

"I am fine for you to call me Symphony. May I call you Joy?"

"Thank you, Miss Wallace. No, you may not. We must always address our customers as Miss, Missus, or Mister, whether we know their names or not. I feel it is a good practice to address each other in this same fashion in order to keep our level of professionalism in constant check."

"Yes, Miss Kiracofe. I appreciate your knowledge and advice."

"Certainly, Miss Wallace. I believe that it is time for Miss Henderson to have a short break."

Miss Kiracofe nodded at the woman sitting at the far end of the telephone board. The woman took off her headphone, rising to leave the room. Symphony noticed that, even as the woman was preparing to stand, there was no change in her posture. Her back remained straight at all times, as if it was being held in a brace.

"Please observe when I answer the next few calls. Listen to what I say and how I sound. Closely watch what I do. You must maintain intense concentration to listen and carry out your task in a swift manner."

Symphony adjusted her posture. She was happy to note that, at least, the chairs had strong backs for support. She imagined that long hours would be horrendous otherwise.

"Number please...Good afternoon, Mrs. Rochester, I am happy to ring your daughter for you. Is that Baldwin 6828? Thank you, Mrs. Rochester. I am connecting you now."

"You have some of the numbers memorized?" Even Symphony could hear the sound of fear in her voice.

"You are not required to do so, Miss Wallace. It is a nice courtesy for some of our more regular customers. Mrs. Rochester is in her late seventies and calls her daughter who lives in Washington, D.C., quite frequently. The number I connected was BAL 6828. That is an urban number with three letters and four numbers. Outside of the larger cities, you will find that the format is only six digits, two letters, and four numbers. I probably don't have to go into too much detail about this. You have certainly used a telephone before."

Symphony gave Miss Kiracofe a forced smile. She thought how to properly answer her question. While phones in the twenty-first century still had numbers, the modern way that they could be stored meant that they were not often dialed directly.

"All my life." Symphony tried to maintain the professional, positive sound that Miss Kiracofe stressed, even though inside she was not positive at all about what she was saying.

"Then, some form of the number system should be quite familiar to you."

"Number, please...Market 7032. I will connect you sir...I'm sorry, sir, that number is busy. Certainly. Thank you, sir."

"Do you offer to take any sort of message if a number is busy?" Even as the words left her mouth, Symphony knew that it was the wrong thing to say.

"No. We do not." Miss Kiracofe paused and stared at Symphony. The power of her stare was almost overwhelming. "I must say, that is a very smart thought though. It shows that you are interested in the customer and his or her satisfaction." Miss Kiracofe looked around them. She lowered her voice. "I have been known to ring back some of our local customers, especially our distinguished ones, to let them know that the line they tried to call had become open. They seem quite appreciative when I do that. Some have made comments to Mr. Smothe when they have seen him. It's a little extra touch of service."

During the hour before five o'clock and the hours between seven and nine, Symphony could barely keep up watching Miss Kiracofe and Miss Henderson navigate the large telephone panel. It was larger than the one she saw on display at the Boyd Museum. Despite being a small community in population, the telephone office in Wytheville was a central one in the region, and had handled calls for smaller communities that surrounded it.

"You've done quite well, Miss Wallace." Miss Kiracofe commended her while they rose from their chairs so that the overnight operator could take over. "You are a little slow making the physical connections of the line to the board. Your speed will develop with time and more familiarity with the equipment. Your diction and elocution is outstanding. Do you have a teacher in your family? Your mother, perhaps?"

"No. My mother is a nurse." At that moment, it dawned on her that both her adopted and biological mothers were nurses. At least, Amburgey was endeavoring to be one at that time.

"And your father?"

"He's a meteorologist." Symphony's thoughts were still on her mothers' occupations when she answered the last question.

"A what?" Miss Kiracofe turned around and gave Symphony a puzzled look.

"A meter operator." Symphony's words came out slowly. Her mind rushed for an explanation. "It has something to do with science and engineering, I think."

"Hmm. I have not heard that term before. Science is an ever-changing endeavor. It's just amazing what people can invent. I read an article in the newspaper a while ago about a man who had invented a machine that could tell whether or not someone was lying. Isn't that amazing?"

"Amazing, indeed." Symphony hoped that man did not decide to pass through Wytheville with his invention any time soon. "Thank you for your patience with me, Miss Kiracofe. I will see you tomorrow evening."

"Good night, Miss Wallace. It's been my pleasure."

"It was so warm yesterday. I can hardly believe that it is early March."

After a hard, sound sleep, Symphony woke up the following morning full of energy. She was already showered and dressed by the time that Amburgey returned from a long night at the clinic.

"I cannot drink coffee." Amburgey mumbled sitting down at the breakfast table. "I really need to sleep. I would go right to bed if it wasn't for the fact that I never got to eat during the night. I don't think I ate anything before I went to work. It's been almost twenty-four hours."

"Fasting can be good for the body." Kathleen, the nurse who was also boarding there, poured her second cup of coffee. "It can cleanse your system."

"I'm not so interested in being cleansed." Amburgey glared at the woman. "I'm more of the likes to be nourished type. Pass the pancakes, Symphony, and those eggs, too."

Symphony knew better than to stand between Amburgey and

her food. It was a trait that she inherited honestly. Symphony never had a problem with her appetite.

"Our seasons are less pronounced in the last few years." Mr. Edgar Barker was the oldest man at the table. "I believe it has to do with changes in our atmosphere that we are not even aware of yet."

"Mr. Barker was a professor at the University of Virginia." Mrs. Bailey passed the plate of sausage and bacon to Amburgey. Symphony snagged a piece of bacon when it went by.

"How interesting!" A good night's rest had made Symphony chatty. Her second morning at the breakfast table in 1924 was feeling more comfortable than she imagined it would. "What did you teach, Mr. Barker?"

"I taught history for thirty-five years." The man's voice was strong and clear. His years of age did not weaken his voice. Symphony wondered if years of lecturing had strengthened his vocal chords, like a singer whose voice grows stronger with age.

"Mr. Barker was the dean of history. Isn't that right?" Mrs. Bailey began to eat from a small bowl of oatmeal in front of her. "Such a distinguished position. We are so honored that he came back to Wytheville to retire. He's almost single-handedly created our local historical society."

"Historical preservation is the backbone of the future. We cannot make tomorrow better unless we remember the mistakes of yesterday."

Symphony thought about the truth in Mr. Barker's words. She was beginning to realize that she might be making the same mistakes that Amburgey and Tyler had made. A chill ran down her spine. It was possible to become stuck in the era of time she now occupied.

"Is something wrong, Symphony? You look sad." Mrs. Bailey reached out and touched Symphony's hand from her seat next to her. "Did everything go well with your first day of work?"

"Yes, ma'am. It was fine." Symphony smiled at the woman. She was fortunate to have found people in this time that cared and were concerned for a stranger. "I am being trained by Miss Joy Kiracofe. She is quite knowledgeable and efficient."

"Lancaster has often spoken of the young lady's dedication and strong work ethic. He was so sorry to hear of her intent to marry." Mrs. Bailey took a long sip of her coffee. "It is the natural progression of life though."

"Mrs. Bailey, don't you think it is unfortunate that good workers who are female must leave their jobs because they wish to marry?"

Amburgey cleared her throat and pinched Symphony on the leg again.

"I'm sure that it does seem unfair, Symphony." Mrs. Bailey set her coffee cup down on its saucer. The action made a clicking noise that seemed extra loud in the quiet room.

"I realize that it is the way of the world, so to speak." Symphony took a deep breath. "I find it to be stifling to productivity. I'm sure that the telephone company has difficulty finding those who can master the workings of the switchboard while maintaining a pleasant manner. Women don't lose their skills and talents only because they put a gold band on their fingers."

Amburgey choked on the food she was eating. Kathleen jumped up to her aid. Amburgey's first drink of water did not seem to clear it. A few moments later, once the initial threat passed, she was still coughing and glaring at Symphony.

"You are young, Symphony. You have much to learn about the rules that this life puts upon women." Mrs. Bailey's answer surprised Symphony. "Fair is not always a word that applies to the female portion of our species. When my Joseph passed, we had a store that we operated together, side-by-side. The store was in his family for two generations, but his brothers had no interest in it. After his death, they did not think that their sister-in-law could operate it by herself. I can assure you that I would have managed it far better than them. It was sold right out from under me. I took Joseph's portion of the sale and bought this house. Thankfully, I was able to turn it into a thriving business that supports me."

"You have done an outstanding job, if I may say so, Mrs. Bailey." Mr. Barker gave his praise. "It is far superior to any such establishment I have lived in, and I have lived in many."

"Thank you, Mr. Barker. My brothers-in-law advised me to remarry while I was still young. I was not interested. The love of my life was gone. I had no use for another man."

"Ah, instead you have had many of us bachelors to keep in line." Symphony could not remember the name of the short, heavyset man in the seat next to Kathleen. She knew that he was employed by the railroad. "You might have had more peace with just one of us, instead of several." The man laughed heartily.

"That is true, Mr. Peterson. I have enjoyed having pleasant conversations with all over the years. You are family." Mrs. Bailey turned back to Symphony. "I do not disagree with your opinion on the matter of what women are allowed to do. In my younger days, when I lived in another part of this country, I marched for the cause of suffrage. I have voted each time I could since women were given the right. Despite that, I do not have blinders on as to how the world works in this time. It is still a man's world. I have seen changes. Perhaps, I shall live to see more."

"I would imagine that these young women at this table do not know that a First Lady came from this town." Mr. Barker looked around. Neither Amburgey nor Symphony showed their knowledge. It was Kathleen who answered him.

"From this little place? I have never heard such."

"Edith Bolling was born in Wytheville in October of 1872." Symphony imagined that they were about to hear one of Mr. Barker's lectures. "Her father was a judge. The family lived on Main Street and Edith grew up in this small town. While visiting her married sister in Washington, D.C., she met Norman Galt. He was a prominent jeweler. They married in 1896 and remained so until his unexpected death in 1908. Edith was introduced to the widowed President Woodrow Wilson in early 1915. Within less than a year, the two were married. She was the First Lady until 1921." Mr. Barker took another helping of pancakes when he finished.

"Mrs. Wilson is from Wytheville?" Kathleen shook her head. She rose from the table. "It's barely been a month since President Wilson passed. I knew that he was a Virginian. It never crossed my mind that she was. Very interesting, Mr. Barker. I'm off to work. See you folks this evening."

"I liked Mrs. Wilson." Mrs. Bailey waved to Kathleen. "The Bolling family still lived here when I first came to Wytheville. Mrs. Bolling, the mother of the First Lady, would shop in our store. She was a pleasant lady, quite distinguished. When Edith became our First Lady, I read the newspaper articles closely for mentions of her. She was flamboyant and fashionable. She enjoyed travel. We didn't fully realize at the time how influential she was on the President. We didn't know how sick he was."

"It will indeed be interesting to see how history remembers this native daughter of our community." Mr. Barker wiped his mouth with a napkin and then rose from the table. "I have a feeling that Edith Wilson had the President's ear long before he took ill. Maybe someday history will reveal the true level of her influence on him and her role in the White House."

Symphony remained silent watching Mr. Barker say his goodbyes. She continued to quietly eat even when Amburgey rose and announced she was going to bed.

"It's just the two of us now, Symphony." Mrs. Bailey poured herself another cup of coffee. "You grew quiet as our conversation continued."

"Perhaps, I spoke out of turn, Mrs. Bailey. I did not want you to think I was complaining about my job or Mr. Smothe. I find it hard to understand why an industrious young woman like Miss Kiracofe has to leave work that she excels in because her last name changes."

"It is a challenge for any woman to understand who has goals and aspirations beyond the socially accepted roles that society has designed for her. I will confide in you that I have taken Lancaster to task on more than one occasion about this very topic. While he willingly complies with the rule, I do not think he completely agrees with it. Miss Kiracofe is not the first capable employee that he has lost to such foolishness. It is equally hard for him to find young women, such as yourself, who do not solely have a mission to work until they find a husband. You will see that it makes the door of employment swing open and closed more often than it should. Learn all you can from Joy. She is probably the best switchboard operator they have ever had. I believe she truly enjoys her work. Her mother told me that she feared her suitor would grow tired of waiting on her. Their engagement is almost two years now. I suppose she finally decided that she loved him more than she enjoyed her job."

"It would be nice to not have to make such a choice." While Symphony knew she lived during a time and in a country where that was not an obvious issue, she still wondered how many women made such choices quietly, one way or another.

"I do not know what your story is, Symphony. I believe that

you turned up on my doorstep rather suddenly. Perhaps you are searching for something. Maybe you needed to make a new start. It really doesn't matter. You are here now. It's up to you to make the most of your time in Wytheville and make the type of change that will most benefit your future." Mrs. Bailey drank the last of her coffee and rose from the table. "Why don't you go out and learn about our little town? I think you will find that a First Lady is not the only interesting person to have passed through here."

"I already know that, Mrs. Bailey. I think I had breakfast with one of the most interesting and enlightened women to ever live in Wytheville." Symphony walked around the long table toward the doorway. "I appreciate your kindness and confidence. To reassure you, I am not in any sort of trouble. This visit to Wytheville is a change of scenery."

"I had no doubt that you were not running from mischief." Mrs. Bailey laughed. "Amburgey is another story. I believe trouble finds her wherever she goes." Mrs. Bailey left the room.

"Perhaps that's why she keeps travelling." Symphony whispered and walked to the front door.

"It looks so different in color." Symphony stood at the corner of Church and Main Streets and looked as far as she could see both ways. "All the photos I saw were in black and white."

"You know what happens if you stand on the street and talk to yourself?" Tyler Gibboney spoke to Symphony over her right shoulder, causing her to jump. "A strange man will come up behind you and scare you."

"That is a self-fulfilling prophecy." Symphony tried to shake off the scared feeling when she turned toward Tyler.

"What type of prophecy?"

"Never mind. I was joking."

"No. I want to know what you mean. I tend to like anything that has to do with prophecies. I consider myself a futuristic type of fellow."

"A self-fulfilling prophecy is a prediction that causes itself to come true."

"Oh, I see. I'm the strange man I predicted. I was the butt of my own joke."

"Exactly." Symphony looked at the clock in the center of town. "It's almost ten o'clock. Don't you have a job, Mr. Gibboney?"

"Yes, I do, Miss Wallace. I am a travelling businessman. Currently, I'm in the travelling phase. Later, I will be doing business." Tyler gave her a wide grin. "How did your first shift of telephone work go? Did you talk to anyone in Europe?"

"No. I believe the farthest away that we had a telephone call from was New York City. I think I am going to like the work, if I can get the hang of moving those long cords from one plug to another."

"I suppose that ladies with longer legs and arms are the most efficient in that aspect. Your voice is crisp and soothing though. I believe your customers will enjoy talking to you, as I have."

There was a lull in the conversation as a Ford Model T car drove by and honked its horn. The 'aaoogha' sound reminded Symphony of the old movies she watched with Grammie Wallace. She wondered what her grandmother would think of Symphony being in the era of her Grammie's childhood.

"Do you think any of that candy is left that I gave the little boy?" Symphony's train of thought was jarred when she saw a little girl wave to her from across the street.

"Not a chance. His mother probably cursed you when she had to try and get him to go to bed."

"I think that she and I are close to the same age. Our lives are so different."

"If I may say so, you seem more like a girl who should be living in the city. I see you in a business suit and heels, working in a tall building in the business district. After work, you meet a group of friends for cocktails, and then go dancing at the latest club. What brought you to this small town?"

"I guess it was my time to come here." Symphony was amazed that she was making such a statement to her time travelling grandfather. "We have to go one place before we go to another. We have to be in one time to get to the next."

"Time. I have a great interest in it. I don't think we challenge it near enough."

"Mr. Gibboney, I am out to take a stroll and learn a little about this new town I live in. You are welcome to walk with me and enlighten me about your theories."

"You are not concerned that your employer might hear that you are strolling with a handsome stranger." Tyler winked and looked behind them.

"Since I know so few people here, everyone is a stranger. I can only tell the truth and say that I was befriended by a kind man who said I reminded him of his sister."

"Indeed. The truth is the best defense." Tyler extended his hand, directing Symphony to walk in front of him. "Since we are going to spend some time becoming acquainted with this town, I believe it would be appropriate for us to be more acquainted. Please call me Tyler. May I address you as Symphony?"

"Certainly. I am not one to prescribe to formality for formality's sake. Sometimes it seems quite impersonal and cold."

"I would agree. I must say I have not been formally introduced to many people here. Those I have met are gentile and hospitable."

"Likewise. True southern hospitality at its finest. I suppose that is because it is a town that frequently has visitors."

"I was not aware of that."

"Uh, I believe I learned that at the boarding house." Symphony scrambled to come up with a way she would know that information. "I believe Mrs. Bailey talked about it."

"It makes sense, especially for those in the deeper South. This mountain air would be cooler in the spring and summer months. It would probably offer a gentler winter than in the North."

"Exactly."

The two grew silent and continued walking. They passed several buildings that Symphony did not recognize from her own time. She remembered that her research revealed many were destroyed. Despite the history that seemed engraved into the very spirit of the Wytheville she lived in, the town in 1924 seemed quite different.

"You seem lost in thought."

"I was thinking about what this town will be like in a hundred years. What is here now that shall remain then? What new structures will replace what we are walking past today?"

"Ever since our ancestors came to this great land, they seem to be preoccupied with changing it. Our buildings get taller and hide the horizon that so lured our forefathers. The descriptions of the beauty of the land from the earliest days contain little details about structures; even homes are only mentioned as places where they found rest and solace." They stopped walking. Tyler continued talking. "I fear that in our quest to make this new world into a country of freedom and opportunity, we are losing the wide open spaces and untouched lands that were so attractive to those first settlers who came here. I can only imagine that our descendants will even build more, until all a town shall be judged by is the length of its streets and what can be found there."

Symphony turned to look at the grand home that was visible from the sidewalk. She knew it did not exist in her time and thought it was the grand house that belonged to the man who in 1924 was Governor of Virginia. Her curiosity caused her to stop a man who was walking by.

"Could you tell me who lives here?"

"Certainly. This is the Trinkle home. I believe that it is currently vacant as Mr. E. Lee Trinkle is currently the Commonwealth's governor."

"Thank you." Symphony smiled. The man tipped his hat and walked away.

"I think it is quite interesting, Tyler, that this little town produced a First Lady and a Governor who served successively. I wonder if they might have been school chums."

"First Lady?"

"Mrs. Wilson. The second Mrs. Wilson."

"Edith Wilson was from Wytheville?" A puzzled look crossed Tyler's face. "I had no idea. I suppose though that I would not have recognized the name of this town before I first came here. It is unusual though."

"There's only one."

"Only one what?"

"There's only one town in the world named Wytheville."

"How could you possibly know that?"

"I…well…Mr. Barker told me." Symphony bit her lower lip and closed her eyes.

"Mr. Barker?"

"Yes. He's a retired professor of history who lives at the boarding house. He makes quite an interesting dining companion."

"I don't understand how he can know that there is only one town in the world named Wytheville."

Symphony knew she had the information to back up the statement. It would be impossible for her to reveal that town officials in the twenty-first century did the necessary research to determine that it was true. She heard one such official tell a story that Symphony thought Tyler might believe. It was worth a shot.

"Mr. Barker says that the pastor of his church suspected that the town's name was unique. While he was travelling in Europe, he sent the Mayor of Wytheville a postcard that was simply addressed with the person's name with the word 'Wytheville' as the only address. It took a couple of months, but the card eventually arrived. Do you know the reason why?" Tyler shook his head negatively. "Because it had nowhere else to go. There is only one Wytheville and it resides in the state of Virginia." Symphony gave Tyler a smug smile. She turned back and looked once more at the grand home.

"To have only been here such a short time, you certainly do have a vast knowledge of this community." Symphony remained silent. "I like that. I'm quite impressed."

The little she read of Tyler's diary told her that she was the one who should be impressed. While his adventures could, perhaps, be described reckless where his family was concerned, the level of bravery that it took to willingly go on his many time travel journeys could not be ignored. Symphony hoped she inherited a smidgen of that same courage.

There were many questions that Symphony was eager to ask Tyler. On that morning, she chose to use restraint and only engage in the chitchat that presented itself while they meandered down the streets of Wytheville. For the most part, she had little recognition of the names of the businesses she passed. With almost a hundred years having passed into the time of her present, Symphony would be hard pressed to find a business that was still in operation. As they paused in front of one business, however, in the center of the downtown district, a name struck her that she knew was aligned with the history that brought her there.

"Victory Merchandise Company, Saul Alper, Proprietor." Symphony read the sign aloud.

"Would you like to go inside?" Tyler looked inside the window. "It looks like a nice store. I've not had the opportunity to make Mr. Alper's acquaintance.

"Yes. Let's do that. It will soon be time for me to go back to the boarding house and get ready for work."

Tyler opened the door. The jingle of a bell chimed overhead, causing Symphony to look up to see the brass fixture attached to the tall door. Walking inside, she saw rows of built-in shelves lining the long walls on each side with counter space in front of it. Down the middle of the floor were tables piled with a variety of items. While the name did not reveal the store's contents, at least to her, it appeared that it was a mercantile-like business that offered many different types of products—a general store.

"Good morning to you." A tall, lanky man walked from the back of the store at a brisk pace. His stride appeared to cover several feet at a time with each step. "How may I help you?"

"Hello. I am new to town and wanted to see what type of goods you had to offer." Symphony ran her finger over a bundle of fabric. "You have quite a selection."

"Only the finest quality of goods shall carry the name Alper. I daresay you will not find any finer merchandise in any store in this town, or for a hundred miles in each direction." The man adjusted his wireframe glasses and ran his hand over his shiny black hair in one smooth movement.

"Are you Mr. Alper?"

"I am indeed, ma'am. Saul Alper, proprietor of Victory Merchandise Company. My family has been in the mercantile business for three generations. The gentleman you see coming toward us is my brother-in-law, Herman Sollod. Herman knows our entire inventory. If we do not have an item you need, we can certainly order it."

Symphony nodded as Herman Sollod walked toward them. Even in height with Mr. Alper, Mr. Sollod's fair features were in stark contrast to his brother-in-law.

"Did you say that you and your husband recently moved to our town?" Mr. Alper looked at Tyler. "I do not believe I have met you before, sir." Mr. Alper walked a few steps toward Tyler and extended his hand.

"Miss Wallace and I are not married." Tyler took the man's hand and firmly shook it. The force of the action made Symphony wonder if Tyler was trying to make a point of some sort with the man. "My name is Tyler Gibboney. I have only recently become acquainted with Miss Wallace. Our shared newness to Wytheville made us logical comrades to learn to navigate the streets and neighborhoods of your fair town."

"I see. What brings you to Wytheville, Mr. Gibboney?"

"Business. I am a travelling businessman. Wytheville was intended to merely be an overnight stop while I waited on the next train. I found it to be quite welcoming and intriguing, so I have extended my visit."

"And you, Miss Wallace? Are you here on business as well?"

Symphony thought that Mr. Alper was being quite inquisitive for a shop owner. She could not afford to have him wonder about her origin though.

"I came to visit my cousin. She boards at Mrs. Bailey's. My intent was to stay awhile and secure employment, which I am happy to say that I have."

"I see. Welcome to Wytheville. As a new resident, you will likely have the need to purchase items that our store could provide. You will see in the back that we have a lovely section of ladies clothing items and accessories as well as a good selection of toiletries. My wife insists that we carry makeup and perfumes." Symphony followed Mr. Alper to the rear of the store.

"I see that you have strategically placed the items that women will be interested in the rear of the store so that they will have to pass by and view all of the other wares." Symphony smiled when Mr. Alper gave her a surprised look.

"Miss Wallace, that statement leads me to believe that you have worked in a store before."

"I have indeed, Mr. Alper. I know the look of a carefully designed floorplan." Symphony hoped that she would not be asked specifics regarding her retail experience. She was not prepared to try to describe the concept of a 'mall' to a rural storeowner of the early twentieth century. "It is a testament to your mercantile talents."

"I must say I am very impressed. What type of employment have you secured? We might be interested in hiring another clerk when spring breaks."

Symphony looked over Mr. Alper's shoulder to the spot where Tyler was looking at men's hats. He rolled his eyes and shook his head in amusement.

"I started employment with the telephone company as a switchboard operator yesterday. I appreciate your kind words, but I believe I will give this new job a chance before I consider any others."

"I understand. That was forward of me, I apologize. It is rare to encounter a lady, such as yourself, in this area who has worked in shop keeping. I was fortunate to marry into a family who were in such a business. Herman and his sister, my wife, began working in their grandfather's store when they were barely old enough to reach the counter. Since the birth of our first child, my wife has not had as much time to devote to our business. I miss a woman's touch in our displays."

"This woman must use that touch on our son and help him to grow to be a great man like his father."

Symphony turned to see a small woman approaching through a doorway that was hidden behind a curtain in the far left corner of the store. On her hip was a toddler with dark curls. The woman drew closer and Symphony could see that she was also carrying an unborn child. The little boy appeared to be around two or three years old. He shook a small rattle. When his big blue eyes met Symphony's, he held the rattle out to her.

"Melvin must see something quite special within." The mother smiled. "He does not offer his precious toy to even his mother."

Slowly, Symphony took the rattle from the little boy's hand. She felt a spark pass through her fingers when the silver metal touched her skin. A cold chill ran down Symphony's spine. Her mind circled back to the story she read before leaving her own time. The fire forced a young family to jump from their second story home. A child was thrown to someone on the ground. Now Symphony knew what drew her into this particular store.

"Are you alright?" The mother's voice brought Symphony back to the present. "You suddenly look pale."

"I'm fine. I just remembered something that I need to do."

Symphony turned to find Tyler, jumping when she realized he was right behind her. The rattle slipped through her fingertips, landing on the top of Tyler's shoe. He bent to retrieve it as Symphony returned her attention to the woman.

"I'm sorry, but I have to go. It was a pleasure to meet all of you." Symphony forced a smile and turned to walk away. She felt the woman's hand on her arm.

"What is your name?" Her voice was soft and melodic, calming.

"My name is Symphony."

"Symphony. The beautiful music of your heart mesmerized my son. It calmed the kicking of the one who grows inside me. My name is Fannie. You shall come back and visit us again. We shall go upstairs and drink tea while these silly men do the business of selling things."

Symphony's eyes locked with Fannie. While she could not make it out, Symphony knew that a silent message passed between them.

Chapter Ten

"NUMBER, PLEASE...YES, SIR. I would be happy to connect you with Remington 4972 in the city of Nashville, Tennessee. Please stay on the line while I attempt to connect you."

On her fourth night on the job, Symphony was allowed to work by herself under the watchful eye of Miss Kiracofe.

"You seem so at ease with the equipment this evening, Miss Wallace. I must say that you are the fastest learner of any of the new operators I have trained. I feel so relieved and confident to be leaving you on this staff when I depart." Miss Kiracofe set down the small paper tablet she was using to take notes on the table beside her. "I recommended to Mr. Smothe that he leave you on evening shift, rather than overnight. I've worried that our evening customers would not get the attention they need. I'm sure you have observed Miss Van Dyke is not conscientious with her duties. I am recommending that she be moved to overnight shift when there are far less calls to connect."

A few minutes of silence passed with the lines quiet. A question that Symphony wanted to ask was dancing on the tip of her tongue, daring her to utter it. She did not want to ruin the moment of praise from Miss Kiracofe. Yet, she knew lulls in telephone calls, such as they were experiencing, were rare.

"I hope that you do not think I am being too nosy. I know that we only have a limited amount of time together before you leave. I would love to know a little about your fiancé. I realize that this type of talk Mr. Smothe does not want us to have. But, we are human, nonetheless, and curious to know about each other's lives. Would you indulge a single girl a little glimpse into your romance?"

Miss Kiracofe pursed her lips and gave Symphony a disapproving look over top of her wireframe glasses that sat on the end of her nose. Despite the expression, Symphony saw a glimmer of whimsy in Miss Kiracofe's eyes. Those eyes darted to each side, like she was searching for something, before they rested squarely back on Symphony.

"John is a quiet man. For every five words he utters, I voice one hundred. Yet, it is in his quiet that he reveals his soul. We met at a church picnic, a few towns away. I was visiting my grandparents for a week in the summer of my eighteenth year. I had no designs on romance. My head was in a book, literally. I made a goal to read as many of the classics as my eyes could consume during that summer— the months before I was to enter Radford College. I grabbed a ham biscuit and an apple from the picnic spread and found a tall oak tree to sit under while I read *Moby Dick* by Mr. Herman Melville."

Symphony watched the woman get lost in her own memories. She imagined that Joy Kiracofe was taking her own time travel journey to a time far closer than Symphony's.

"All of a sudden, a shadow was blocking my sunlight. I looked up and saw a tall, thin, young man looking down at me. He had on a pale blue shirt with dark blue pants, white suspenders, and a straw hat like someone would wear in a picture show. Despite the fact that he was interfering with my reading, I was intrigued by this unusually attired fellow standing before me."

"A man that comes between a woman and her book is indeed a brave soul."

"Indeed. I would rather get lost in the nourishment of the words of a story than in a banquet of food."

Miss Kiracofe's slender form made Symphony wonder if the woman might truly be making a literal statement. During the brief time they worked together, Symphony frequently saw the woman eating an apple on her break, huddled in the corner with a thick book on her lap.

"Without so much as an introduction, the young man sat down next to me by the tree and proceeded to ask me what I was reading. When I told him, he began to ramble on about his theories regarding the hidden meanings in different parts of the story. I had to hold my hand up to get him to stop talking. I did not want him to reveal the details of the ending of the story before I had a chance to read it for myself." Miss Kiracofe furrowed her brow in a look of irritation.

"It sounds like you met a kindred spirit that day."

"I did." The whimsical expression returned. "I did not let it hinder my goal of an education. I only allowed John to visit me once a month. The rest of the time we corresponded through letters. I completed my studies to become a teacher, and then returned home to live. We became engaged almost two years ago. I wanted to be sure and I wanted him to become more established."

"What does he do?"

"He is a law clerk for a judge in a neighboring county. John is the senior clerk now."

"May I ask why you are working here, a telephone operator, instead of teaching?"

"There have not been any openings nearby. There is a teacher retiring soon at a school near where John and I plan to live. I am promised the position."

"I'm sure you shall make a wonderful teacher. You have made it so easy for me to understand this job. Your patience is extraordinary."

"You are a good student, Miss Wallace. I've learned patience because most of those who I have trained have not taken their duties seriously enough. It can be a trying experience to teach someone who only wants to learn enough to be paid. I hope future generations will be different."

Symphony wondered how Miss Kiracofe would feel about the modern workforce. Her patience might wear thin if she was teaching in Symphony's time.

"You asked me about my intended so I shall give you a bit of unsolicited advice." Miss Kiracofe's voice took a serious tone. "Seek someone who you have enough in common with to be compatible, but not enough to become bored. I believe that marriage should be a lifelong mystery with clues gradually presenting themselves to help you understand your beloved's soul. Find someone who would travel to the end of time for you, or with you, if necessary."

The mention of travelling in time caught Symphony off guard and intrigued her. It made her wonder if Miss Kiracofe knew something she was not revealing. She seemed to be daring Symphony to ask a forbidden question.

"Do you believe in the possibility of time travel, Miss Kiracofe?" Symphony held her breath and waited for the woman's reaction.

"There are those who have theorized the possibility. I read some of the work of a Mr. Albert Einstein who has some interesting speculations about time."

"It may be the stuff of fiction and fairytales." Symphony chose to remain silent about the mention of Einstein. "Yet, in a vast universe, isn't anything possible?"

"I would agree. If we do not allow our minds to dream beyond our knowledge, how can we ever expect to understand the mysteries that surround us?"

Before Symphony could respond, the ring of a call interrupted their discussion. She wondered if Miss Kiracofe was so caught up in the conversation that she forgot who was supposed to be handling the calls. Several came in with quick succession over the next fifteen minutes with only short lulls between. There was a complicated overseas call later that was handled by Miss Kiracofe with Symphony standing close beside her to listen to the details and to learn how it would be transferred. It was the call that closed out their shift.

"You did an excellent job this evening." Miss Kiracofe picked up her belongings. Symphony waited in the doorway. "I enjoyed our chat." Symphony smiled and continued walking with her. "Symphony?" Turning back toward her, she saw Miss Kiracofe's face light up in a smile. "Please call me Joy."

THE FOLLOWING DAYS flew by in quick succession. To her surprise, Symphony was left to handle the evening switchboard shift on her own. Multiple workers quit on dayshift and Joy was moved to that timeslot to train three operators at once. The young woman looked harried each afternoon when Symphony took over. She always stayed a few minutes for a quick chat.

Working opposite shifts meant that Symphony saw little of Amburgey. It began to distress her that she seemed to be living in 1924 without learning anything to further solve the mystery of Amburgey's obsession with time travel.

"You are spending this evening with me. We are going out."

It was a Friday morning—February 29, 1924. The night before, Symphony completed nine straight nights of work. On Sunday evening, she would begin her normal schedule of five evenings working with two off. She lost track of the number of days straight Amburgey worked, including some including double shifts. Influenza hit the town in recent days causing more patients to come to the clinic each night. They were both exhausted.

"I don't know. I was planning to get as much extra sleep as possible." Having returned to their upstairs room after one of Mrs. Bailey's hearty breakfasts, Symphony looked longingly at her bed. "What is there to do here on a Friday night?"

"It's nothing like the world we are used to, but there's more than you might expect. I was thinking that we would have dinner somewhere, and then catch whatever the show is at the Opera House."

"What is an opera house exactly?" Symphony stretched out on her bed while Amburgey changed into her nightgown. "Somehow I don't think it's only women with high voices performing. That would seem rather limiting in a small town like this." Her body relaxed into the mattress; Symphony noted that second helping of pancakes probably was not a good idea.

"I don't know exactly. I think it's really an entertainment venue. Kind of like a modern concert theater. I've only been there once, but I've read the posters about upcoming acts. There seems to be a variety of types of entertainment including theatre, comedy, music, movies, and even circus-like events. It's Friday night, there's bound to be something fun. I want fun. I need fun." Amburgey collapsed onto the other twin bed. "I might as well enjoy myself. I'm deeply concerned that you are going to marry Tyler Gibboney and make my existence impossible."

"Good grief! I'm not going to marry Tyler. I've told you that our friendship is purely platonic. Besides, it would be virtually impossible anyway."

"And why is that?" Amburgey sat straight up in the bed and looked Symphony squarely in the eyes. "Why is it impossible?"

"Ah." Symphony's mind was not helping her get out of that blunder. Her pancake fog was making her say dangerous things. She would have to come up with a lie. "I think he might already be married." Even though her heart started beating again, it did not mean that Symphony was relieved.

"Married? It never occurred to me that he might be married in this time. Did he say something about having a wife? That would help explain why he kept coming back to this time. He seemed devoted to my mother. It's hard to imagine he was living a double life."

"If your father had a life in this time and in a time in the future, he was living a double life. I shouldn't have said anything about him being married. I don't have anything to substantiate that." A sick feeling began to form in the pit of Symphony's stomach. It was not pancakes. It was regret.

"Then, why did you say it?" Symphony could see tears forming in Amburgey's eyes. "I'm so tired. I'm so worried. I have to work to live in this blasted time, and it doesn't leave me much opportunity to search for what I'm trying to find. I thought it was good having you here. Someone to talk with about this stuff. Maybe I was wrong." One of the tears slid down Amburgey's face. She squinted her eyes in anger. "I don't even know why you are here."

"I made it up. I'm sorry. Tyler never said anything about being married. I don't want you to think I'm interested in him. I'm not going to steal him from your mother. That's the furthest thing from my mind. You have helped me very much. I wanted to help you. If I get to know him, I can help you find out what you want to know."

"Why would you think that?" The expression on Amburgey's face remained unchanged. The trust was gone from her eyes. "He's my father, yes. He's not who I am looking for."

"Oh, I thought you said that your father disappeared and you thought he travelled back in time."

"He did. He's the reason I knew that I could travel. He's not the reason I chose to do so. I know that I shouldn't really occupy the same time and space with him here. It's unnatural. It could mess up my future. He taught me that much before he left. Dad told me not to ever connect with him in the past, if I could prevent it."

"Then, why are you here? Who are you looking for?"

"I'm looking for the man of my dreams."

"The man of your dreams?" Symphony furrowed her brow and then lay back down on the bed. "Can't you go to sleep and find him?"

"That's the thing. I found him in my dreams. Then I found a photograph of him. It was like I instantly fell in love. My heart recognized this man from my dreams. I knew I had to find him."

"You had to find him, even if that meant the danger of travelling to another time?"

"Yes. Isn't that how true love is supposed to be?"

Symphony stared at the ceiling. Amburgey revealed more than Symphony anticipated. The information made more questions fill her head.

"Is that why you were in 1950?"

"Yes. The photo of him made it impossible to tell what

time period it was from. It was black and white, but without any identifying factors like a vehicle or some item that would indicate in what era it was taken. I took it to a friend of my stepfather's from a local university. He was a history professor. He said that he could not determine when it was taken. Sometime after the invention of photography, and before the color film era was all he could offer. That's a lot of years."

"Do you have a way of determining what time frame you travel to?" It was the first time that Symphony felt brave enough to ask such a question.

"Not exactly. The first time I travelled, I ended up in the late seventies. I knew that was not a time I was going to find the man in. I got out of there as quickly as I could. Luckily, the clock was in exactly the same place where I last used it."

Symphony wondered how she could find out that location. She did not think that the clock was in the Rock House before it became a museum.

"I didn't plan to go to 1950 either. But that trip gave me an idea about how I could pinpoint the time frame a little better. It was really genius. It's probably how you are doing it, too."

"How's that?" Symphony thought the way she was ending up in the different time frames was anything but genius.

"After I returned from 1950, I realized that I spent the previous couple of weeks immersed in a project at school that was about the 1950s. It started as a history project that our teacher spilled over into other classes, culminating with a 50s themed prom during my junior year. When I got to thinking about it, I realized that my trip back to the late 70s was because of all of the disco albums I listened to at my aunt's house during a two-week summer visit."

"So, if you immerse yourself into a former time, that's where the portal will lead you. Hmmm, that's interesting, and helpful."

"At least, it is how it worked for me. I read something that hinted about that in my father's journal. It didn't make sense until I experienced it for myself." Amburgey stretched and yawned. "I cannot stay awake any longer. I want to have enough energy to have fun tonight. I think I can trust you again. Get out of here now so I can get some rest. Wake me up at four o'clock." Amburgey crawled under the covers and closed her eyes. "Get out. I need quiet." Without opening her eyes, Amburgey shooed Symphony away with her hand.

"Okay. I'll go out and see if I can find out anything about Tyler, so you can avoid him."

Amburgey grunted a response. Symphony quietly gathered her coat, hat, and purse. Before she could get out of the room, she heard Amburgey's steady breathing turn into a snore.

When Symphony reached the downstairs, she found Olivia, Mrs. Bailey's housekeeper, cleaning up the breakfast table.

"If you are looking for Mrs. Bailey, she's gone to do the grocery shopping."

During her time living in the house thus far, Symphony had not interacted with Olivia more than in a casual greeting. She learned from a conversation with Mrs. Bailey that Olivia graduated from a college in the North with a degree in education. A sudden debilitating illness forced Olivia to come home to Wytheville to care for her mother. In 1924, Wytheville barely embraced professional opportunities for white women. In order to help support herself and help her mother, as an African-American woman, Olivia had to take the housekeeping position.

"I wasn't looking for her specifically. I have a question. Maybe you can help me." Olivia stopped stacking the dishes and looked at Symphony. "This may sound strange. I have a few hours to myself and thought I would go exploring around town. I'm used to living in an area with lots of museums and libraries and such. I have this silly obsession with clocks. I wondered if you knew if there were any unusual ones in the hotels or other buildings nearby."

"Clocks? You like clocks?" Olivia's left eyebrow rose and gave Symphony a questioning look.

"Yes. It's silly. I'm sorry to bother you." Symphony began to walk away.

"No. Funny thing is you asked the exact right person that question. Makes me think you know more about me than you are saying." Olivia picked up a pile of dishes and walked through the swinging door into the kitchen.

"Oh, no. I didn't realize you knew anything about clocks." Symphony was almost hit by the door when it flew back toward her. "Do you like clocks, too?"

"Not especially." Olivia did not turn around and started washing the dishes she carried to the sink. "I've been around clocks more than most people have, more than I wanted to be actually."

"Why is that?" Symphony picked up a dishtowel from the counter and took the first dish out of Olivia's hand after she rinsed it.

"My father is the only person for miles around who can repair clocks. Our house is always full of them, big and small."

"How interesting!" Symphony's eyes grew big with shock and excitement.

"It's far from interesting when you are trying to sleep and a dozen clocks chime a few minutes apart." Olivia laughed. Symphony thought her laughter was a beautiful sound, melodious. "To answer your question, there are some very nice clocks in some of the hotels here as well as the bank buildings. I think one of the most unusual is within First National Bank. You should go and take a gander at some of them. If that's not enough time watching for you, I'll take you home with me one evening and you can see my Daddy's collection."

"Thank you, Olivia. I appreciate the information. I hope your mother is doing better. It's a shame that you aren't able to pursue the profession your education prepared you for."

"Well, Miss Symphony, sometimes you have to do what's right for others before you do what is right for yourself. My mother scrubbed floors for my education. I believe I can do the same for her. You get on out of here and enjoy the weather. It's not the warmest February day I have ever seen, but it is mighty close. It's an extra day, too, like a bonus."

"I'm sorry. What do you mean?"

"It's February 29—leap year day. It only happens once every four years."

"Yes. I forgot. I remember reading once that it is the day that a woman can ask a man to marry her. Do you have a beau you'd like to propose to, Olivia?"

"Hush your mouth, child. Don't even think about such nonsense. Why would I want to complicate my life with a man? I intend to remain a single woman all the days of my life. I'm going to go back up north and teach mathematics. I want to be a professor one day. Only man I ever plan to answer to is a boss man or my Daddy. You take your leap year nonsense and go find you a fellow to ask."

Olivia pushed Symphony out the door. Symphony peeked back at the woman once she was out of her direct sight. She watched Olivia return to the dining room. She rubbed her forehead and her shoulders slumped before picking up the last of the dishes. Symphony hoped that Olivia's dream came true one day.

Symphony left the porch of Mrs. Bailey's boarding house. The sun shined bright in the sky. Its brightness was deceiving. Symphony pulled her felt hat down tighter on her head and buttoned the top button of her coat. The edge of what would soon be a March wind lifted up the last remains of dry leaves on the sidewalk.

"This will shake that pancake fog out of my system." Symphony walked up the block toward Main Street. "I sure wish Jason was here to give me a warm hug while we walked."

Jason walked through her dreams almost every night; Symphony did not allow herself to think about Jason much during the day. There was a special pang of longing that came with missing someone who was almost a hundred years away. It was sadness cloaked in fear. He would not be happy when he found out she travelled in time again. The thought that she might not be able to return to her own time hung around her heart like an anchor. She would welcome his chastising, if she could just get home to receive it.

Up ahead on the street, she saw two people—a man and a woman. The man was yelling at the woman and waving his arms in the air. Symphony stopped walking and watched, not wanting to eavesdrop, yet being concerned for the woman's safety. A few seconds later, the man suddenly started pushing the woman and she fell to the ground. The man appeared to continue to talk to himself walking away in the opposite direction. Symphony watched him until he was out of sight. Then, she frantically ran toward the woman, reaching her right when she began to try to rise.

"Are you okay?" Symphony grabbed the woman's arm and helped her continue to rise to her feet. "I saw that man push you down. We should call the police."

"No. No. You can't do that. He would be very angry."

"He already looks like he's angry. He attacked you. Do you know him?"

"Yes. I know him."

"Then, it should be easy for the police to find him. You would be able to identify him."

"NO! No police. He'd kill me."

Symphony looked at the woman, taking in her appearance and demeanor. She was about Symphony's height, but far skinnier. The woman's face was drawn and pale with dark circles under her eyes. Staring back at her, the woman's beautiful green eyes showed no sparkle. To Symphony, it appeared there was no emotion except the fear that perhaps was making her hands tremble.

"I am fine. I have not been hurt. I thank you for your concern." The woman gave Symphony a curt nod and began to walk away. Symphony noticed a limp hindered her stride.

"Have you hurt your ankle or foot?" Symphony caught up with her. "I can go with you to the clinic. I have a friend who works there. I'm sure someone could help you."

"No. It is an old injury. I was not hurt." The woman kept moving, stumbling and almost losing her balance. Symphony grabbed the woman's arm to steady her.

"At least allow me to walk with you to your home. Is it nearby?"

A pained look crossed the woman's face. She closed her eyes and let out a sigh. Symphony hoped it was a sigh of resolution that would allow her to help. The woman merely opened her eyes and nodded.

"I am just a couple of blocks away on the back side of Main Street."

Without any further discussion, the woman continued walking toward the intersection ahead. Still limping, she accepted Symphony holding on to her arm. Looking both ways before crossing, Symphony also searched the street in both directions for the man. He was nowhere in sight. After walking another block, they made a left turn and ventured another block and a half before the woman pointed to the back door of a building.

"I live there. I thank you for your concern."

"May I ask your name before I leave?"

"My name is Cecelia. Cecelia Washington."

"It was nice to meet you, Cecelia. My name is Symphony Wallace. I am staying at Mrs. Bailey's boarding house. It's just about a block and a half from where I joined you on the street. I work as a switchboard operator at the telephone company. If I can ever help you, if you ever need a place to go—"

"You are very kind. I have told you, I am fine. It was just a silly argument. I lost my balance and fell. I have to get inside. I have much to do. Thank you."

"Who was the man, Cecelia? Please tell me."

"He is my husband, Miss Wallace. Please leave me alone."

Without another word or any eye contact, Cecelia opened the door, stepped inside, and quickly closed it behind her. Symphony stood there for a moment, grasping Cecelia's words and their meaning. The movement of a curtain brought Symphony back from her thoughts, and she quickly walked from behind the building, up the alleyway beside it toward Main Street. In her time, a mural covered the brick of the building honoring a woman whose life was far better than Symphony imagined Cecelia's was. She turned to her right, and walked down the street. She noticed that the front of the building where Cecelia lived was Saul Alper's Victory Merchandising Company. It was a coincidence Symphony could not ignore.

Standing facing the store, Symphony looked up the street to see the imposing structure that housed First National Bank, the building where Olivia suggested that Symphony might find an unusual clock.

"That can wait a few minutes." Symphony whispered under her breath. An older woman stopped in front of her.

"Were you speaking to me, dear?" The woman's hair was white and arranged in a bun on top of her head. She wore a long burgundy coat with a black fur collar and carried a matching purse. In a word, the woman looked like money.

"No. I'm sorry. I'm always talking to myself. It's a silly habit I developed as an only child. I was saying that I was going into this store—Victory Merchandising Company. Do you shop there?"

"Oh, certainly, my dear. It is a lovely establishment. The owners are courteous, and their products are of the highest quality. You will not be disappointed."

"Thank you."

Symphony smiled at the woman before walking toward the door of the store. Before she could reach for the knob, the door flew open and a man came rushing out. In his haste, he almost knocked the woman down.

"Slow down, Herman." The woman's voice was an octave higher. She reached for Symphony's arm. "You are not a youngster running out to play."

While the incident itself was far from comical, Symphony had to hold back a giggle. She saw the bug-eyed reaction of the man. He looked mortified. His embarrassment seemed to increase while trying to help the woman by taking hold of her arm.

"Let go of me." The woman swatted him with her free hand. "Can't you see that I am using this kind young lady to steady myself?"

Symphony did not notice that the man dropped a bag on the ground until the woman pointed it out.

"Mr. Alper will be quite upset if you lose today's bank deposit on the ground in front of the store."

Herman gasped and quickly scooped up the bag. He briefly made eye contact with Symphony before sprinting down the street.

"Herman lacks confidence. It will hinder his success in life." The woman shook her head. Symphony watched him go down the street.

"Thank you for helping me, young lady. My name is Wilma Snyder. What is your name, dear? I don't believe I have met you before."

"My name is Symphony Wallace, Mrs. Snyder. I'm pleased to meet you. I recently moved here. I am staying at Mrs. Bailey's boarding house and working at the telephone company."

"Keeper of secrets. That's what you are." Mrs. Snyder laughed heartily. "You are better off being a stranger in that line of work. You will not know the difference between the truth and the lies that travel over those lines." The woman waved at a gentleman crossing the street. "Symphony, you ring my house sometime and come visit me. I live on Hickory Lane. We will have some tea and talk about good literature. You like good literature, don't you?"

"Most certainly, ma'am. I am passionate about reading."

"Delightful. You visit me soon. I look forward to getting to know Wytheville's newest resident."

There was a twinkle in her eye when she smiled at Symphony. In a split second, Mrs. Snyder encountered another woman on the street. They immediately began to converse. Symphony watched the two women in animated conversation and thought that Mrs. Snyder reminded her of a teacher she had in elementary school—the teacher who sparked Symphony's interest in reading. Little did she know, the long journeys to other worlds, and different times were an imaginary dress rehearsal for the real adventures in Symphony's future.

Turning back toward the store entrance, she wondered why she crossed paths with the friendly woman and how she might fit into the mystery Symphony was trying to decipher. The jingle of the bell on the door brought her back to the reality of the moment. She walked on inside.

"Hello, Miss Wallace, so nice to see you return to our store." Saul Alper briskly walked toward her. "You had so little time with us the other day. How can I help you?"

Symphony forgot that a second visit to the store so soon might indicate that she actually wanted to purchase something. Idle browsing might not be as common in 1924.

"How are you, Mr. Alper? I am in need of a couple of items. I have not received my first check from the telephone company yet. Would I be able to set up an account and make some purchases on credit? I could offer a down payment."

"Certainly. A job with the telephone company is like money in the bank."

"Thank you. I need a nice pair of shoes."

"Saul, you take Melvin, and I will help Miss Wallace."

Symphony looked behind her to see Mrs. Alper standing nearby, holding her young son. The child looked like he was fresh and clean from bathing. She put him in her husband's arms and walked to Symphony.

"It's so nice to see you again, Miss Wallace."

"Please call me Symphony."

"Symphony, I am Fannie. What can I help you find today?"

"I need a nice pair of shoes and some nylons." The word 'pantyhose' was in her mind. She hoped 'nylons' was an acceptable word of the time.

"I do not know what nylons are." Fannie looked puzzled. "Do you have them on?"

Symphony pulled up her skirt and pointed to her legs.

"Stockings! We have a lovely selection over in the corner."

"Yes, of course." Symphony breathed a sigh of relief. "We call them nylons back home."

Fannie led her to a series of wooden drawers below a long counter. She opened one. Symphony saw layers of stockings carefully stacked between tissue paper. Fannie lifted up a pair that was a beautiful charcoal gray color. Symphony ran her hand over the luxurious silkiness of the material.

"It's lovely. It feels expensive."

"Yes, it does. The stockings are reasonably priced. We do not charge extra for luxurious beauty." Fannie winked at Symphony and handed the pair to her. "I am pleased that you have returned to our store. I was hoping that we would have a chance to talk again."

"It is quite a process to establish yourself in a new town." Her short time in Wytheville in multiple time periods taught Symphony that what she said was true. "When I arrived here a couple of weeks ago, I was not prepared for several things I have encountered. Needing a new wardrobe is one of them."

"Moving to a new place can be challenging. I moved here with Saul after we first married. This is a friendly place, yet people can be hard to get to know. I am happiest in my home upstairs with my little family."

"Someone mentioned that your brother is part of the business." Symphony handed the stockings back to Fannie. "I would like two pairs of those in gray."

"Yes. Herman lived here before Saul and I were married. He is the reason I met Saul. The two were friends in college. Herman only attended a year or two, and then came home to help support our mother. While they were still in school, Herman brought Saul home one weekend. I liked him instantly."

"Love at first sight."

"Hmmm, I'm not sure I would say love. I did find him attentive and charming. We began to exchange letters. When Herman returned home, he and Saul continued to keep in touch. After our mother passed away, Saul invited him to come to Wytheville and work in the store." Fannie put the stockings on the counter and led

Symphony back to the shoe section. She motioned for Symphony to sit down and put her foot up on the shoe-fitting stool. "I would guess that you wear a size seven."

"You would be correct."

"Do you see any that you like in particular?"

Symphony pointed to a black Mary Jane pump with a wide buckle on the top. It had a low heel that would serve well for work, but the buckle added a little accessory that made it dressy.

"Excuse me for a moment while I go find your size."

Symphony watched Fannie walk to the back of the store and disappear through a curtained area. A few seconds later, she heard the bell chime on the front door and she watched Herman hurry through it. He did not appear to see her when he briskly walked the length of the store until he almost walked past her.

"Oh. Hello. Good day, ma'am."

"Hello." Symphony smiled. Herman's expression changed from serious concentration to growing embarrassment. "That Mrs. Snyder is a talker, isn't she?" Symphony thought that a lighthearted response would ease Herman's awkwardness with the situation.

"That would be true, quite a friendly lady."

"Herman, you've returned. I see you have met Miss Wallace."

"I think I was introduced to Mr. Sollod when I was in the store previously."

Symphony watched Fannie's glance move between her and Herman. She continued to approach Symphony with a box of shoes.

"Let's try these and see how they fit."

While Fannie sat down on a bench in front of her, Symphony could see Saul Alper approaching them from the back room. His son was not with him.

"Melvin finally fell asleep." Saul smiled at Symphony. He directed a question to his brother-in-law. "Did you see him?"

"I did not." Herman's voice was deep and serious. "I saw the curtain move. Cecelia would not open the door."

"Do you know Cecelia?" Fannie whispered to Symphony. She slid the right shoe on her foot. Symphony's expression must have shown a change at the mention of Cecelia's name. "You look concerned."

"I'm sorry. I should not be listening." Symphony tried to change her expression. She strained to hear what the men were saying, but they moved further away from where Symphony and Fannie were seated.

"It is not as if they were being quiet. Men do not always know the meaning of discreet." Fannie held out the left shoe for Symphony to try on. "It is a sad situation. Her husband is involved in crimes. We know this, yet we cannot do anything."

With both shoes on, Symphony stood up and began to walk up and down the aisle. The shoes fit perfectly. Their style made her feel like she was in an old movie. A smile crossed her lips at the thought.

"You like them. They fit well?"

"I do like them. They fit perfectly."

"Come sit back down and I will box them up for you. Do you need anything else today?"

"Just the stockings. I will be back soon to find some more items."

The words so freely left her mouth. It was such an automatic statement. In her heart, Symphony hoped they were not true. She needed to learn whatever the knowledge was that she had come to 1924 to gain. She needed to get back to her own time, her real life.

Symphony did not realize that she had methodically taken off the shoes and given them back to Fannie until the woman returned to her with the box and the bag of stockings.

"I can see from your expression that you are worried about Cecelia." Fannie sat down beside Symphony. "It is a grave situation.

Her husband is not a good man. You've only been in Wytheville a short time. How do you know Cecelia?"

"I met her today." Symphony looked around and lowered her voice. Saul and Herman were no longer within sight and there were not any other customers in the store. "I saw her husband push her down in the street. They were arguing."

"I would not stand for it. My father taught me from a young age to never tolerate a man who raises his hand to a woman."

"What sort of crime is her husband involved in?"

"We are certain he is involved in some petty theft. Saul thinks he might also have been involved in more serious crimes elsewhere. They rent a couple of rooms from us on the backside of this building. Saul tried to get rid of them. I worry about Cecelia though. I fear that she does not have anywhere to go. Later this afternoon, I will go to visit her. I will take her some of the stew I have cooking. She may be carrying a child, I am not sure."

"She is so thin. I could see that despite the coat she was wearing. She is pale and frail."

"Cecelia lost a child about a year ago. I think she is not healthy enough to carry one to full term. I try to take her food or invite her to come and eat lunch with me. She cannot nourish a baby, if she is not nourished herself. I will not reveal what you told me about earlier today." Fannie reached over and squeezed Symphony's hand and rose from her seat. "Someone who is concerned about a stranger is someone with a good heart. We shall be friends, you and I. Maybe we can help Cecelia together."

Symphony followed Fannie to the counter and signed the bill of sale for her shoes and stockings. From the back, she heard a wale of crying.

"My little man demands attention. You will come back again

soon. It does not have to be to purchase something. We are friends now." Fannie started walking in that direction. "You will come and visit and tell me about your new life here."

An exasperated Saul came out from the back with the baby in his arms and immediately handed the child to his mother. Fannie waved at Symphony. She watched Fannie disappear into the back.

"Thank you for shopping with us today, Miss Wallace. Please do return. My wife enjoys your company."

"Thank you, Mr. Alper. Have a good day."

Symphony briskly walked to the door. Before she could open it, the door flew open and Cecelia's husband entered. The word 'devious' entered Symphony's mind. She saw a sinister expression cross his face when he looked at her. His gaze made her feel uncomfortable and she quickly exited the open door.

She did not look back. Symphony wanted to shake the feeling of foreboding that was overtaking her. If she could travel to the past, could she see the future? She already knew what history recorded would happen in only a few short days. The historical accounts only contained snippets of the story. Ominous details loomed between the lines in the lives of those who history would not remember.

Her brisk walk took her right to her original destination, the front door of the First National Bank. She opened the tall door and walked into the high-ceiling lobby, in doing so it crossed her mind that she had been there before. She could not imagine how because she did not think the building still stood in her time, yet there was something familiar about the structure that she could not put her finger on.

"Good afternoon, ma'am. Welcome to First National Bank. May I help you?" A short middle-aged man in a blue suit with a plaid vest approached her. He looked to be in charge.

"Hello. I have recently moved here and started working at the telephone company." To Symphony's ears, her introduction was beginning to sound like a broken record. "I will soon need to open a bank account. I thought I would stop in and see what I needed to do." Her ability to create fiction from the truth of her situation was becoming a skill.

"Excellent. We would be happy to welcome you to our family of customers. My name is Samuel Roberts. I am the assistant bank manager. Allow me to give you a tour of our bank."

"Oh, lovely. I enjoy touring interesting buildings."

A jolt of excitement passed over Symphony while following him around the bank. Taking in the grandeur of the structure's interior, she was amazed at the beauty of the arches of the high ceiling and the marble columns that were interspersed. It did not look like the small town bank she imagined.

"This is our vault." Mr. Roberts pulled open the large heavy round door. It resembled ones she saw in the old banks of Charleston during her youth. "As you can see, your money will be quite safe with us. Where did you live previously, Miss—?"

"Wallace. Symphony Wallace. I am from West Virginia, near Charleston."

"An area rich in the natural resource of coal. It makes for a prosperous economy."

Symphony knew that it would not take a century passing to change that statement. It was a different world in her time and one that no doubt changed for the banking industry as well.

"If you will follow me back to this corner, you can see a seating area where our clients can wait for one of our staff to help them with their accounts."

Large, comfortable-looking, straight back chairs in rich brown leather were separated by wooden end tables. She almost gasped when in the far corner Symphony saw what she was looking for—the unusual clock that was her time portal. There was a part of her that wanted to clutch the pendant that hung beneath her blouse and touch that clock—and spin far, far away, back to her own time.

Instead, she sat down in one of the not-as-comfortable-as-they-looked chairs and waited while Mr. Roberts went into the teller area and returned with a pleasant looking woman he introduced as Miss Brooks.

"Miss Brooks is here every day, Monday through Friday. When you return with your first check, please ask for her and she will assist you with opening your account."

Symphony was not paying too close attention as Mr. Roberts made the introductions. Her gaze was still longingly preoccupied with the clock in the corner. Realizing her rudeness, she turned toward Miss Brooks and extended her hand in greeting.

"It's nice to meet you, Miss Brooks. My name is Symphony Wallace." As their eyes met, Symphony went back in time to her past and her first college roommate. "Pam Brooks."

"Why, yes. How did you know Pam was my name? It's really Pamela." The young woman giggled. "But, I despise it."

There it was. In the middle of a confusing and unusual day in a time that fit like someone else's shoes—there was a snippet of something that was uniquely hers, a friend who was more like a sister. Symphony took a deep breath, ready to turn her back on the clock, for now, and go back to the business that brought her to 1924, whatever that was.

Chapter Eleven

"THAT WAS REALLY A GOOD SHOW." Amburgey commented while walking out of the Opera House. "Let's go up to the Blue Ribbon Lunch and have some dessert. Before you ask, they open on nights when the Opera House or one of the theaters has a show. They have the best butterscotch pie I have ever eaten."

Symphony sneered at the mention of butterscotch.

"How can you not like butterscotch? It's like smooth heaven."

"It's an acquired taste. I've not acquired it. Surely, they must have other flavors of pie."

"I suppose. All the more butterscotch for me."

Symphony buttoned her coat. The temperature dropped a few degrees while they were watching the show.

"I found the clock." The words spilled out of Symphony's mouth before she thought about what she was saying.

"What?"

Several steps ahead of her, Symphony turned around to find Amburgey stopped on the sidewalk. She walked back to where Amburgey stood.

"I found the clock. You know...*the* clock."

"You make these random statements to me. You give me these slivers of information. Yet, you never really tell me who you are or why you are doing this. For all I know, you were sent to find me for some reason. It's hard to trust you, Symphony Wallace." Amburgey crossed her arms and stood still. "I've told you why I am here. I think it's about time you came clean with why you are."

"It's quite complicated, Amburgey."

"And my situation isn't? Not everyone can do what we can. It's dangerous and stressful. It's scary in a way that few people can comprehend."

"Okay. I will try my best to explain my situation to you." Symphony let out a sigh and bit her lip. "I don't think we should do it over pie though. Someone might overhear our discussion."

"There can still be pie. We will get it to go." Amburgey walked briskly up the street.

"Do they do that in 1924?" Symphony almost had to run to keep up with her.

"You've had sandwiches to go since you've been here."

"Well, sure, sandwiches." Symphony was amazed at how silly her question sounded. "But a pie is different."

"We will buy a whole pie if we have to." Amburgey let out a huff and kept walking.

"But, I don't like butterscotch."

"Symphony." Amburgey stopped at the door of the Blue Ribbon Lunch. Before opening the door, she turned and gave Symphony a hard look. "Stop talking and wait outside."

"But—"

"I'm warning you."

Symphony remained outside and watched Amburgey go into the restaurant. There were few people out on the streets of Wytheville that night. It did not matter to Symphony; most of the faces she might see were strangers to her. The time she spent exploring earlier in the day yielded no information regarding Tyler Gibboney. She did not see him and the few people she asked did not seem to know him.

"Evening, ma'am." A young man in a suit and hat stopped in front of the door to restaurant. A pretty woman about her age was on his arm. She smiled. "Aren't you the lady who came into the diner earlier today asking about Tyler Gibboney?"

"Yes." Symphony looked from the man to the woman. She did not remember seeing either one of them before.

"My girlfriend's brother works at the train station." The man took hold of the woman's hand that was tucked around his arm. She smiled again and stepped closer to him. "When I went to pick up Dorothy this evening, I asked him if he remembered Tyler Gibboney. He did and said that he remembers the man buying a train ticket to New York a few days ago."

"Oh, so he has left the area."

"I suppose. Gerald said that the man bought the ticket and was waiting for the train to arrive when the strangest thing happened. Gerald said that the man went into the telephone booth and he swears that he disappeared." The young man looked at his girlfriend and the two shrugged their shoulders. "Gerald's not one to tell tall tales. He had no explanation though." The young man tipped his hat at Symphony. "I thought you would want to know." He and his girlfriend continued to walk.

"Thank you." Symphony watched them walk away.

"Who were you talking to?" Amburgey suddenly came out of the door carrying a box.

"I think I may know what your father's time travel portal is."

"What?"

Symphony grabbed the box from Amburgey's hand when it started to fall.

"I learned a valuable piece of information. I think that Tyler Gibboney is gone for a while." Symphony turned to walk down the street in the direction of the boarding house. "It seems he may have travelled via a telephone booth."

"No way! My father would not do something so clichéd."

"It's clichéd to you because of the time you are from. Maybe he's being a trendsetter in this era."

"But…what a minute? How did you find this out?" Amburgey caught up with Symphony and began to walk backwards in front of her in order to face her while they talked.

"You told me to stay outside. I stayed outside."

"And this information, it beamed down from the sky?"

"No, it walked right up to me and said hello." Symphony gave Amburgey a big smile, and then started to walk faster.

"I don't buy this. I left you outside for less than five minutes. There's no way that someone happened upon you like that."

"Like I 'just happened' to find you in 1950 and 1924." Symphony stopped and looked Amburgey squarely in the eyes. "Things happen, especially to me, and you, for that matter. Don't judge. We're going back to the boarding house and eat pie. There better be something other than butterscotch in here. I am going to tell you as much as I can about why I am here. I don't know all of the answers."

Symphony resumed walking. She was about to turn the corner to head down Church Street, when she realized that Amburgey was not with her. She was standing in the middle of the sidewalk looking up at the stars. Symphony watched her for a few minutes before walking back. When she got closer, the light of the moon revealed tears on Amburgey's face.

"What's wrong?"

"I'm silly and reckless and stupid. I'm risking my life to find a man who doesn't even know I exist. If I ever do find him, he might be in love with someone else and I might get stuck a hundred years away from everyone who loves me." Amburgey's quiet tears turned to loud sobs. "I'll end up like my father, lost in time."

"I have more questions than I do answers." Symphony set the box down on a bench nearby and took hold of Amburgey's shoulders. "I can't tell you how I know this. I'm pretty sure you will find him. I'm not going to tell you that everything is perfect, because I don't know that. I do know that you will find love, and you will lose love. But your story isn't over yet. There's still time to write the ending."

"You promise?" Amburgey wiped her eyes and nose and took a deep breath.

"I can't promise things I don't know. I can't tell you how I know the things that I do. It's a jumbled mess complicated by time travel. But, I think something incredible happens to you and there is more to look forward to in the future, if you can just find your way home." The words came out of her mouth, but they pierced Symphony's heart. She knew then why she was making these journeys. It was less about knowing what happened. It was not about finding her mother in the past. It was all about finding her in Symphony's future.

"You're a smart kid. Your mother must be proud."

The words made tears form in Symphony's eyes. She quickly turned away and retrieved the box of pie.

"Let's get back to Mrs. Bailey's place. It's getting late. Maybe everyone will already be asleep and we won't have to share this pie."

"I don't know. I think Mr. Barker has sugar sonar. The week before you arrived, he got so excited about a chocolate cake that Olivia was baking that he pulled a chair up to the stove and waited for it to come out of the oven."

"Didn't it have to cool before she could frost it?"

Symphony and Amburgey resumed walking. Suddenly two cats streaked by them yelping as they passed. They turned and looked back down the street in the direction they came, watching the cats scamper down a side alley.

When they turned back around, a man was standing in front of them. They both jumped backwards. The light of the moon reflecting on the glass of a storefront gave Symphony a glimpse of the man's face. Even in the darkness, there was no mistaking him—it was Cecelia Washington's husband.

"Good evening, ladies."

"Good evening." Amburgey spoke the words slowly and carefully while Symphony remained silent.

"You are out a little late. Do you need any assistance?" Mr. Washington looked over their heads and up the street behind them.

"No, thank you. We are just fine. You have a nice evening." Amburgey took hold of Symphony's arm and pulled her into a fast walk. Symphony started to turn and look behind her. "Don't turn around. Keep walking. That man has quite the reputation in this town. It's not a good one."

Once they proceeded around the corner and part of the way down Church Street, Amburgey slowed down and briefly looked behind them.

"I don't think he's following us, but keep walking."

"I saw him earlier today. He pushed his wife down in the street."

Symphony looked straight ahead. The path was getting darker as the clouds covered up the moon.

"Cecelia has visited the clinic several times, I am told."

"I tried to get her to go today."

"The police left instructions to be notified if she comes in again. Her husband will be arrested. While we are living in a time when some tend to look the other way to such family violence, the police chief does not. I am told that he experienced such treatment firsthand in his own childhood home and has zero tolerance."

With the Bailey house in sight, their pace slowed. The temperature turned colder since they left the Opera House. With a breeze on her face, Symphony could feel it chapping from the cold. The house was dark except for a lone light on the porch—a beacon of refuge, a welcome.

"When I was old enough to understand, my parents explained to me that I was adopted." After each of them ate too much pie—apple for Symphony, butterscotch for Amburgey—Symphony began to tell her story in the solitude of the kitchen. "They told it in a matter-of-fact way, like everyone was adopted. Always emphasizing that their life together was not complete until I appeared in it."

"They sound like wonderful people. You are lucky. I'm sure that it turns out differently for some." Amburgey paused to take a drink of water while Symphony gathered their dishes and walked to the sink. "What do you know about your parents?"

"Very little." Symphony chose her words carefully. "I do not know much about the time surrounding my birth or even if my parents were married." The thought struck her that she wondered why she had not pressed Nadia for such information. "I was given up for adoption when I was about a month old." Symphony turned on the faucet and waited for the water to slowly come out of the pipe.

"I don't understand how a mother can give up a child. It seems so permanent to disconnect yourself with someone who you literally carried inside you."

Symphony bit her bottom lip. By her best calculation, her mother was within a couple of years of making that fateful decision. Hearing Amburgey speak about her opinion regarding the matter told Symphony that the young woman she was with now was a far different one than the one who gave birth to her. Symphony had to know what happened that changed Amburgey so much. It had to be something drastic, if the woman was speaking the truth now.

"It's a question I often ask myself, not because I suffered because of it. I cannot imagine a better childhood than the one I had. I often wonder if her choice brought forth something positive in her life, or if it haunted her with regret." Symphony felt the water trickle over her fingers while she washed one of the small plates.

"Haunted. I'm not sure that I would want to live a life that was haunted. It would be better not to exist at all."

Symphony turned to face Amburgey. She slung the water that her hands were in, and it flew across the table and hit Amburgey in the face.

"Hey, watch it."

"No. You watch it. Don't talk like that." Symphony's heart began to race. Her mind followed the path that Amburgey's words described. Her greatest fear was that Amburgey *was* dead. She shuddered at the thought that Amburgey could have taken her own life.

"I'm only speculating. I don't know what your mother did. Maybe she's sitting in some white-picket fence life wishing you would find her. There's got to be ways to do that. Records you could search. It would probably be more beneficial than hopping through time. What does this time travel have to do with your mother anyway?"

"She was a time traveler." Symphony turned back to face the sink. Letting out a sigh and closing her eyes, she began to methodically dry her hands. She had to be careful.

"How do you know that? It's not like there are records of such." Amburgey grew silent for a moment. "Are there?"

"She left a trail. Some of it was accidental. Some was deliberate. I think she left clues that she knew her child would find—if the child ever decided to look for her."

"Are you finished with those dishes?"

"I guess." Symphony turned back to face Amburgey.

"Then, sit down." Amburgey waited for Symphony to do so. "Let me get this straight. Your mother was a time traveler. She gave you up for adoption. How did you learn she was a time traveler? Did she leave you information about that?"

"Not really. I was left on the steps of a church about fifty miles away from where I was born. There was a letter left with me, a photograph, and this pendant." Symphony pulled the necklace out from inside her shirt.

"Yes. I remember that pendant from when we were together in 1950. It's magic, isn't it?"

"Magic. What is magic?"

Symphony looked down at the pendant. As many times as she had examined it in her life, she still sometimes saw something different within it that she had not seen before. This time it was a tiny speck of blue near the center of it. The color reminded her of winter pansies. She looked up and realized that Amburgey was waiting for her to continue.

"I could not imagine that time travel even existed until I suddenly found myself in 1950. Even being here now, in another time, does not make it any more of an understandable experience. If this pendant contains magic, it cannot be the only way. For me, it is the combination of this pendant and that unusual clock. Somehow, I do not believe that is the whole story. I think there must be something within us that makes it possible. I do not think that I could just give this to another person and it would work for them."

"I believe you are right about that. It must be genetic in some way. My father passed it to me. I think there might be other members of his family with this gift.'

"Gift. Curse. It's hard to find the right word to describe it." The feelings came out of Symphony quickly and bluntly. It was the truth of her heart. "Am I correct that the clock is your time portal?"

"Yes. In our time, it resides in an unusual location, don't you think?"

"Hmmm. What do you mean unusual?" Symphony looked down at the design of the cloth on the small kitchen table where they sat, trying to seem nonchalant about Amburgey's question.

"This isn't the first time that I've tried to talk to you about our time and you were evasive. Aren't you travelling from the 1980s?"

"No." Symphony looked Amburgey squarely in the eyes. "I'm travelling from a later time than that."

"Then, how are we ending up here at the same time?" Amburgey stared intently at Symphony. She could almost physically feel the look.

"I'm not sure, Amburgey. I don't know if it is safe for us to speculate about that. It would seem that there should be some rules to this stuff."

"Maybe we are related."

"That could be possible." Symphony was growing more nervous about where the conversation was going. "I told you earlier that I think Tyler Gibboney might be using a telephone booth for his portal. Did you know that already?"

"Not exactly. He would only tell me that he used something that could be found almost anywhere. I think my mother forbade him to give me that much detail. She is adamantly against time travel. I don't guess I can blame her. It took the love of her life away."

"That's a good reason." Symphony thought to herself that twice time travel took a loved one from Nadia. She had to make sure that she was not the third person to leave Nadia's life that way. She needed to be more careful.

"I still find it incredible to believe that there are so many people in the little town of Wytheville who can time travel. If you are from a later time than mine, it means you are from the future. Maybe I know your mother in my time. What's her name?"

"Amburgey, I don't think we should be talking about this. We are mixing up times, and that might be against the laws of time travel. Let's just stick to why we are each here."

"You're right. My father talked about that in his journal. It's actually almost a guide to how to time travel. Only problem is that he leaves out several key parts. I'm sure that is because of promises he made to my mother. He told me that if I ever travelled myself that I should do everything in my power to not interact with him. He said that close relatives travelling from different times could interfere with each other's futures."

"What do you mean?" Symphony's head began to throb and she felt a sick feeling rising in her stomach. It felt like fear.

"In his journal, he talked about one trip that he made when I was still a toddler. He accidentally went to the future and unknowingly interacted with someone in his family."

"Unknowingly?" Symphony took a deep breath.

"Yes, apparently it was someone that he did not recognize."

"What happened?" Symphony let out the breath and closed her eyes.

"He wrote that he saw the person change before his eyes. It messed up something with the person's existence. He didn't elaborate any further. Before he disappeared, I heard my parents arguing one morning. He kept telling my mother that he had to try and undo the harm he'd done. When I asked my mother about it, she said that he was filled with guilt and could not seem to do anything to make it right."

"Forgive me. But I've got to ask. Knowing all this, why have you travelled in time?" Symphony opened her eyes and saw that tears were running down Amburgey's face.

"It's like an addiction, Symphony. I have to find this man. It's ridiculous, I know. My heart is so full of love for someone who I have never met. It's like we are connected through time. I think I will go crazy if I don't find him."

"What will happen if you do find him?"

"We will live happily ever after, of course."

"Just like your parents did."

"It's a fairytale. But it's mine, and I'm going to do everything in my power to achieve my happy ending."

"Be careful what you wish for."

"Well, isn't that something? You sound like you read my father's journal. That was the last sentence."

Chapter Twelve

SYMPHONY SLEPT LIKE THE DEAD like her Grammie would say. Her dreams were tormented with life in her time intermingled with situations she experienced in 1950 and 1924. Her final dream before awakening the following morning was filled with the sound of shattering glass. The beautiful multi-colored pieces fell around her. She sat straight up in the bed hollering and found that she was alone.

"There was something quite familiar about that." Symphony rubbed her eyes and stretched swinging her feet out of the bed and onto the wood floor. Feeling the coldness on the soles of her feet reminded her of the first weeks she lived on the top floor of the Rock House. "It was shards of glass like I saw at Cybelee's."

Putting on her robe, she gathered a few toiletries and a washcloth to head to the bathroom. Amburgey's bed was still unmade leading her to believe that her mother might be downstairs. Her theory was

204 ROSA LEE JUDE

validated when she met Amburgey in the hallway a few seconds later.

"The dead has arisen." Amburgey was holding a water glass with a dishcloth around it. "Note to self, bring a big coffee mug with me on my next trip. Those little teacups to hold a full mug of coffee? It's ridiculous. It's one swallow when you need coffee like I do." Amburgey put the index finger of her free hand to her mouth to send a signal to be quiet. "Mrs. Bailey doesn't know about this coffee in a large glass arrangement. Olivia and I have an understanding. I hope you are heading to take a shower. You look rough. What did we do last night?"

"We had too much pie and conversation. Sometimes that can be worse than a night of drinking." Symphony turned to open the bathroom door. "You don't look so hot either. Have you even combed your hair?"

"You should know better than to talk to me before I have absorbed my coffee. Don't be surprised if our room door is locked when you return." Amburgey took a long drink from her glass and stomped the rest of the way down the hall.

A few minutes later, Symphony let the warm water of a shower cascade down her body, her mind slipped back to what Amburgey revealed the night before. Tyler encountered a close relative on a trip to the future with some serious consequences. Symphony wished she made the time to read his journal in its entirety when she first found it. She imagined that the person he encountered had to either be Amburgey or herself. Not knowing how far into the future he journeyed, she had no way of knowing what happened.

After toweling off and wrapping up in her robe, Symphony rubbed the steam off the small bathroom mirror and looked closely at her face.

"I wonder if time travel can age you." Dark circles under her eyes and faint lines at the corners of the mouth seemed to have sprung up overnight. An image flashed before her mind. A face she could not see. "No. It couldn't be."

"Symphony!" Amburgey was suddenly banging on the door. "Open up."

"What's wrong? You scared me." Symphony opened the door. The look on Amburgey's face silenced her. There was fear in her eyes.

"The police chief is downstairs. He wants to talk to you. It's about Cecelia Washington. I told him you were taking a shower, and that I'd bring you down to the station later. He said he would wait for you to get ready. He's sitting in the parlor now."

"What do you think he wants?"

"He says that he is investigating an incident he heard about that occurred yesterday. I told you that he has zero tolerance for spouse abuse. You better get ready. He's not the kind of person to keep waiting."

"I understand."

Symphony gathered her belongings and followed Amburgey back to their room. While she dressed, her mind clicked through the interaction she saw between Cecelia and her husband. She needed to be clear about what she saw.

After dressing, Symphony pulled her still-wet hair into a bun, and applied a light dusting of face powder, and then a dab of lipstick.

"You look fine. He's not here to take you on a date."

Amburgey's efforts to calm Symphony down by joking did not lead to the desired effect. The few minutes it took Symphony to dress only increased her anxiety.

"It will be fine. Just tell him the truth. Cecelia deserves for someone to stand up for her."

Symphony nodded and headed for the door. After she opened it, she turned around to ask Amburgey to go with her. The woman was already on her heels.

"You don't have to do this alone. I'm going with you."

For a split second, Symphony saw Mariel, the mother that raised her, standing there. Those would be her words. Her eyes focused and she saw that it was actually Amburgey standing before her. Symphony wondered if she would have received the same level of support she was feeling now if Amburgey raised her.

They were silent walking down the stairs. When they reached the parlor, the police chief stood up. Symphony noticed an expression of worry on Mrs. Bailey's face. The woman gave Symphony a slight smile and pointed for her to sit down.

"Miss Wallace, I'm Chief Norman. I'm sorry to bother you on a Saturday, but I need to ask you a few questions."

"Yes, sir. I understand." Symphony sat down in the chair opposite of Chief Norman.

"I understand that you witnessed an altercation between Mrs. Cecelia Washington and her husband, Cephas. Is that correct?"

"I saw a man push Cecelia down on the sidewalk near the corner of Church and Spring Streets. I was told later that the man was her husband."

"What happened prior to him knocking her down?"

"I could not hear what was said. I was too far away. But I could hear him yelling, and she seemed to be trying to respond to him. His voice was much louder than hers. He sounded agitated." Symphony paused and took her gaze from the Chief to Mrs. Bailey. The woman nodded encouragingly.

"Please continue, Miss Wallace. What happened next?"

"The yelling went on for a few minutes. Mr. Washington was gesturing and throwing his hands up in the air. He pushed her on the right shoulder and Cecelia stumbled backward a little. She regained her balance and walked back toward him." Symphony took a breath. "The expression on her face looked like she was pleading with him. He started to walk away from her. Something she said must have made him turn back around. This time, I saw the back of his hand hit the right side of her face. She stumbled again, but did not fall." Symphony took a deep breath, and looked toward the window, like she was lost in thought. "I just realized that I was walking closer to them at this point. I guess what I saw transpiring made me unconsciously do that. I could hear what he said when he pushed her down to the ground."

"What was it?" Chief Norman was sitting on the edge of his seat. "What did Washington say to his wife?"

"He said that no one would miss her. He would make her disappear and no one would miss her." Symphony turned to look at Amburgey in the doorway. "I didn't remember that part until this minute. I guess I was too caught up in the emotion of it when it was happening."

"No one would miss her. You're sure that's what he said." Symphony could feel Chief Norman's stare.

"Yes. I'm sure."

"Then, what happened?"

"He pushed her down again and kicked her. A few seconds later, he walked away. I waited until he was out of sight before approaching Cecelia. She was trying to stand when I got there."

"Did he look back?" Mrs. Bailey joined the questioning. "I'm sorry, Chief."

"No. It's fine. It's a good question." Chief Norman smiled at Mrs. Bailey. "Please answer that, Miss Wallace."

"No. I watched him until he turned the corner. I kept looking back in that direction while I was helping her. He didn't look back at all."

"The reason I knew to come and question you was because someone told me that they saw you helping Mrs. Washington back to her home. Did she appear to have any serious injuries?"

"No. She was limping. I think she might have sprained her ankle. I tried to get her to go to the clinic. Amburgey works there." Symphony looked in her direction. "I knew they would help her. She refused. I encouraged her to allow me to call the police. She emphatically told me no." Symphony took another deep breath and looked down at her hands on her lap. "She indicated that he would be very angry if she involved the police. She said he would kill her."

"Thank you, Miss Wallace." Chief Norman stood up. "I appreciate you taking the time to talk to me."

"I should have contacted the police myself." Symphony rose and faced Chief Norman. "I've only been here a couple of weeks. I don't know a lot of people. I was trying to mind my own business."

"Don't beat yourself up, Miss Wallace. Most people don't like strangers interfering in their family life. But, most people aren't Cephas Washington. That man is in a class by himself." Chief Norman turned to Mrs. Bailey. "I apologize for barging in on you, ma'am."

"It is perfectly fine, Chief Norman. I wish there was not such an incident for you to have to investigate."

"Miss Wallace, if you happen to have any further contact with Mrs. Washington and learn any information that might be helpful, please do me the kindness of giving me a call. I understand that you have access to a telephone line every evening." Chief Norman smiled briefly. He walked toward the door.

"Chief Norman, may I ask you a question before you go?" Symphony followed him.

"Certainly, ma'am."

"What prompted you to come and question me?"

"It was the result of another incident that happened overnight. Mrs. Washington was found sitting outside of her apartment in the early hours of this morning. She was almost frozen to death. Apparently, Cephas locked her out of the apartment. Saul Alper found her huddled in the alley. She was barely conscious. He immediately took her inside of his store. While Mrs. Alper was helping to warm Mrs. Washington, Saul contacted me. We admitted her to the clinic for observation. This isn't the first time something like this has happened. It's no secret that Mrs. Washington had a miscarriage last year. One of the nurses at the clinic told me that she's pretty sure that happened by Cephas' hand as well. I will be arresting him whenever I can find him."

Symphony clutched her heart and tears started to run down her face. Behind her, she could hear Mrs. Bailey muttering under her breath.

"It takes a weak man to be abusive to a stranger. It takes a coward to do so to his own family. I'm going to introduce Mr. Washington to how serious this lawman takes such behavior."

Chief Norman tipped his hat, and then walked out the screen door. Amburgey walked around Symphony and closed the inside door. Images flashed before Symphony's eyes of a small frail woman huddled in the cold. A tall man stood over her laughing.

"I bet it was Marguerite who told the Chief about what happened to Cecelia."

"What?" Symphony blinked her eyes and tried to focus on Amburgey. "Who's Marguerite?"

"She's a nurse at the clinic. She works dayshift. She is one tough lady." Amburgey looked over Symphony's shoulder before she whispered. "Marguerite is the spitting image of that woman who played Alice on the *Brady Bunch*. I swear she could be that actress' mother."

"Why are you talking about a TV show in a time without television? This is serious, Amburgey. Cecelia almost died. I could have prevented that."

"Symphony, stop it! This is not your fault. You said yourself that you tried to get her to call the police and you tried to take her to the clinic. This is not something that just happened in the last couple of days. Her husband probably has been abusive to her for their entire marriage. I told you that Chief Norman is serious about this type of stuff. He will get Cephas. The Chief will put him under the jail."

"What are you two out here whispering about? It's time for lunch. I tried to get the Chief to stay and eat with us. As you can see, he has pressing matters on his mind." Mrs. Bailey put her arm around Symphony. "You did a fine job telling him what you knew. Chief Norman is a tough member of law enforcement. He and his officers will find Cephas Washington, and they will make sure he gets what he deserves. Amburgey, you go upstairs to the gentlemen's floor. I told Mr. Barker and the others to wait in their sitting area while the Chief talked to Symphony. I'm sure they are famished."

Mrs. Bailey began to walk toward the kitchen as Amburgey climbed the staircase.

"Symphony, you come help me serve. Olivia is off today. You are in for a treat. I made my chicken and dumplings. I won a prize for this recipe at a state fair contest when I was in my late teens."

Symphony followed Mrs. Bailey to the kitchen. She half listened to the woman recount the story of her winning recipe, the other half of Symphony's mind was elsewhere. Rather than thinking about this older woman's memories of a happy day, Symphony thought of the young woman huddled in a small bed fighting for her physical health and, no doubt, her sanity. Symphony wondered why she crossed paths with her on this visit to 1924. How would Cecelia Washington's life fit into the mystery that brought Symphony to the Wytheville of this time? She wondered if she would ever know.

"We must remember the words of the Apostle Paul in his Letter to the Romans when he wrote, 'Love worketh no ill to his neighbour: therefore love *is* the fulfilling of the law.' What does this passage mean to you?"

Symphony stared straight ahead, trying to listen to the sermon of Reverend Isaiah Perry on Sunday morning. At the invitation of Mrs. Bailey, she and Amburgey joined their landlord for the mid-morning service.

Gazing up at the domed center of the sanctuary, Symphony admired the beautiful circular stained glass window at the apex. A delightful elderly gentleman she met upon entering the church told Symphony that the church was built only a few years earlier in 1916. He said that the structure was built upon a big spring that was an early water source for the town, and it was still visible in the basement.

"As we close our service, I ask each of you to join me in prayer for a young woman who has spent many years in our church and who is going through a time of tribulation and heartache. Lord, please send a shield of protection on our sister, Cecelia Washington. I remember the many summers she spent in this community as a child, visiting her beloved grandparents who were anchors of this church, Joseph and Caroline Gibboney—"

Symphony heard nothing after that. She and Amburgey almost broke their necks quickly turning to look at each other.

"What was your father's sister's name?" Symphony whispered to Amburgey.

"Cecelia." Amburgey put her hand over her mouth. "It never even occurred to me when you said her name. Dad took her to the future to escape an abusive husband."

The congregation stood and began to sing the closing hymn. Symphony looked again at the beautiful ceiling. Now, she knew why her path crossed Cecelia Washington's. It seemed that no matter what, she was drawn to members of her time-travelling family. Each piece of the puzzle should make the picture clearer to view. Instead, Symphony felt more confused about what it all might mean.

"THAT WOULD EXPLAIN why my father was here. Cecelia is nothing like he described her to be."

Upon returning from church, Symphony and Amburgey went to their room for a few minutes to discuss what they learned.

"This is obviously a low point in her life." Symphony took off her new shoes, and rubbed her feet. "You said you never met her, right?"

"No. I don't think when my father took her to the future, he intended for her to stay there. I remember him telling my mother about how dangerous her husband was. He said that she disappeared into the future. It all makes sense now."

"I can see why she didn't want to stay in 1924. I don't understand why she cut ties with Tyler. That part doesn't make sense if he saved her from her former life."

"Nothing about my family makes sense. Be thankful you aren't a part of it."

Symphony turned away to hide her reaction. She did not need to give any further reasons for Amburgey to question her motives or not to trust her.

"I'm going to go back downstairs and see if lunch is ready. I would like to get a short nap in before I have to go into work this afternoon." Symphony put her shoes back on.

"Good idea. I forgot that you have to start your week this evening. I'm looking forward to another day off before I have to return to the clinic. I saw one of the nurses at the church. She said that two of the dayshift nurses quit this week. I will probably have to work longer shifts because of it." Amburgey stood in front of the mirror and looked closely at her face. "Do you think I look anything like Cecelia?"

Symphony looked at Amburgey and thought about her question. She remembered that Tyler had said she reminded him of his sister. Symphony could not say that she noticed the details of Cecelia's features on Amburgey's face in the short time they were together. What was striking was the dark circles under the woman's eyes, and the fear within them.

"I really couldn't say. I only saw her briefly. Do you think we should go to the clinic and see her?"

"I thought about that yesterday while the police chief was here. I wonder if it might embarrass her for you to do so, considering what you saw. Maybe, we should ask Mrs. Bailey what she thinks. If Cecelia is associated with the church, Mrs. Bailey should know her."

"That's true. I can't imagine that she will want to go home once she is released."

"She probably doesn't think she has anywhere else to go." Amburgey joined Symphony at the door. "Maybe we can help her feel differently."

"Would that be messing with time?"

"You keep talking about stuff like that. What do you know that I do not?"

"I know enough to be afraid."

"Reverend Perry's sermon this morning spoke of loving your neighbor. Do you believe that applies whether the person is in a good situation or a bad?" Once everyone filled their plates and began eating, Symphony directed her question to Mrs. Bailey.

"Certainly. When our neighbor is in unfortunate circumstances, it is even more of a reason to help." Mrs. Bailey squinted looking at Symphony over the top of her glass of iced tea. "Why do you ask?"

"We know that Cecelia Washington was injured and is probably still recovering in the clinic. I was wondering if we might show some neighborly love by inviting her to come and stay here for a while when she is released. I would be willing to help pay for her room and board." Symphony bit her bottom lip waiting for Mrs. Bailey to respond.

"I would help, too." The expression on Amburgey's face showed worry.

"I will help the woman. She's in bad shape." Symphony turned to see Kathleen, the nurse who also boarded there in the doorway behind them. "I don't think I'm speaking out of turn by saying this. Chief Norman may have told you." Kathleen sat down in her normal spot at the table. "Her injuries were extensive with bruises on her back and legs. She had some minor frostbite. What we are most concerned about is how malnourished she is, especially because she is carrying a child."

Haunted by the Fire   215

"Oh, my goodness." Mrs. Bailey gasped. "That's all I need to hear. Kathleen, can you help us arrange for her to be brought here when she is able to leave the hospital?"

"I'm sure that Chief Norman would be happy to help make that happen. He already has been talking to Dr. Chitwood about seeing if she could be moved somewhere safe. Her husband has not been found yet."

"I'm going to call the Chief right now and tell him my intentions." Mrs. Bailey rose from the table. Passing behind Symphony, the woman squeezed her shoulder. "You have a good heart, young lady. I took you to church this morning. You obviously took the sermon to heart better than I did. You too, Miss Grumpy." Mrs. Bailey smiled and patted Amburgey on the top of her head while walking by.

"We will need to stand guard over this house until her husband is found." The older man who sat next to Kathleen at the table, who was normally silent, spoke. "I'm going upstairs to clean my gun."

"You do that, Mr. McClintock."

Kathleen patted him on the hand and he rose from his chair. Everyone was silent watching as Mr. McClintock carefully laid his cloth napkin over his half eaten plate of food.

"You tell Miss Olivia to save that for me. I will be back down to finish it once I've gotten my gun ready to protect Mrs. Washington."

Symphony watched the others' reactions. Mr. McClintock left the room.

"Is there something I don't know about Mr. McClintock?"

"Mr. McClintock was a police officer, Symphony. He was the sheriff in a neighboring county for many years until a cold December day shortly before Christmas in 1908." Mrs. Bailey returned to the room joining the conversation. "On that day, his only son was shot and killed on Main Street."

"Here in Wytheville?" Amburgey looked around the table.

"Yes. Walter McClintock was our Chief of Police." Mr. Barker responded. "He and a couple other officers were attempting to arrest two brothers on robbery charges. The officers approached the brothers on Main Street, in front of the courthouse, and told them they had warrants for their arrest. One of the brothers pulled out a handgun and opened fire, striking Chief McClintock. Despite being mortally wounded, the Chief was able to return fire and he killed the suspect. The other brother was taken into custody and later convicted of murder. Walter was thirty-nine years old and was only chief for a year."

"Wow. How very sad for Mr. McClintock and his family." Symphony took a deep breath.

"The day after his son's funeral, Mr. McClintock turned in his own badge." Mrs. Bailey's gaze seemed to fall on something far away. "I remember hearing that he said his wife worried about him and their son all their married life. She'd been through enough. I imagine that he will station himself outside of whatever room we put Mrs. Washington in, with his rifle cocked and ready, laying across his lap."

"Once a law man, always a law man." Mr. Barker nodded his head and rose from the table. "I believe the other gentlemen here and I will be happy to take turns relieving him."

"Glad to hear that. Mr. McClintock is not a young man. His health is frail. His wife died two years ago. He's lived here ever since. It will give him something to focus his attention on—a purpose that befits his talents." Mrs. Bailey looked around the table. Symphony could see the concern in her eyes. "I was able to speak with Chief Norman. Mr. Washington has not been found. He will ensure that Cecelia is brought here in a secretive manner."

"That's not going to be easy to do." Amburgey began helping Olivia take the dishes into the kitchen.

"I'm sure Chief Norman has his ways." Olivia spoke up. "He's a smart man. This isn't the first time he's hidden someone from harm."

Symphony heard a tone of conviction in Olivia's voice. She wondered what the woman knew or, perhaps, what firsthand experience she had with the subject.

"How do you think he will do it, Olivia?" The excitement in Amburgey's voice reminded Symphony of someone watching a suspense movie.

"What's the best way to hide someone? In plain sight. I imagine that poor Cecelia Washington will be overcome by her injuries and sadly pass way." Olivia shook her head. A smile crossed her face. "They will call the undertaker to come and retrieve her. That way, she can be covered up and carried right out of the front door."

"Olivia, if I didn't know better, I would think you participated in such yourself." Mrs. Bailey winked at Symphony. She bumped Olivia, who was gathering plates beside her. "That's exactly what the Chief told me that would be done. Cecelia will be taken in the hearse to the funeral home, in case someone is watching. Then, they will put her in a disguise, and bring her here later. She will stay here to build up her strength. Later, she will be taken somewhere far away to start a new life. No one seems to know where her family is from. We can help her contact them, if she still has any."

A look passed between Symphony and Amburgey. Only they knew just how far away Cecelia would eventually go.

Chapter Thirteen

B Y THE TIME THAT SYMPHONY WOKE up the following morning, Chief Norman's plan was carried out. While working at the telephone company on Sunday evening, she connected several calls for him while he tried to find any of Cecelia's family. The grandparents who Mrs. Bailey mentioned were long since deceased. Their daughter, Cecelia's mother, was dead as well. Symphony opened her eyes to find Amburgey staring at her.

"She's here. We've got to find my father."

"What?" Symphony's mouth opened in a huge yawn. It was the soundest night of sleep she had experienced in 1924. "You told me that you were trying to avoid Tyler."

"I was. His sister needs him. Maybe it's time for him to take her to the future."

"It may be. It's not our job to write the story though. It will happen when it's supposed to."

"You are so nonchalant about everything. What's the good of travelling back in time if we can't help make something happen? I'm following my instincts on this one. My inner compass says that I need to find Dad so he can rescue his sister."

Symphony was stunned to see that Amburgey was already dressed for the day. Because of the overnight hours that she worked at the clinic, Amburgey normally slept until almost noon to keep her inner clock on the same schedule.

"Did he ever tell you that you were a part of the process of helping his sister?" Symphony stood up.

"No." Amburgey continued sitting on her bed while Symphony put on her robe.

"Maybe that's because you aren't a part of it." Symphony picked up her toiletry bag and opened the door. "I suggest that you leave the situation alone."

"Is that what you're doing?" Symphony stopped. "If that was really true for you, I don't think you would be talking to me in 1924. Don't lecture me about messing with time, Symphony. You are doing the same thing yourself."

Symphony continued walking out the door and down the hallway to the bathroom. Every task she had to complete in the next few minutes was done in a harried, non-thinking manner. She didn't stop moving or begin thinking until a stream of hot water showering down safely surrounded her. Only then, did Symphony allow her emotions to come to the surface. She slowly sank down to the floor of the tub and began to sob.

"She's been sleeping ever since she arrived." Mrs. Bailey spoke quietly with Symphony outside of the door of the bedroom where Cecelia was resting. "I thought it would be best to put her on the same floor with me. It would be easier for the doctor to visit her and not be too far for the poor girl to walk downstairs when she is able."

Mrs. Bailey's boarding house was a huge structure. Symphony did not think that the home still existed in her modern time. The house had four full floors and an attic. She and Amburgey's room was on the top floor, 'the ladies floor,' as Mrs. Bailey called it. Directly below them was 'the gentlemen's floor.' Mrs. Bailey's personal area was on the second floor. It was the first time that Symphony was in that area of the house since she arrived, aside from walking up the staircase. Like the two higher floors, the area had three bedrooms and a large sitting room. One bathroom was on the end of the hall.

"I'm surprised at how large this house is. How old is it?"

"It is very spacious, even for the time. It was built in the 1830s by a family that was quite involved with railroad and lumber. They were one of the richest families in Virginia at one point. They had eight children and wanted a spacious home."

"Has Mr. McClintock been there all night?" Symphony nodded in the direction of the stairs.

A straight back chair was placed at the top of the staircase, across the hallway from the door to the bedroom occupied by Cecelia. Mr. McClintock sat there, his head bobbing occasionally while he unsuccessfully tried to fight sleep. As predicted, his rifle lay across his lap.

"He has been. Mr. Barker is finishing his breakfast and will be up shortly to relieve him. Mr. McClintock was quite a dedicated lawman in his day. I expect nothing but vigilance from him while he guards Cecelia." Mrs. Bailey quietly opened the door so that she and Symphony could peek inside. "I fear that she will have a long recovery. The poor thing is as weak as a kitten."

Quietly, Symphony and Mrs. Bailey tiptoed into the room. While similar in layout to the one she occupied with Amburgey, the room seemed more spacious since it only contained one full-size bed. The bed was placed near the window. The morning sun was peeking in and cast a shadow on the wood floor. Under a beautiful quilt lay a small figure, huddled in a ball. Symphony could only see wisps of the woman's hair and the pallor of her skin. A chill went down Symphony's spine thinking about what the woman had endured. It made perfect sense why her brother wanted to whisk her into another time. Mrs. Bailey adjusted the covers and tidied up a few things before they crept back out and saw that Mr. Barker was now stationed at the guarding post. After some words of greeting to him, Mrs. Bailey continued talking with Symphony.

"Why don't you go downstairs and have breakfast with Mr. McClintock? I'm sure he would enjoy having some company. I believe that you two are the last ones who need to eat."

Symphony nodded and walked down the two flights of stairs to the bottom floor. When she entered the dining room, she found that both Mr. McClintock and Chief Norman were sitting at the table. They rose at the same time.

"Good morning, gentlemen. I was not expecting to see you, Chief Norman." Both men sat back down after Symphony did so. "You must have had a busy night. I hope you found Mr. Washington."

"I have not, ma'am. I fear that someone in this community is hiding him, probably against their will. I've had men going door-to-door in town looking for him. Later today, we are going to start searching out in the county."

"Are people being told that Cecelia passed away?"

"Well, Miss Wallace, let's just say that we are not correcting folks who come to that conclusion. Her injuries could have certainly led to a mortal wounding. From the looks of her, she's not completely out of the woods yet. We are treating this like a case of attempted murder. When you lock your wife outside in the cold of winter, your intent speaks for itself."

The door to the kitchen swung open with Olivia backing her way in carrying two plates of food.

"Sleeping beauty finally rose from her long nap, I see." Olivia placed steaming plates of food in front of first, Chief Norman, and then, Mr. McClintock. "I made those eggs exactly the way you like them, Mr. McClintock—hard on the edges and runny in the middle."

"Oh my, Olivia, they sure look good. How will I ever eat three of them though?" For the first time, Symphony saw Mr. McClintock smile. His grin was missing a few teeth, but it was beautiful all the same. "That's more of a breakfast for a working man like the Chief here."

"He gets a plate like yours too. You men are working law, and need a good breakfast to give you the stamina you will need." Olivia patted Mr. McClintock on the back. "I'll be back with yours in a minute." Olivia nodded to Symphony. "I'll bring you some of my apple butter for your biscuits, Chief."

"Is it your momma's recipe?"

"Of course." Olivia filled the Chief's coffee cup.

"Then, you might as well bring the whole jar. I could eat it by itself with a spoon."

After Olivia returned to the kitchen, Symphony watched the two men eat. Both plates were filled to the edges with eggs, fried potatoes, country ham, grits, and slices of tomato. Between them was a plate of hot biscuits wrapped in a towel. Symphony's mouth watered watching them. Like in 1950, food tasted better in 1924 than she ever experienced in her own time.

"Before we moved her, I was able to talk to Mrs. Washington. She confirmed everything that others said. She was afraid to go to the police because of what she thought Cephas might do to her. Cecelia understands now that I am going to get her away from here, whether I find her husband or not. I'm sure it would put her mind more at ease if I could tell her that he was in custody. I think that there is surely a place in this great big country that we can take her where he can't find her ever again."

Symphony took a long drink of water from the glass in front of her. She wondered if this was actually the timeframe from which Tyler took his sister away.

"Miss Wallace, you didn't happen to take any calls last night concerning Cephas Washington, did you?"

"No, sir. Only the ones you made, Chief. It was actually a rather slow evening for telephone calls. I did hear some folks chatting about the situation." Symphony looked down at the napkin in her lap. "I'm embarrassed to say that I listened to those conversations a little longer than I should have."

"I believe I asked you to do that, young lady. I'm presuming that you heard some gossip about the situation."

Olivia returned with a bowl of apple butter that she placed in the center of the table and a full jar that she set in front of Chief Norman. He gave her a big smile. Walking around the table to Symphony, she placed a plate in front of her.

"Thank you. The eggs look delicious."

"Scrambled and fluffy, like little yellow clouds. That's what I used to tell my momma. It's how I like my eggs, too. Eat up. These two still look hungry. Just because they are lawmen, doesn't mean they might not try to steal your food."

Mr. McClintock looked up from his almost clean plate and shook his head in agreement.

"That was mighty good ham, Miss Olivia. Is there anymore back in the kitchen? I'd like to make a ham biscuit with honey like my Rose used to make me."

"Yes, sir. There's plenty. You want anything else, Chief?"

"No. I'm good. This is my second breakfast today. I couldn't resist your good cooking."

Symphony started eating her breakfast. She couldn't help watching the Chief slather a biscuit with apple butter. She wondered how different their jobs were from the officers who came after them in the decades since. She was sure that both men would be surprised at the technology that was commonplace in modern police work.

"Has Mr. Washington been in trouble with the law before?" Symphony broke the silence at the table. Taking her first bite of a hot biscuit slathered in butter, she rolled her eyes back in her head with pure pleasure.

"Yes. Apparently, he has quite the reputation for stealing. He came here with the railroad. I've been told that employment was a front for petty theft. It seems that on certain train trips, people were reporting items being stolen from their belongings—small things that could easily be slipped into a pocket, like a piece of jewelry or a liquor flask, or outright cash. The railroad company investigated and discovered that Cephas was working on each of those trips. He was a ticket taker. It was a part of his job to go up and down the aisles and converse with the passengers. His personality is such that he could be the charming sort, when he wanted to be. Apparently, he charmed some folks right out of their valuables."

"Why did he end up staying here? Did he have a family connection to Wytheville? I'm sure there are many train depot towns, big and small, where he could have landed."

"I believe he met Cecelia in another town. When she mentioned about the summers she spent here with her grandparents, Cephas probably thought that she came from a rich family. Her grandparents were quite well off when Cecelia was a child. They fell on hard times shortly before their deaths, and lost their home and savings."

The thought passed through Symphony's mind that the people Chief Norman was referring to were her own great-grandparents. It was bizarre for the concept to sink in.

After Chief Norman finished talking, he drank the last of his coffee and rose from the table about the same time that Olivia re-entered the room with Mr. McClintock's ham and honey.

"Thank you for the delicious meal and this jar of apple butter. I've got to get back to looking for Cephas. Tell Mrs. Bailey I will drop back by this evening to see how Cecelia is doing. If she needs me before then, have her call the office. Unless something major happens, I plan to have an officer patrol through here every hour or so to keep a look out in case Cephas gets wind of what we've done. I'm leaving the safety of this house in your capable hands, sir."

Chief Norman shook hands with Mr. McClintock. Putting on his wide brim hat, he tipped it to Olivia and Symphony as he walked toward the door.

"That's as fine a man as you will ever meet. My heart was broken over the reason he became the Chief here. I cannot think of a better lawman to walk in my son's shoes."

Mr. McClintock went back to eating his ham biscuit with honey. Symphony respected his silence and continued to eat her meal without conversation. A few minutes later, after he drank the last of a glass of milk, he stood up, nodded at Symphony, and left the room. Symphony picked up the remaining dishes on the table and joined Olivia in the kitchen.

"Olivia, I thought I would help you with all of these dishes."

"I can always use some help." Olivia stood at the stove adding ingredients to a huge pot of soup. "I'm about finished with this soup."

Symphony had not been in the kitchen too many times. Watching Olivia, she noticed the unusual stove. It reminded her of one that was on display at the Boyd Museum. She thought it was going to be incorporated into a new educational exhibit that was being planned.

"My goodness! This is a Hughes Electric Range." Symphony ran her fingers across the brand name on the appliance. She remembered doing the same thing when she first saw the similar one on display.

"Mrs. Bailey paid a pretty penny for it, I've been told. It took me some time to get used to cooking with it." Olivia continued to stir the soup.

"It's the first stove to include burners and an oven in one appliance." Symphony opened one of the white enamel oven doors and peeked inside. "It's strange how they make the doors white and the rest of it is black."

"How come you know so much about stoves?"

Symphony cringed. Her nervous chatter got her in trouble again.

"I have an uncle that sells appliances."

"Does he sell clocks? You seem to be interested in them, too. Did you find the clock you were looking for?"

"I did. It was in the First National Bank, exactly like you said."

"Uh huh. I've heard that clock is quite special." Olivia put the lid on the top of the soup pot. "My Daddy says it has parts that work and others that don't, but the clock still keeps perfect time all the same. He says it must have a deal with time, like some people have a deal with the devil."

"Oh, that's interesting." Symphony rolled up her sleeves and began to wash the dishes she saw soaking in the sink.

"Interesting, huh? I find it interesting that both you and Miss Amburgey have an interest in clocks. That doesn't seem to be the normal hobby of young ladies like yourselves. Why are timepieces interesting to you?"

Olivia brought the cutting board she was using to the sink. Wiping her hands on a towel, she stared at the side of Symphony's face. Symphony could feel her gaze like someone had lit a match next to her cheekbone. She dared not look the woman in the eye for fear that the truth would come pouring out.

"I told you. I like clocks."

"Uh huh. You like clocks. You like them or they like you?"

"Oh, Olivia. How could a clock like me?" A nervous laugh escaped Symphony, followed by a snort. "You have such a crazy sense of humor."

"More like I have a keen insight into things that aren't quite like they seem. I heard Amburgey tell Mrs. Bailey that you and she are cousins. I think you are closer kin than that."

Symphony could not stop herself from looking at Olivia that time. Nor could she control the shocked expression she knew was on her face.

"Aha! I knew it."

"Why are you saying that? Do you think we look alike?"

"It's less about the looks and more about the disposition. If I didn't know better, I would think you were mother and daughter. But that can't be unless you two know more about time than the telling of it."

A pain shot through Symphony's hand. She turned back to the sink. The water was red. She dropped the glass when Olivia guessed the truth and did not realize it had broken.

"Lord, child, you've cut yourself." Olivia grabbed Symphony's arm and pulled it out of the water while wrapping a towel around the cut on her hand. "Hold that tight while I go and get some medicine and bandages."

Symphony looked down at her hand in stunned silence. How could she be so careless? It was even more frightening to think about what Olivia might be able to figure out about the reality of the relationship between her and Amburgey. Olivia was either wise beyond her years or had wisdom from experience she probably did not care to share.

Within a couple of minutes, Olivia returned with a box filled with first aid supplies and bandages. They sat at the small table in the kitchen where Olivia first carefully cleaned the cut, and then tightly secured a cloth bandage. There was silence between them. Symphony could feel an unspoken presence, like a fog hanging over the room.

"My goodness. What has happened here?" Mrs. Bailey walked into the kitchen through the swinging door.

"Symphony was helping me with the dishes and broke a glass." Olivia made eye contact with Symphony and shook her head. "We were talking nonsense and she was distracted, I guess. I don't think it needs stitches, but it bled quite a bit."

"I can see that." Mrs. Bailey moved over to the sink area and was looking at the bloody water. "Are you sure we don't need to take her to the clinic?"

"I don't think the cut is too deep. I've bound it tightly. Maybe the doctor can look at it when he comes to check on Mrs. Washington later. You favor your right hand, I believe. This cut on your left should not prevent you from working." Olivia gathered up the rest of supplies and rose from the table. "I've got lots to clean up in this kitchen before I can go home to my family." What began with a stern look to Symphony, ended with a wink and a knowing nod as Olivia encouraged them to leave the kitchen.

"Thank you." Symphony stopped at the door while Mrs. Bailey walked out ahead of her. "I'm sorry that I made a mess."

"That mess can be fixed. I encourage you to be careful, Symphony. Some messes have permanent consequences."

Looking out of the front window, Symphony saw that while it looked cold outside, the sun was shining. She did not see anyone else in the downstairs area and made her way up the steps. Symphony thought she might gather her coat and hat and go for a walk around town. It was still a couple of hours before she would need to report to work.

Mr. Barker nodded to her from his post at the top of the second level landing. An open newspaper covered his lap with Mr. McClintock's rifle in clear view within easy access next to him. She thought she might be hearing deep snores when she walked up past the gentlemen's floor. Mr. McClintock was surely resting after the long night and large breakfast.

Entering her room, she found Amburgey, still fully dressed, stretched out on the bed. Symphony tried to quietly gather her stuff. She saw Amburgey slowly open one eye, and then the other.

"Did you eat two breakfasts?" Amburgey sat up in the bed. "What happened to your hand?"

"I had a little accident in the kitchen." Symphony bit her bottom lip. She wondered about telling Amburgey about her conversation with Olivia. "I think Olivia is suspicious. She seems to know a little about time travel."

"That wouldn't surprise me. History will tell you that Olivia will become one of the smartest women to ever come from this area. And her father, his relationship with clocks is something out of a magical story."

"What do you mean?" Symphony sat down on the edge of her bed, opposite Amburgey.

"They call him the Clock Man. He can fix any timepiece that's put in front of him. But that is not all. People say that he can look at a clock and make it stop. He can tell stories about where a clock was and situations that occurred near it."

"The Clock Man. Do you think it's the piece of machinery that he connects with or time itself?"

"That's a good question. I would think it might be hard to separate one from the other. The clock marks the time, but time has to pass through it."

"We pass through time. We've passed through a clock." Symphony allowed her thoughts to have voice. "It's not the same for all time travelers though. We know that telephone booths are at least one portal that Tyler uses. I've heard stories about time travelers using closets, cellars, or even plain doors."

"It is strange that you and I both use the same clock. I made up a story about us being related. I wonder if we have a connection somehow. If something about our ending up in the same time period is not simple coincidence."

"I wonder." It was the only thing Symphony could think of to say that would not incite more questions from Amburgey. "Olivia thinks there is a connection between us. Maybe her father knows more about time than clocks."

"I've been waiting for you to come back upstairs." Amburgey began putting on her shoes. "I want to go and look for my father."

"Amburgey, I really don't think that is a good idea. It could be dangerous for the two of you to be in close contact, especially if he doesn't know about your existence yet." Symphony closed her eyes and shook her head. Her words tasted bitter. She thought about the secrets that Amburgey did not yet know. "I don't think he is in Wytheville now. We can't be sure when he took Cecelia to the future. We don't want to interfere in what is to happen or has happened. I'm going for a walk before it's time for me to go to work. Why don't you come with me? We can do a little exploring and see what the town looks like. I bet we can find some places that still exist in our own times."

"I probably should depart sooner than later. It's not like I'm any closer to finding my mystery man either. Maybe I should give up."

"You can't give up." Symphony's voice went up an octave. She felt a surge of panic pass through her. She had no idea if the man in Amburgey's photograph was her father. It seemed like a logical deduction though. "Do you have the photograph with you? If I knew what he looked like, I could help you look."

"Certainly. It's my time travel token." Amburgey went to a drawer and dug around in her belongings.

"What?" Symphony's hand immediately went to the pendant hidden under her blouse.

"Like your pendant. I have to have this photo with me in order to travel in time." Amburgey pulled the photo out of the drawer and gazed at it.

An ice-cold chill passed over Symphony. A pain shot through her head with piercing accuracy. The room spun for a moment. Amburgey turned the photo around for Symphony to see. Something was happening. Her eyes began to focus on the photo, and the image of the man became clearer. It was like she was seeing it for the first time, even though it was in her possession all her life. There was something familiar about the face that Symphony never realized before—something hauntingly familiar.

"You still haven't explained your reaction to seeing my photo."

Symphony and Amburgey briskly walked down Tazewell Street in the direction of the Rock House. Symphony wanted to see what the structure was like almost one hundred years before she lived and worked in it. She stopped on the corner of Tazewell and Monroe and studied the building.

"Why are you staring at this house?" Amburgey stopped next to Symphony and looked at the structure. "Does it mean something to you?"

Symphony furrowed her brow. She searched her mind for the timeline of the structure. She thought that the Town of Wytheville purchased the Rock House some time during the late 1960s. She did not know when it opened for tours or how frequently it was open in the early years. She seemed to remember Marcella telling her that Allison was hired in the 1990s to oversee the museum operations. If Amburgey was from the early 1980s, the Rock House might not be open to the public yet in her time.

"It's quite unusual, don't you think?" Symphony decided that it was better not to dwell on any significance. "Most of the houses are wood or brick. This is made of rock."

"Well, yeah, I guess. Some of the big buildings on Main Street are made of stone, like that bank we need to visit."

"Yes, they are stone though. Smooth surfaces. This looks more like rocks."

"I guess that makes it a rock house then." Amburgey giggled at her joke. "I can't remember if it still exists in my time. Does it in yours?"

Symphony watched Amburgey tilt her head and stare at the building again. She could almost see the wheels turning while Amburgey's mind searched for the image in her memory.

"I think it does." Symphony pointed to the left. "Let's walk this way and loop back to Main Street. I think there is an alleyway about a block down."

Amburgey followed as Symphony headed further down Monroe Street. Approaching the alley that led back to Main Street, Symphony realized that it was the location of the apartment where Cecelia lived.

"Amburgey, look! There's someone lurking around the door to the apartment." Symphony pulled Amburgey back and peeked around the corner of the building. "We don't want him to see us."

"Surely, it's not Cephas. He wouldn't return here in broad daylight. Let me see." Amburgey inched her way around Symphony, hitting a bucket that was sitting in front of the building they were hiding behind. It began to roll down the street, making a racket. "Crap! That person will see us."

The man turned around and was walking toward them. In full view, Symphony realized that it was Saul Alper. He waved when he recognized Symphony.

"Shew, that scared me. It's the owner of the building."

"Oh yeah. He owns the store in the front. He has an adorable son. He and his wife brought the baby into the clinic early one morning before first light. He had the croup. I wished that I had a humidifier from modern days to help—"

"Hello, Mr. Alper." Symphony interrupted Amburgey when Mr. Alper got closer to them. "I guess you must think we are silly hiding around this corner."

"Considering the tragedy that occurred here, I am not surprised to see people lurking around while the murderer is still on the loose."

"Murderer?"

Symphony elbowed Amburgey in the ribs.

"Yes, Amburgey. Didn't you tell me that there was a young woman who was brought into the clinic with injuries that led to her passing?"

"Oh, yes. It is so sad. Is this the area where she was found?"

"I am saddened to confirm that, ma'am. The police are searching for the scoundrel who left his wife to die in the cold. The man is trouble. Against my better judgment, I continued to allow them to live here. My heart was sympathetic for the woman's plight to be saddled with such a worthless creature." Mr. Alper shook his head. "My wife was wondering when you are going to visit us again. I do not mean for purchasing items. My Fannie enjoyed your conversations, Miss Wallace."

"She is delightful. I will visit soon. Do you know Miss Amburgey Gibboney, Mr. Alper?"

"Yes." Saul nodded. "Miss Gibboney was most helpful when we brought our Melvin into the clinic in the wee hours of the morning. We were beside ourselves in fear. He could hardly breathe. The doctor and nurses were able to ease his discomfort and our worried souls."

"I hope that the police can find this man who treated his wife so badly. What is his name again?" Symphony was careful to guard that they had any other knowledge.

"Cephas Washington. I cannot imagine that he has travelled too far in this cold. The Police Chief thinks that he might have forced someone to conceal him. It is possible that he hopped a train as well. That is the way he came to our town. You found me checking to make sure there was not any evidence of his return. My brother-in-law and I are going to aid in the search for him this afternoon. He must be brought to justice. Mrs. Washington was a long-suffering child of God to have put up with him for so long. May she rest with the angels." Saul took off his hat and bowed his head. Returning his hat to his head, he began to walk back in the direction of his building. "You ladies be careful out in this weather. Even with the sun shining, it does not take long for it to become too cold if you do not keep moving."

"Thank you, Mr. Alper. Give my best to Fannie. I look forward to seeing her and Melvin again."

A pain shot through Symphony's skull. It must have caused her expression to change, because Amburgey took hold of her arm.

"Are you okay? You look like you are in pain."

"The cold must be getting to me." Symphony put her hand flat against the wall beside her to steady herself. "Why don't we go to one of the coffee shops nearby?"

Amburgey continued to hold Symphony's arm while walking past the apartment where Saul stood. On the windowsill was a flowerbox filled with winter pansies. The purple, blue, and yellow flowers peeked out. Symphony did not remember seeing them when she brought Cecelia home. A pile of straw was under the windowsill. The configuration of the straw made Symphony wonder if that was where Cecelia lay huddled in the cold. A feeling of immense sadness overcame her, and she felt tears well up in her eyes.

"It's so incredibly scary." Amburgey seemed to be reading her thoughts. "Cecelia must be made of some strong stuff to have survived that night of cold with her other injuries." Amburgey turned and looked behind her. "I've got to be more careful. We don't know who might be listening. I sure do hope I get to meet her someday. Meet her as a member of my family."

They found a small table near the window at the Blue Ribbon

Lunch. Symphony felt chilled to the bone and ordered coffee with a piece of apple pie. The restaurant was unusually busy. After a few minutes of looking around, she realized that most of the patrons were men with guns strapped to their sides.

"Do you think that Chief Norman called in help from neighboring communities?" Amburgey leaned across the table and whispered. "We don't have this many police officers locally."

"I made at least a dozen telephone calls for him last evening. This must be some of the results. Surely, with all of these people looking, they will find him."

"We can hope. But, you know a snake like Cephas Washington can slither in and out of a lot of places. He could be hundreds of miles away by now." Amburgey looked around again and whispered even softer. "Maybe she will be years and years away before they find him."

"Let's hope that he doesn't have the ability to travel the same way." The sharp pain returned to Symphony's head. This time, it was so severe her reflex was to grab hold of the side of her head. "Ouch."

"That's it. I've seen you do that one too many times. We are going to the clinic." Amburgey drank the last of her coffee before lying a quarter on top of the bill. "I cannot get used to paying so little for things. Ten cents for a slice of pie and coffee. It's like we are in another world." Amburgey winked. "Oh, wait. We are."

Symphony forced a smile and rose to her feet. She felt lightheaded but would not dare let Amburgey see that.

"I'm really fine." Symphony put on her coat and hat. Her gloves fell to the floor. Before she could reach to pick them up, a handsome young man quickly retrieved them.

"Here you go, ma'am. Those pretty hands will get cold without these."

Flashing her a big smile, the man looked like he had just walked out of a movie. He made her think of Garon Fitzgerald in his early Hollywood days. She missed her friend.

"You have excellent timing, Collin. I was just about to take my friend to the clinic. You can help us." Amburgey put on her coat and hat.

"I've told you that I'm fine. We don't need to bother this gentleman."

"Gentleman is a stretch, Symphony. This fellow is a medical student doing his residency at the clinic. He's also a big flirt."

"Don't pay any attention to what she says." Collin offered Symphony his arm. "I've got a Model T out front and would be happy to drive you to the clinic and examine you personally."

"You can drive her, slick. We will let someone else examine her." Amburgey glared at Collin.

"I really don't want—" Symphony started to speak, but Amburgey raised her hand.

"You don't want to make me mad so you are going to go willingly. That's what you were going to say, right?" Amburgey tilted her head and raised her eyebrows in a questioning manner. "That's what I thought. Go get your car, Collin. We'll meet you out front."

Collin released Symphony's arm and disappeared out the door. Symphony was about to protest further when she realized that Chief Norman was walking toward them. He began talking to a group of men and did not see them.

"We've got some maps for you outside and have divided you into pairs. I don't think that it is advisable for anyone to search alone. Washington may be armed. At the least, I do not think he will surrender willingly. You might need back up."

Before Symphony could say anything to him, Chief Norman

began talking to some of the men individually, and then went back out the door.

"Cephas Washington doesn't stand a chance with all of these men looking for him." Amburgey leaned in from behind Symphony as they made their way out with the group. "All of these men look tougher than him."

"Anyone who leaves his wife out in the cold deserves the same treatment himself." A tall man dressed in black stated to another man in front of them.

While he was holding the door open for Symphony and Amburgey to pass, Symphony got a good look at him. Collin was waiting with the door of his Model T opened for them to jump in.

"Did you see him?" Amburgey whispered into Symphony's ear once they were inside.

"He was the spitting image of—"

"The man in black himself. I could hear him singing in my ears." Amburgey laughed while they waited for Collin to get into the driver's seat.

"I hear a train a coming..."

"You can't possibly hear the train. The depot is at least two miles from here." Collin jumped in and closed the door. "I think you really must have hurt your head if you are hearing trains."

After a long pause, Symphony and Amburgey could not hold it in any longer and burst into sidesplitting laughter. Collin shook his head and drove down the street.

"I APPRECIATE YOU dropping me off at work, Collin." Symphony took the man's offered hand, and then she climbed out of his car in front of the telephone office. "The doctor said I'm fine. I probably have the beginnings of a head cold or a sinus infection."

"There is no sense in you having to walk in this cold. I am happy to drive you."

"It was nice to meet you." Standing awkwardly in front of the business, Symphony extended her hand to shake Collin's. "It is about time for my shift to begin. Thank you, again." Symphony smiled and turned to walk down the sidewalk into the building. She almost reached the door when she heard Collin.

"May I call you one day soon and ask you to dinner?" The tone of Collin's voice was a mixture of overconfidence and schoolboy shy.

"I am flattered by your kind offer. I am afraid that I must decline." She turned to face Collin. "I have a boyfriend back in my hometown." Symphony saw the smile leave his face.

"Certainly. My mistake. I'm sorry. I hope you get to feeling better." Collin hopped back into his vehicle before Symphony could say anything else.

Symphony was surrounded when she entered the building.

"Was that Collin Gleaves who brought you to work?"

One of the dayshift switchboard operators, a blonde named Thelma took hold of Symphony's right arm. At the same time, the front desk secretary, a redhead named Helen, took hold of her left.

"Yes. I was at the clinic and he offered to drive me here."

"He's a dreamboat." Thelma cooed and made her eyes flutter. "I'd love for him to be my jelly bean."

"Jelly bean?" Symphony furrowed her brow.

"You know, jelly bean, beau, boyfriend." Thelma shook her head and rolled her eyes. "He's the bee's knees."

"My sister, Caroline, dates his roommate. Collin comes from a wealthy family. They got a lot of clams." Helen chimed in as they continued walking down the hallway.

"Clams? Is his family in the seafood business?"

"Are you trying to be funny or are you that dingy?" Thelma was not mincing any words. "His family has a lot of clams. That means they are rich. He's not a dew dropper though."

"From the look on her face, Thelma, I don't think Symphony knows what a dew dropper is either." She cackled. Symphony thought it sound like a hen. "A dew dropper is a lollygagger. You know, a deadbeat who doesn't work. Caroline says that Collin is a hard worker. Maybe that's why his family has so much money. They are workers."

"Are you going to date him, Symphony?" Thelma seemed eager for an answer.

"No. I am not."

"He sure was looking at you like he wanted to take you to a show." Having released Symphony's arm, Thelma now elbowed her in the ribs and winked. "You are probably a Mrs. Grundy."

"Yeah, Mrs. Grundy!" Helen joined in the laughter. "Oh, I don't think she knows that one either, Thelma."

"A Mrs. Grundy is a prude, a fire extinguisher." Thelma suddenly stopped talking.

Back in the switchboard area, Symphony closed her eyes and shook her head. Mr. Smothe was coming down the hallway and the other women scattered. He nodded to Symphony when he passed.

"Those girls are going to get themselves in trouble if they keep up that silly talk." Joy Kiracofe came up behind Symphony, startling her. "I didn't mean to scare you."

"I've got to admit that I barely understood what they were talking about. We don't use those types of slang phrases where I come from."

"It's all the rage to say a bunch of gibberish without saying what you mean. They think they are modern city girls because they read *Cosmopolitan* magazine, and go to the picture shows every Saturday."

"It's so good to see you. I thought that you were not coming back. Aren't you supposed to be getting married?"

"I will be getting married on April 20. It will be Easter Sunday. Mr. Smothe asked me to come back for a couple more weeks since he lost two more daytime operators. These girls he's been hiring don't understand the meaning of work. He's lucky to have you."

"I'm happy to see you again. The last week was frightful." Symphony put on her headset and took a call. "Number, please. How may I connect you?" After a brief pause, she continued. "Good afternoon, Mrs. Thacker. No, I do not know if they have apprehended him yet. Chief Norman is working hard to find him. Did you wish me to make a call for you? You have a good evening, too."

"It's atrocious what that Mr. Washington did to his wife! May her soul rest in peace."

Symphony had no way of knowing if Cecelia truly ended up getting any peace. Everything indicated that the woman did get a change of scenery in her lifestyle, if nothing else.

"Miss Kiracofe, I appreciate you agreeing to help us in our time of need." Mr. Smothe re-entered the room. "Miss Wallace does need to give her undivided attention to our customers though. I think it's time for you to go home."

"Yes, sir. I was leaving." Joy winked at Symphony. She picked up her handbag from a small table in the corner and took her coat off the peg beside where Symphony hung hers. "I hope you have a good evening of pleasant callers, Miss Wallace."

"Thank you, Miss Kiracofe."

While commonplace in the beginning of their relationship,

their formalness now seemed almost comical. A bond formed that Symphony knew would last the test of time.

Chapter Fourteen

FROM SUNRISE TO SUNSET OVER the next three days, Chief Norman sent out teams of men in different directions in search of Cephas Washington to no avail.

"It's as if he's vanished into thin air." The Chief sat at Mrs. Bailey's breakfast table on Thursday morning. "No matter how many people we question in every direction, no one saw him. He's either a master at evading our possé of men, or he's found himself a hole and climbed in. If he managed to somehow get on a train, it's hard to tell where he could be by now. One thing is for sure; sooner or later someone will find him. I've sent a wanted poster for him out as far as I can."

"How did you have a photograph of him?" Amburgey's question seemed a little out of place, causing all eyes at the table to turn in her direction.

"We found one in Cecelia's belongings when we cleaned out

the apartment." Chief Norman gave Amburgey a long hard look. His gaze was piercing. "They had photographs made when they got married. There were individual photographs of each of them, and then one together."

Symphony looked at Amburgey out of the corner of her eye. Her lips were tightly closed, and she was rocking slightly back and forth in the chair. Symphony thought she looked like a child who got in trouble and was trying to remain quiet.

"Cecelia was able to walk a little down the hallway yesterday and today." Mrs. Bailey drew the conversation in her direction. "The doctor was here this morning. He was pleased to see the progress she has made."

"Did he say how soon she might be able to travel? I've promised her that I would get her away from here as soon as possible." Chief Norman held his cup up for Mrs. Bailey to refill it.

"I think that will be quite some time yet. She's still weak and unstable on her feet." Mrs. Bailey filled her own cup before setting the coffee carafe down. "I see a great deal of fear in her eyes. But, there are glimmers of strength, too. That strength will get stronger each day."

"The longer she stays here, the greater the chance that someone will figure out she is still alive." Mr. Barker spoke from his seat across the table from Symphony. He had remained silent in the conversation up until that point.

"Mr. Barker, I do not believe there is anyone in this house who shall betray this confidence. Do you?" Mrs. Bailey gave him a stern look and kept the same expression while she slowly looked around the table.

"I do not, Mrs. Bailey. But, what about those who visit this house?"

"There will be no new boarders or visits from strangers. Deliveries will come to the kitchen door, as always, without any access into the interior of this house. I've never tolerated the loafing of deliverymen. There's no use in allowing it now."

"What about the young ladies receiving gentleman callers?" Mr. Barker seemed to be relentless with his questions.

"With no offense intended to the young ladies who board here, it is not like there are gentlemen coming to our door every evening to call on them. I think that Kathleen, Amburgey, and Symphony all have good sense, and they will be cautious if either of them have a date." Mrs. Bailey looked at each of the three young women.

"You don't think that Cecelia will try to leave, do you, Chief?" Kathleen spoke the question that Symphony was thinking. "It's not uncommon for people to flee from safe conditions when they experience as much anxiety as she has."

"I hope not, ma'am. I've thought of that myself. She is afraid. That's one of the reasons that I wanted her to stay here. I knew there would be a strong support system from Mrs. Bailey and all of you good people. If we can get her strong enough, I plan to be one of the people who personally escort her to a new life."

"Where do you plan to take her?" Symphony watched as Chief Norman furrowed his brow at her question.

"I do not plan to tell anyone that, Miss Wallace. It's not that I do not trust you. I believe that the fewer people that know, the less likely that Cecelia's whereabouts could get back to Cephas. We don't know if he has friends here. We need to continue to let this community believe she is dead."

"I understand. I'm sorry I asked. What can we do to help you?"

"Take care of Cecelia. Give her some encouragement. Most of all, keep this secret. Her life depends on it."

———◦⚬◦———

"Thank you for working an extra shift, Miss Wallace." Mr. Smothe greeted Symphony upon entering the telephone company building on Friday afternoon. "We've had many operators quit lately. I had no one else to call when our weekend girl was put in the hospital."

"You're welcome, sir. I did not have plans for the evening."

The truth of the matter was that Symphony intended to spend the evening with Cecelia. The woman seemed stronger and Symphony thought she might entertain her by reading from one of the popular books of the day. Mrs. Bailey had an extensive library. A perusal of it earlier in the week caused Symphony to discover that *The Prophet* by Kahlil Gibran was published in 1923. Symphony read the collection of poetic essays while in college and thought the passages might be inspirational for Cecelia.

"That surprises me, Miss Wallace. A young woman as comely like yourself should have a list of suitors for a Friday night on the town."

"That is kind of you to say so, sir. But, as I recall, this company discourages the hiring of women who are interested in courtship or marriage." Symphony turned away from Mr. Smothe. She didn't want him seeing her roll her eyes.

"That is certainly our policy, although recently, I found out, it is quite difficult to enforce."

"Perhaps, if you focused more on the quality of workers, and less on their personal lives, everyone might have a more amicable experience." Symphony put on her headset. Mr. Smothe followed her around. His hovering was getting on her nerves. "I mean no disrespect, sir. It is only the observation of a dedicated employee."

"You have a brazen streak that I underestimated. It must be the positive influence of Miss Kiracofe and your lovely cousin, Miss Gibboney. How is she doing?" Mr. Smothe's face lit up.

"I saw Joy just the other day. She was filling in here on dayshift. Her wedding approaches in a few weeks, I believe." Symphony enjoyed intentionally evading his question.

"Yes, Miss Kiracofe. She was kind enough to help us out during our shortage of workers. I was referring to how Miss Gibboney was doing." A look of annoyance crossed Mr. Smothe's face.

"Amburgey is fine. Working hard every night at the clinic. We have no shortage of phone calls; the clinic has no shortage of sick people. There's a call coming in, sir. I better answer it."

The evening was busy with an unusual number of difficult and complicated telephone calls passing through the switchboard including several made by Chief Norman to locations in other states. Symphony dared not listen to the Chief's conversations, although her curiosity begged her to do so.

A new operator was brought in to potentially relieve Symphony a little early. The young woman lost a connection with two long distance calls right when Symphony was preparing to leave, she decided it would be best to stay until the seasoned overnight operator came in. When the overnight operator failed to show up, Symphony reluctantly agreed to work a second shift to insure that no calls were lost.

"I assure you that we will properly compensate you for these extra shifts." Mr. Smothe's voice seemed frantic when Symphony called to inform him about the woman who did not show up. "Connect me with Miss Wellington's home number and I will see if she might come in early for the morning shift. She is one of my most dependable operators."

After Symphony made the call for him, she took off her headset and stood up to stretch.

"Juliet, I am going to go use the restroom and walk outside a moment for some fresh air. If I do not, I will not make it through the next few hours. Please be very careful if you connect any calls."

The timid young woman shook her head and went back to looking at the board in front of her. It appeared that Juliet was trying to memorize the words over each of the connection spaces. Symphony could not understand why Juliet was released from training without already learning all of the connections.

After leaving the restroom, Symphony opened the back door of the building, and then walked outside. Bitter cold hit her in the face and made her catch her breath.

"This will certainly wake me up." Symphony rubbed her hands over her arms while walking up and down the short sidewalk. Taking in another deep breath, she caught a whiff of something. "That smells like smoke. It must be coming from someone's woodstove or fireplace. This is a good night for a fire."

Returning to the inside, Symphony could hear Juliet talking to a customer.

"I am happy to connect you, Chief Norman. Have a good night." Juliet turned to Symphony. "You look cold."

"It's frigid out there."

"My Daddy says we are going to have a mighty cold March. He says that five Saturdays in March is a sign of cold weather."

"I've never heard that before." Symphony walked over to look at a calendar that hung on the wall near the door. "There sure are five Saturdays and five Sundays in this month. That is unusual." Symphony tilted her head. She looked closer at the dates. "I can't seem to keep track of what day it is. I feel like I am forgetting something."

"It's March 8. I know because today is my mother's birthday."

"Happy Birthday to your mother. I hope she has a nice day." Symphony kept staring at the calendar.

"She's had a lot of really nice days for the last ten years." Juliet grew silent for a few moments. "I would guess that every day is like her birthday where she is."

"Oh, where is she?" Symphony, lost in her personal thoughts, automatically asked the question.

"She's in heaven."

Juliet's response shook Symphony out of the fog of her thoughts. The matter-of-the-fact manner, in which the young woman responded, made a sad feeling pass through Symphony. The grief of loss was a normal emotion.

"I'm so sorry, Juliet. I'm sure that never gets easier."

"Thank you. My mother was sick most of my life. It was like she had a cold that she could not shake. It just got worse and worse, as I got older. Momma got weaker, until one day her poor little body gave up. As much as I miss her, and wish I had her with me now, I would never be so selfish to want her back the way she was. Part of her was already in heaven long before the rest of her joined. I feel her with me every day. I'm going to name my first daughter after her."

"I bet she had a beautiful name. She gave you one."

"Her name was Shenandoah. Given to her to honor the land on which she was born. There was only one person who was allowed to call her anything shorter and that was my father. He called her 'his Shanny.' He would have walked through fire for her, and he did the night our little farm house when up in flames."

Flames. Fire. March 8. Suddenly, it hit Symphony what she forgot. This was the morning of March 8, 1924. The smoke she smelled was not someone's stove. It was a blaze brewing on Main Street—the Great Wytheville Fire.

Before Symphony could say another word, Juliet answered a call from the Alper residence.

"Oh, my. Yes, I will do that immediately." A scared expression was on her face when Juliet turned to Symphony.

"There's a fire." Symphony's tone was calm.

"How did you know that? That was Herman Sollod. He says that they are trapped on the second floor of their building. We've got to call the fire department."

"Yes. You do that. There's a list of emergency numbers on the clipboard."

Symphony looked at the clock; it was four-thirty in the morning. Her mind raced with what she could do to prevent the devastation that would make this day a turning point in Wytheville's history. Before she could say anything, another call came in. Symphony put her headset back on and answered.

"Number, please."

"Symphony. This is Mrs. Bailey. I need to reach Chief Norman as soon as possible."

"What's wrong, ma'am? You sound scared."

"I am. Cecelia has run away." Mrs. Bailey's voice cracked.

"What?" Symphony felt like her heart stopped.

"Something woke me up, and I decided to check on her. Her bedclothes were left on her bed. She had dressed and snuck out."

"How did she get past Mr. McClintock in her weakened state?"

"He must have fallen asleep. She is so tiny. Her step would be light. He's out there himself in this frigid weather searching. I fear what might happen to both of them. Get me the Chief!"

Without another word, Symphony sprang into action. The Chief answered his home phone on the second ring.

"Chief, this is Symphony. I have two things to quickly tell you before I connect you with a call. Herman Sollod called in a fire at the Victory Merchandise building. The Alper family is trapped on the second floor. We've contacted the fire department and your office." Symphony paused a second and took a breath. "Your call is from Mrs. Bailey." Symphony looked around and saw Juliet answering another call. "Someone is missing from the house. I'm connecting you now."

Symphony finished the connection. Quickly scanning the list of telephone numbers on a clipboard next to her, she found the one she was looking for, and made the connection.

"Mrs. Blevins, this is Symphony at the telephone company. I need to speak to Amburgey. It's an emergency."

"This can't be good if you are calling me in the middle of the night." Amburgey quickly came to the phone.

"Be careful how you react to what I'm about to say. You are not alone."

"Okay."

"There's someone missing from the boarding house."

"No!" Amburgey screamed.

"The building that she used to live in is on fire."

"You have got to be kidding."

"I wish I was. I think we need to get down there. I think we are supposed to be a part of what happens."

"How can you know that?"

"Do you trust me?"

"Of course, I trust you."

"Then meet me at the apartment. And, Amburgey?"

"Yes."

"Be careful."

She disconnected the call with one hand, and then tore her headset off her head with the other. Turning around, she found herself face-to-face with the morning relief operator that Mr. Smothe said might come in early.

"There's a fire in the middle of Main Street. You are going to be swamped." Symphony did not give the woman time to greet her. "Juliet still needs help with long distance calls, but she is improving." Juliet heard Symphony's comment and gave her a big smile. "I'm sorry, but I've got to go. I have a family emergency."

Symphony threw on her coat and dashed down the hallway toward the front of the building. The cold wind slapped her in the face, and a sudden gust almost knocked her off her feet. Regaining her balance, she quickly walked down the path to the sidewalk that paralleled the street. It was just one block up to Main Street, but with the strong wind, her pace was slower than she liked. The streetlights in 1924 Wytheville were few and far between, and rather dim in comparison to her time. Approaching the intersection, she could see the flames of the fire shooting up from the Alper building in the center of town. She was looking at the building and not where she was going and ran right overtop of Amburgey.

"Slow down. We've got to go around the block to get to the apartment. We can't go through the alleyway." Amburgey tried to turn Symphony in the opposite direction.

"We can't do that. We don't have time."

"Don't have time for what?"

"You've got to trust me. Come on." Symphony grabbed hold of Amburgey's arm, and started across the street, walking toward the fire.

"What's wrong with you? We shouldn't be walking into the fire. It's dangerous, and we will get in the firefighters way."

"I know this sounds crazy, but we've got to catch the Alper's little boy."

"What? Catch their little boy? Symphony, what is wrong with you? We need to get to Cecelia's apartment and see if she is there."

"No, Amburgey. You don't understand. If we aren't there, no one will catch Melvin. I know it. I can't tell you how, but I know!"

"You know? I've thought you were strange all along. Now, I think you are crazy." Amburgey jerked away from Symphony's grasp and held up her hands while she backed away. "You do what you want. I'm going to go see if I can help my aunt. We *know* that she *is* in danger. Or, have you forgotten that?"

Symphony watched Amburgey give a glaring look before she turned, and ran back up the street toward the corner. This was not the way it was supposed to play out. Tyler said in his diary that Amburgey would be the one to catch Melvin. Symphony shook off the feeling of helplessness and frustration, and turned toward the burning building. She ran toward the back of the building where she saw two people jumping together from a window above. Symphony held her breath and watched them land on the street below. From the historical accounts she read about the event, Symphony thought that Paul jumped first, and then the child was thrown to him. Something was different. She held her breath getting closer to the scene.

"Throw him down, Fannie. I will catch our son." Paul shouted to his wife.

"We told her to let us jump first, and then we could catch the both of them." Herman was grasping his right arm and grimacing in pain. "I think I broke my arm in the fall. Paul can barely stand."

Before Herman could finish talking, Paul's leg collapsed under him. He was on the ground. Symphony looked around. No one else was in sight. Looking back up at the second story, she could see the flames pushing Fannie toward the window. Spreading rapidly, it looked like there was fire all around the woman except at the spot where she stood clutching her son. Symphony knew for a certainty why she was there.

"Fannie, throw Melvin to me. I will catch him."

Hearing Symphony's voice, Fannie's eyes opened wide, and a brief expression of hope flashed on her worried face. She nodded clutching her son, and then she kissed him. Symphony saw the woman wrap him tighter in the blanket, covering his face so that all that could be seen was a bundle of cloth.

The two men stood behind her. Symphony looked up at Fannie. Their eyes locked in an unspoken message.

"Go ahead. I'm ready. Trust me, Fannie. I am here for you." The words were true. Tears rose in Symphony's eyes, and ran down her face. She wiped them away and held out her arms. "Send Melvin to me."

In a split second, Fannie released her son. He came falling down. Symphony felt it was happening in slow motion. Her eyes never left the bundle. He grew closer and closer, and landed right in her open arms. A flash of déjà vu overcame her. She remembered the dream she had. Symphony pulled the child close to her chest and said a silent prayer of thanksgiving. Again, Symphony locked eyes with Fannie.

"You two get ready to catch Fannie. I will hold Melvin. Hurry, the flames are growing stronger."

Symphony moved out of the way. Removing the blanket away from Melvin's face, he began to cry. Quickly, Symphony pulled the chain of her necklace until the pendant was visible and put it into his little hands. Melvin stopped crying and tugged on the chain before putting the pendant in his mouth.

"Jump, Fannie. It's time to jump, my darling." Paul shouted encouragement to his wife.

Fannie looked behind her, and then climbed on to the ledge of the window. Holding tight to the frame on each side of her, Symphony could see the woman take a deep breath, and then jump. She shot down like a rocket into the waiting arms of her husband and brother. They all toppled down to the ground. There would be bruises and broken bones, but the family was still intact—safe and sound, whole.

"My baby, my baby." Fannie jumped up and limped to Symphony. Taking Melvin in her arms, Fannie showered him with kisses. A few moments later, she pulled Symphony into an embrace. "You are our lifesaver. You were sent to us by God Almighty. We are blessed."

"I'm so happy that all of you are alright. It looks like your building will not be." All of them moved into the street where firefighters asked them to get out of the way.

"A building can be rebuilt, Miss Wallace." Paul Alper pulled his wife and child into an embrace. "I have but one family. I am thankful that my brother-in-law is a light sleeper. His warning saved us all."

"It was the grace of God. I heard a noise in the downstairs and got up to see what it was. I guess it was the beginning of the fire."

Symphony wondered if the noise came from the apartment. She needed to get back there and check on Amburgey.

"I'm glad you are safe. I've got to go and find Amburgey." Symphony began walking toward the corner.

"Symphony, wait!" Fannie handed Melvin to his father and slowly walked to Symphony. "It is the early morning. Why were you out in the darkness? How did you come to be here to help us?" Fannie looked deep into Symphony's eyes.

"It was fate that brought me here. I saw it in a dream, and now it is so." Symphony dared not tell Fannie anything but the truth.

"This is a pendant of protection." Fannie took Symphony's pendant in her hand and ran her finger over the smooth front surface. "This was made with love and magic—a shield and protection for the one who would wear it. Everything within it has meaning." Fannie held it in her hand; she returned her gaze to Symphony. "Thank you. I will never forget you, Symphony Wallace."

Before the lump in her throat could turn into tears, Symphony pulled Fannie into a hug. Letting her go, she quickly ran up the street. Symphony dared not to look behind her. She knew they had said goodbye.

It would be another hour before the sun rose on that frigid March morning. The Great Fire, it would later be called, was lighting up the darkness of the early morning sky. Symphony headed toward the fire on the backside of the building; the light grew brighter with each step she took. She heard the loud voice of Tyler Gibboney long before she could see him in the alleyway in front of the apartment where Cephas and Cecelia Washington lived.

"You should not be here!"

Tyler sounded angry. Beside him stood a frail Cecelia. Amburgey was facing them with her back to Symphony.

"You!" Tyler moved around Amburgey and pointed at Symphony. "I have not figured out who you are, but you need to stay away from Amburgey. This is the third time I have seen you together. There is something about your presence with her that is wrong. I cannot determine what it is. She needs to get away from here. You both need to leave."

"I've told you that I know who you are." Amburgey did not look at Symphony. "Why can't I stay with you and travel with you?"

"We should not be together outside of *our* time. I don't know how to make you understand this. You are jeopardizing your life by doing so." Tyler placed his head in both of his hands. "This is ludicrous. We are breaking more rules of time than I can count. I've come to take Cecelia away. I'm here to save her life. I cannot be worried about what I am doing to your life in the process." Tyler stopped and walked closer to Amburgey. He raised his hand to touch her face, and then withdrew it, like he was touching something hot. He backed away.

"I don't understand any of this, Tyler." Cecelia moved closer to her brother and took hold of his arm. "These women live where I was hidden. They helped me. Who are they? What is all this talk of time?"

"It is fine, Cecelia. All will be fine. We are going to leave this place and go where Cephas can never hurt you again. Do not be afraid. Maybe you will meet these women again, in a later time." Tyler turned back to Amburgey. "I hope we meet again, Amburgey, when it is right for me to know you at this age. I hope that nothing happens here to jeopardize that. You need to go home. Nadia will not be happy."

"I don't understand why I can't go with you." There was desperation in Amburgey's voice. "You could help me find him."

"I don't want to know who this *him* is. You are still a little girl in our time." Tyler turned to Symphony. "Symphony, I have no idea who you are." Tyler turned back to his daughter. "That's right, you heard me. I am telling her not to reveal her identity. There must be a connection. It's a dangerous thing to mess in time. I've learned that the hard way. Cecelia and I are leaving now. Do not follow us. Do not tell anyone you saw us. I don't care if you have to lie to the police. You did not see us. We were not here. I know what they did to protect her. I appreciate it. I'll handle it from here on."

Symphony walked up behind Amburgey and put her arm around her. She could see the tears rolling down her face. Amburgey did not pull away.

Cecelia looked tired and confused. She took her brother's hand and started to follow him. As they walked away from the burning building, Symphony thought she saw Cecelia wave. The thought crossed her mind that the woman was waving to a life she was leaving behind. She had no idea how far away she would go.

"I know he is right." Amburgey broke the silence and sniffled away her tears. "I'm reckless and stupid. I should not cross paths with him. I've probably jeopardized both our lives."

"You're adventurous and impetuous. A time animal that cannot be tamed." Symphony's attempt at humor was lame to her ears. "The two of you didn't self-destruct. It must be okay."

"I've read things, Symphony. There are books out there if you take the trouble to go looking. Travelling through time is not a problem if you stay away from your own ancestry. Start messing with people who make up your gene pool and you might alter yourself in ways that aren't visible to the naked eye. Each of our existences is layers upon layers. If you re-arrange your history, you might lose an important part of yourself."

"If that's true—" Symphony stopped herself before she said anything further.

"Dad is right. You can't tell me who you are. Maybe, I will figure it out on my own one day. From what he said, this isn't the last time we will meet."

The sun rose, and with it the reality of what was happening in front of their eyes. Symphony and Amburgey began to walk further down the street, and away from the spreading fire. Symphony knew from her research that the path of destruction would keep intensifying that day. Despite the devastation to the business district, it was comforting to know that no lives would be lost in the tragedy.

Reaching Main Street, they covered their faces with handkerchiefs and began to walk in silence down Church Street to return to Mrs. Bailey's boarding house. Symphony knew they needed to tell Chief Norman something. He would continue searching for Cecelia otherwise. His relentlessness was apparent. They needed to tell a plausible enough story to convince him to call off the search.

Upon returning to the boarding house, they found a flurry of activity. Amburgey marched directly up the stairs without a word. Sensing that she needed some time to herself, Symphony took off her coat and hat, and then followed the noise to the dining room and kitchen area.

Around the table sat most of the residents in a loud debate regarding how Cecelia left unnoticed.

"Exhaustion must have overcome Mr. McClintock for him to be so soundly sleeping that he did not hear Cecelia go by him." The lines in Mr. Barker's face seemed to have deepened overnight. "He insisted on being the one to guard her for the largest duration of the day."

"That was entirely too long a period for a man his age." Mrs. Bailey walked around the table pouring coffee. Olivia entered through the swinging door with a couple of platters of food. "I should have put my foot down."

"Good morning, Symphony." Olivia seemed to be the only person to notice her presence. "You look like you worked a double shift." Olivia walked around her and placed the food on the table. "Did you walk through the fire or try to help put it out?" Her voice sound like she was joking, but the look on her face showed that the odor was stronger than Symphony realized.

"My goodness, Symphony. You have soot on your face. How in the world did you get that at the telephone company?" Mrs. Bailey stopped pouring and stared at Symphony. "Mr. Barker, I thought you said that the fire was in the center of Main Street. Has it spread that far?"

Before Mr. Barker could answer the question, the front door slammed and seconds later, the sound of Chief Norman's heavy boots could be heard clomping toward them.

"I'm sorry to barge in, Mrs. Bailey. With all the chaos of last night and today, I don't have time to have good manners. I came to see if you heard anything from Cecelia or saw Mr. McClintock. He seems to be missing now as well. Most likely, it's the stubborn, ornery lawman in him that doesn't think he needs to answer to anyone else."

"No, Chief. I am beside myself with worry about what has become of that frail woman and that old man. Sit down. Have a quick cup of coffee and a bite of breakfast."

"Mrs. Bailey, I really don't have the time—"

"Sir, you may be in charge outside of that door. Don't forget. I knew your mother, and I diapered your backside when you were a snotty nosed boy. I'm going to be your maternal constituent for a moment, admonish you to take five minutes to rest, and get some nourishment in you. You can't find either of them if you are exhausted yourself."

"Yes, ma'am." Chief Norman shook his head, took off his hat, and sat down.

Olivia put her hand on the swinging door and started back into the kitchen.

"You don't have to continue searching for Cecelia." Symphony came out from around the corner. Olivia stopped dead in her tracks.

All eyes moved in Symphony's direction. The clatter of silverware against the dishes and the clang of cups hitting saucers ceased. A silence hung in the air like someone hit the 'pause' button.

"What do you mean, Symphony? I don't understand." Mrs. Bailey sank down into a nearby chair. She looked like she was preparing herself for bad news. "Explain to us what you mean."

"I saw Cecelia leaving with a man." Symphony walked toward the table.

"Who was he? Where were they going? Do you think it is someone who is connected with Cephas?" Chief Norman stood up and his chair tipped over behind him.

"No, I don't think he has any connection to Cephas. Quite the opposite."

Without needing to turn around, Symphony felt Amburgey standing behind her. It was like an electric current connected the two of them. Symphony turned her head slightly to allow her peripheral vision to glimpse at Amburgey. Her eyes were slits focusing on Symphony. She could almost feel the glare.

"You are going to have to explain yourself further, young lady." Chief Norman reached down to the floor to reset the chair in its place. "Why haven't you given us this information sooner?"

"I just got here, Chief." Symphony closed her eyes, and thought for a moment before she continued. "When I heard about where the fire started, I was worried about the Alper family. I left the telephone company and ran down the street. They were jumping from the second story window. It was terrifying to watch. I caught their little baby boy in my arms."

Amburgey came closer to Symphony and touched her arm. The gesture caused pent up emotions to come to the surface.

"Symphony. They threw their child out the window to you?" Olivia's voice was barely above a whisper.

"They had no choice. The fire spread so quickly that jumping out the window was their only chance to survive."

"The Alper family is fine. Paul and Herman have some broken bones. Thankfully, they woke up in time and could escape through the window." Chief Norman seemed anxious. "I want to hear about this man who took Cecelia. I need a description so that we can locate them."

"Chief, I don't think you need to look for them. I am certain that Cecelia left willingly. She knew this man. He was not a stranger to her. He was here to rescue her." Symphony looked the Chief squarely in the eyes.

"You cannot be certain of that. Cecelia might have been threatened into acting like she was going along with it." The Chief put his coat on and started for the door.

"She told me that he was coming." Amburgey's sudden statement caused all eyes to shift toward her. "I've been spending quite a bit of time with her. She confided in me that a man who she trusted and loved was going to come and get her. He was going to take her somewhere so far away that no one would ever find her again. She begged me to keep her secret."

"Why would she need to keep that secret?" Chief Norman walked back to Amburgey. "We would help her if we knew she had a place to go."

There was silence for a moment. Symphony could almost see the wheels turning in Amburgey's head trying to decide what to say.

"She thought that there was someone in this house that had a connection to Cephas."

"What? That is ridiculous." Mrs. Bailey rose from where she was sitting and approached the Chief and Amburgey.

"I agree. It makes no sense. Cecelia was abused by Cephas

for a long time. It affected her mental state—her ability to think rationally."

"That's possible." Kathleen spoke up for the first time. "People who are treated badly for long periods of time sometimes have trouble separating fact from fiction." Kathleen paused. "Amburgey, was it me whom she distrusted?"

Amburgey did not actually respond. She merely raised her eyebrows. She smiled in a neutral, yet affirmative, manner.

"Why would she think it was you?" Mrs. Bailey looked worried and confused.

"Because about a year ago, before she lost her baby, Cecelia and Cephas came to the clinic several times. He had a strange growth on his back that had become infected. Cephas paid too much attention to me. He was quite flirtatious with me, even with Cecelia sitting right there. It made me so uncomfortable that I asked another nurse to take care of him from then on." Kathleen looked at Amburgey. "He was treated by Bertha after that."

"I bet he learned something from that experience." Amburgey laughed heartily. "Bertha was a nurse in World War I. She might possibly be the tallest woman I have ever seen. She looks like a linebacker on a football team."

Amburgey's eyes grew big. She looked at Symphony who nodded her head. Symphony's father was a serious football fan. She knew that football was already a popular sport even in the early twentieth century.

"Cecelia probably thought that something happened between me and Cephas." Kathleen continued her story. "He does have a reputation for being seen with other women. In my case, it couldn't be farther from the truth. Just the thought of him, it makes my skin crawl. He's a thug."

"Well, I guess that would make sense. I still don't understand why Cecelia could not confide that in me or Mrs. Bailey." Chief Norman picked up his coffee cup and held it out to Olivia. She complied with his request. "I thought she would have trusted us."

"I think Cecelia was mostly scared. She might have had some uncertainty regarding whether or not this man would actually come." Amburgey glanced momentarily in her direction, but Symphony could not determine why. "There may not be many men in her life that she trusted."

"Her grandparents were wonderful folks. Her grandfather was the salt of the earth." Mr. McClintock's voice came from the hallway. Everyone turned in his direction. "Cecelia had no reason to fear him."

"Mr. McClintock! We were so worried about you. Where have you been?"

Mrs. Bailey rose and started to walk toward the man. Symphony noticed that Chief Norman made a slight shake of his head, and she stopped.

"I've been trying to right the wrong of my actions. I failed." Despite the man's words, his head was still held high with his gaze planted straight on the Chief. "I've tarnished the legacy of my son with the man who followed him."

"Mead, you did no such thing. Walter stood on your shoulders for most of his career. You and I both know that. Heck, all of us young men who wanted to wear a badge stood on your shoulders. We would still be standing on them if it weren't for the fact that the weight you were forced to bear was too heavy."

"I failed my assignment." Mr. McClintock held out his rifle to the Chief.

"Nope. I'm not taking it. That was Walter's. It is yours. You are seventy-five years old and you have a bad heart. You fell asleep. From what I am hearing now, it sounds as if Cecelia Washington had a plan of her own. I wish she made us privy to it. It would have saved a lot of time and aggravation on a day that was full of tragedy and heartache." The Chief looked at Amburgey and Symphony. "I'm going to trust that you are telling me the truth, young lady. I'm going to stop looking for a woman who I've passed off as dead anyway. I'm going to continue to concentrate on finding that no good piece of—"

"Language." Mrs. Bailey gave Chief Norman a stern look.

"I'm going to concentrate on apprehending the perpetrator of the crimes against Mrs. Washington right after the fire that is destroying our downtown is under control. So far, there has not been any loss of life. It sounds like Miss Wallace might be responsible for saving one of our youngest citizens from harm. You better get some rest, Symphony. If you think that telephone lines were busy last night, I bet it will look easy after tonight."

"I'm supposed to be off, Chief."

"Wasn't that true about last night too?"

Thinking about what he said, Symphony looked at the grandfather clock in the corner. It was about to chime nine times. So much happened in such a short period of time.

Chapter Fifteen

DESPITE THE HORRENDOUS TRAGEDY of the Great Fire, the sun rose on Sunday, March 9, 1924. The reality of the destruction sunk in and stories began to be passed around about how the fire consumed the downtown.

"The fire wiped out about two entire blocks." Mr. McClintock took the gentlemen of Mrs. Bailey's house out in his vehicle after breakfast that morning to view the destruction. "It destroyed about twenty businesses on both sides of Main Street."

"The fire crossed the street?" Amburgey asked while passing a bowl of mashed potatoes to Symphony. Churches cancelled their morning services, but it did not prevent Sunday lunch from occurring. "How does a fire do that?"

"It's the wind, Amburgey." Mr. Barker responded. He took a slice of ham from the platter. "It picks up some embers and blows them. When they land, a new fire is ignited."

"Jake Chambers at the bank estimated that it was over $200,000 in loss." Mr. Peterson was normally the quietest person at the table. The fire, however, seemed to incite in him a desire to be in the discussion.

Symphony recalled seeing an article, in the Museums archives, from the *New York Times* that ran the day after the fire that highlighted the over $200,000 loss. As part of her research, she calculated that it would be over $3 million in modern value.

"It was mighty fortunate that Pulaski's fire crew could come and assist." Mr. McClintock took a biscuit from the plate Mrs. Bailey offered. "Somebody told me they had to lift the fire truck driver out of the seat when he arrived. It was so cold driving that open fire truck over the mountain that he almost froze to the seat." He shook his head. "I guess that's why they made it here so quickly. Someone told me they drove the twenty-eight miles in a record thirty-five minutes."

"Wythe Motor Company had over thirty new Ford cars stored in the second story of Sexton Hall. One of the bystanders told me that the fire weakened the joists, and the floor just gave away with all those cars crashing down below." Mr. Barker shook his head in amazement. "What a sound that must have made!"

"What a strange place to store cars!" The phone rang and Mrs. Bailey rose to answer it.

"It's a good thing they keep money in steel vaults." Mr. Peterson joined the conversation. "The structure of First National Bank survived, since it is brick. The interior was completely gutted by the fire though. That will cost some money to replace all that beautiful woodwork they had."

"First National Bank?" An ice-cold feeling travelled through Symphony's veins.

"Yes. Is that where you kept your money, Miss Symphony? I'm sure it's still safe in the vault."

Without saying a word or looking at her, Symphony felt Amburgey's hand reach under the table and clasp her own.

"Yes. I opened an account at First National Bank a few days ago, Mr. Peterson. They had a lot of beautiful furnishings." Symphony swallowed hard and gasped for air. "And a really unusual clock."

Glancing at the swinging door that led to the kitchen, Symphony saw Olivia stop and turn around to face her.

"That was a mighty pretty clock they had there." Olivia's voice was calm. "My Daddy kept that clock making perfect time. It had a long history attached to it."

"I remember that clock." Mr. Barker stood up at the same time that Mrs. Bailey re-entered the room. "It sat way back in the corner near the vault. I think it was originally in the old Boyd Hotel on Main Street. That's another building that has its share of stories."

Symphony looked at Amburgey. There was fear in her eyes.

"That clock was mighty prized by my Daddy." Olivia walked around and behind Symphony, reaching over her to pick up an empty bowl. Symphony felt Olivia's strong hand squeeze her shoulder. "I think that clock is visiting my Daddy in his shop."

"Oh, that's wonderful!" The words came gushing out before Symphony could stop them. "I mean that it would be horrible for such an antique to be lost."

"That was Reverend Perry who called. He is organizing a food and clothing drive to help those who lost their homes in the fire."

"Lost their homes? I thought it was just businesses that were lost." Amburgey stood up and began to follow Olivia out of the room.

"It was buildings that were lost." Mrs. Bailey picked up several bowls of food. "But there were several apartments in those buildings.

Everyone got out with his or her life, but some didn't get to take much else. Olivia, I'm going to go up to the attic and get some of those clothes that boarders left behind through the years. There's quite an assortment of things up there. It's time to put them to good use. Will you help me carry the boxes down, Amburgey? Symphony can help Olivia clean up the kitchen."

"Yes, ma'am." Amburgey exchanged glances with Symphony. A smile crossed both of their faces. "I'd be happy to help with that."

Amburgey followed Mrs. Bailey while the rest of the boarders dispersed into other parts of the house. Symphony and Olivia moved back and forth from the dining room to the kitchen carrying dishes and leftovers in silence until everyone had left.

"Is it true? Does your father have the clock?" Symphony blurted out the question once they were both in the kitchen.

"Yes, he does. My Daddy told us last night that a man called him midday on Friday and told him that the clock at First National Bank needed fixing. He didn't leave his name. He just hung up. Daddy got in his truck and went to the bank. The manager told him that the clock was fine. But he and Daddy went back and looked at it. Sure enough, it was stopped, and there was a crack in the glass on the door. The manager told him to go ahead and take it to repair over the weekend."

"That's a mighty strange story, Olivia."

"It is that, Symphony. I was hoping you might know something about it."

"I do not. I am quite relieved to hear it though."

Olivia walked toward the small table in the kitchen. She pulled out one of the chairs and sat down, pointing to the chair on the opposite side for Symphony to sit in.

"I figure it will take Mrs. Bailey about an hour to go through those boxes upstairs. Maybe, a little longer since she has poor Amburgey as a captive audience for her stories." Olivia laughed softly. Symphony saw a beautiful young woman who was trapped in a life of duty. "I think that should be enough time for you to tell me how it is that you came to be in this house in 1924. You can't fool Olivia. My eyes are wide open to the possibilities of the universe. I don't think you arrived here on the train."

Since her experience with time travel began, Symphony learned something. You had to have someone to talk to about it, or you would go insane. In her own time, there were friends she could confide in. During her two trips to the past, Symphony learned it was dangerous to have such discussions with anyone even talking to Amburgey about some aspects was a risk she could not take.

Sitting before her was an educated young woman of the present, who happened to have a connection to the clock. Symphony did not believe in coincidences. This was one of her Grammie's signs. She needed to heed it.

"It all started when I moved to Wytheville, the year was…"

"I feel like you have read one of those classic adventures I used to read in the library."

A half-hour had passed. Symphony recounted all that she experienced since moving to Wytheville. Olivia was silent for the telling of it. Her face was void of emotion or judgment. Symphony told of her experiences in 1950. She saw compassion in the woman's eyes when Symphony explained who Amburgey really was to her.

"I knew you were closer kin than cousins. It's not so much that you physically favor each other; you do in subtle ways. It's more your general personality, your manner." Olivia rose from the table and went to the sink to begin washing the dishes. "Growing up in a house of clocks made me have an unusual interest in time. It's complex and simple. We don't value time like we should. We think we have an unlimited reservoir of it. It's foolish for me to say this. I believe you, Symphony. I'm going to help you. That clock is going to sit in my father's workshop until they get the bank back in operation. I don't think you or Amburgey need to stay here that long. You've had a couple of close calls already. You are long overdue in 1924. It's time for you to go home."

"I'M SO HAPPY that I saved these things. They will come in handy for those in need."

An hour and a half later, Mrs. Bailey and Amburgey returned from the attic with several overflowing boxes of clothing.

"Waste not, want not. That's what the old people tell us." Olivia bit her lower lip and glanced at Symphony. "Why don't you let me load all that stuff in my car? I can drop it off at the church on the way home."

"That would be kind of you, Olivia. I'd like to stay at the house in case Chief Norman comes by with a report. I'm going to work on a big pot of my Brunswick stew to take to the church later for a supper they are having."

"I think that I'm going to go upstairs and rest for a while." Symphony tried to subtly motion for Amburgey to go with her.

"I could use a nap, too. I tossed and turned all night."

"You girls had a rough couple of days." Mrs. Bailey pointed to the boxes. "Please help Olivia get those into her car. I will call the Reverend and tell him to be expecting Olivia."

Putting on their coats and hats, they all picked up a box and headed to Olivia's car in the rear of the house.

"Make sure you bring whatever you need for the trip." Olivia handed Symphony a small slip of paper. "Here are the directions to my house. Amburgey should know the way."

"What?" Amburgey looked confused.

"I'll explain in a minute." Symphony pulled Olivia into a hug. "I don't know if I will get a chance to do this later. Thank you for listening to me, Olivia. You can't possibly know what it means."

"No. I don't expect I can. I doubt my life will ever have the adventures that yours has." Olivia hugged Symphony back and got into the car. "Don't dilly dally. None of us knows how much time we have."

Symphony closed Olivia's car door and watched the woman pull away. A feeling of apprehension lingered thinking about Olivia's parting words.

"What in the world was that about?" Amburgey questioned her before the car was out of sight.

"Let's go upstairs and rest, like we said we would. I've got something to tell you."

Walking through the house to the staircase, Symphony heard music playing on Mr. Barker's Victrola. The scratchy sound was in stark contrast to what Symphony was used to hearing in her time. Yet, there was more than nostalgia in the sound she heard that afternoon. There was a feeling of closure knowing that her time in 1924 might possibly be drawing to an end.

"Spill it, kid." Amburgey had not closed the door to their room before she blurted out. "What have you gotten me into now, without my permission?"

"You need to gather up whatever you want to take with you. Make sure you have the photograph of your mystery man."

"You are barking instructions. That isn't explaining to me what you have in mind." Amburgey sat on her bed with her arms folded in front of her. "Explain. Now."

"You heard Olivia say that her father has the clock. It's in his workshop. That clock is our ticket out of here. Before the bank decides to take it back and lock it away in storage while they rebuild, we need to catch a ride back to our times. That clock didn't end up there accidentally. I think someone intentionally damaged it so that Olivia's father would have to get it out of the bank before the fire could destroy it."

"Who in the world would do that? How would anyone know that the fire was going to destroy the bank?"

"It had to be someone who knew about the Great Fire of 1924 long after it happened. Who do we know that could do that besides you and me?"

"Dad." The realization of what Symphony was trying to tell her finally clicked.

"Tyler probably knows more about what we have done while we've been here than we do. History will never tell it this way, but my theory is that Tyler set that fire in Cecelia's apartment. Who knows if that is the way it originally happened? Maybe he changed history a little bit. The fact is that he used the fire as a diversion. It helped him get Cecelia away from here without the possibility of being stopped."

"Wow. He must really love his sister to go through all that danger."

"Amburgey, I think that your father may have started out travelling in time as a grand adventure. Somewhere along the way, it became a mission to save people he loved. Maybe that's why he left you and your mother when he did. It could be all because he is protecting you from something."

"I bet my travels have botched up what he was doing. He looked so angry the other night. From the age he looks to me, I think it was not too long before he disappeared. He really physically looked like the father I remembered."

"That may be true. I think we owe it to him to use this opportunity he has given us. He's opened the door. We better go through it."

"WE ARE GOING to be frozen in time, if we don't soon reach Olivia's house."

Symphony and Amburgey walked almost an hour in the March cold to the little farm owned by the Clock Man on Reed Creek. Amburgey carried the singed suitcase that in Symphony's time held her mother's favorite things.

"We couldn't ask someone for a ride. We are going to come up missing soon. I don't want Olivia to have to try to explain that." Symphony thought she saw the farmhouse in the distance.

"I know. I would like to be able to feel my toes before I take my trip home."

"Before we get there, I want to talk to you about something." Symphony kept walking, turning slightly to see Amburgey's profile beside her. "Tyler said that he saw us together three times. That means we are going to travel again."

"Yes. I heard him. I don't know. This trip was scary on levels that I never even imagined. Coming face-to-face with my father and interacting with him gave me a feeling inside unlike any I could begin to describe. I felt something change inside of me. Like it was a physical change that occurred in my body. Maybe, I should forget this guy I've been searching for and try to live a normal life."

Logical common sense told Symphony that she should agree with Amburgey, encourage her to give up time travel. Gut instinct told Symphony that her existence would be in jeopardy if that happened.

"Tyler didn't tell you not to travel again. He must have known some details about the outcome of that trip."

"I guess. Maybe. I will let fate decide." Amburgey pointed to a gate ahead of them. "This has got to be it."

Symphony turned to see the face of a clock on the gate in front of the old farmhouse. Above it the words 'Clock Man' were painted on a simple sign. Below the clock were three words 'Take Your Time.'

"It's about time you two got here. What did you do, walk?"

Looking toward the house, they saw Olivia on the front porch.

"Yes, we did."

"You have got to be kidding me." Olivia walked down the porch steps. "It's March. That was several miles. I thought you would catch a ride here or borrow Mrs. Bailey's car." Olivia got behind them with one hand on Symphony's back and the other on Amburgey's, pushing them up the porch.

"We are going to leave from here. Disappear." Symphony whispered. They stopped outside the front door. "I didn't want anyone to know where we were. It would make it bad for you and your family if you were known to be the last people that saw us."

"Miss Symphony, you are smarter than I give you credit for. Bless you, child, for thinking of my family and me like that. Bless you both for coming into my life. The stories I will have to tell my grandchildren." Olivia pulled them both into a hug. "Now, let's get you inside. I make the best hot chocolate you have ever tasted. It will warm you up in no time."

The heat from a large fireplace instantly hit them when they walked over the threshold. The house was simple in comparison to Mrs. Bailey's large fine house. What it lacked in grandeur, it made up for in comfort—this was a home, in every way it could be.

"That old man snoring in the rocking chair is my Daddy—Isaiah Johnson. He was born a slave on this very farm. He will die on this land, a businessman. There is no one better at fixing time pieces than that old grump right there."

"I heard that Livy. I'm not too old to take a hickory switch to your backside."

A broad smile crossed Isaiah's face. He opened his eyes and stood up from his chair. Tall and slender, a little hunched over, no doubt from years of leaning down to look inside the clocks that surrounded him.

"You've come to meet my clocks."

The man's voice was smooth and deep; reminding Symphony of a favorite actor of her time whose voice was heard on many commercials.

"Yes, sir. We would be most happy to make their acquaintance, and yours." Symphony extended her hand to Mr. Johnson. He hesitated at first, and then took it in a gentle handshake.

"Nice to meet you, sir." Amburgey shook his hand as well.

"My Olivia has spoken of you both. She says you are fine Southern ladies."

"I'm not sure about that, sir. If the truth be told, we are probably more trouble than we are worth." Amburgey's statement caused Symphony to give her a questioning look. "Trouble seems to not have any difficulty finding me."

Symphony walked around the room, looking at the many clocks that hung on any available space on the walls or sat on tables. Despite the smallness of the room, she estimated that every bit of fifty clocks were visible—all keeping time.

Symphony noticed that Olivia slipped into another room while her father was talking. She returned a few minutes later.

"Mama's sleeping. I think it would be a good time for you to take the girls out to your workshop."

Isaiah Johnson moved toward the front door with Amburgey following him. Olivia pulled on Symphony's sleeve to make her stop.

"After we are out there for a few minutes, I'm going to ask Daddy to go check on Mama. That's the only way to get him out of that shed. He will talk to you all night otherwise. That's when you two can do your leaving."

Symphony shook her head and turned to follow Amburgey. She felt Olivia tug on her sleeve again.

"I'm mighty proud to know you, Symphony Wallace. You look me up in the history books when you get back to your time. If I've made anything of myself before I die, I'll try to leave you a message." Before Symphony could say anything else, Olivia pulled her into a strong embrace, kissing her on the cheek when she was done. "Let's go."

Isaiah's workshop looked old and rundown on the outside, but the inside was neat and spotless. It was also surprising devoid of clocks considering what they had seen in the house.

"I know you all are thinking, where are all the clocks?"

Isaiah chuckled sitting down in a chair at his workbench. It reminded Symphony of an architect's drawing table.

"Those clocks in my house are all pieces of other clocks. I save all the parts—good and bad. When I have time, I put parts together and make new clocks. Ones of my own designs. The clocks in the shed here belong to others. They are in the process of being fixed."

"That makes sense." Amburgey walked over to a long table where three mantle clocks were sitting in various states of repair. "How many are you normally working on at once?"

"I'd say I average having about fifteen to twenty in my shop at any different point. People come for miles around to see the Clock Man."

"He's being modest." Olivia chimed in. "People come from states around, and those who don't come ship them here on the train. Mama always kept track of Daddy's customers. I do it now. We've got books full of names. Thousands of people have sent their clocks to him to fix through the years."

"Wow!" Symphony's eyes grew big looking around the room. Her eyes lingered on a tall clock in the corner with a sheet overtop of it. "How long have you been the Clock Man?"

"All my life, young lady. My GrandPappy was a slave on this land, and he fixed clocks, too. I learned by sitting at his feet and watching. I started being paid to do it when I was sixteen in the back of a shop on Main Street. That shop went out of business, but clocks kept breaking. I was working at the sawmill and people would stop to see me and bring their clocks. I started taking them home and fixing them at night. More and more people came until I figured out that as long as I did a good job, I was going to have business. That was over fifty years ago."

"He lives the life, I tell you." Olivia walked over to her father and hugged him. "He works on his clocks in the morning, and sits on the creek bank in the afternoon, fishing and snoozing."

"It's not always been that easy for me. But, I've come to the point where I can ask a fair price for my work because there's no one else for at least a hundred miles who can fix clocks like I can."

Symphony and Amburgey sat down in front of Isaiah and listened to him tell stories about his clocks for almost an hour. It was mesmerizing in a way that Symphony would never have imagined, hearing about the life of a piece of machinery that marked the passing of a human life.

"Daddy, why don't you show these ladies that beautiful clock in the corner?"

"Oh, my goodness. That lady almost lost her life in the fire the other night." Isaiah walked over to the corner and pulled the sheet away. "I was her knight in shining armor."

Amburgey grabbed Symphony's hand when they saw the clock revealed. Automatically, Symphony's other hand rose to clutch the pendant around her neck. She felt something similar to a jolt of electricity pass between her and Amburgey.

"Do you know anything about this clock, Mr. Johnson?" Symphony released Amburgey's hand.

"I do. As a matter of fact, I know quite a bit." Isaiah stood next to the clock and ran his hand down the side of it. The action caused a cold chill to run down Symphony's spine. "This clock was made the year I was born, 1855. It was built by William Joel Sebastian. He made it for his bride. Legend has it that she never knew it was for her. William worked at the Boyd Hotel on Main Street, tending bar. During his free time, he liked to craft things from wood. He became quite good at making clocks, especially these tall grandfather style ones. Some say he learned it from his grandfather, a German immigrant. Considering the style and craftsmanship, it would make sense. I do know that most of the parts of the clock came from another time piece, straight from Germany."

"My goodness. How do you know so much about it?" Amburgey walked toward the clock.

"Nobody knows a clock, like a clock man. Now, there are clock men who make clocks, and clock men who repair them. I am both. So, I know all the secrets and the secret hiding places."

"Within the clock?" Symphony joined Amburgey.

"Yes. Clockmakers like to leave a little history in their clocks, a little piece of themselves. In this case, William left a letter in the clock. Maybe it was for his bride to read later. Maybe it was for his grandchild to find someday. Maybe it was only so that an old clock man would know a little about the creator of this beauty."

"What did the letter say?" Symphony noticed that the damaged front glass was removed.

"Mostly what I told you already. It's been several years since I read it."

"What happened to the letter?" Amburgey stepped away from the clock and toward Olivia.

"It's still in there. I put it right back where I found it. It will be waiting right there, just in case there's ever the possibility for whoever it was intended for to read it."

A wave of excitement passed over Symphony. She would love to get her hands on that letter.

"Has working on clocks all these years made you understand time any better, sir?" It was a question Symphony had to ask.

"You learn a lot about time when you work on the device that keeps account of it. An hour can seem like a second when you are having a good time or working hard. A second can seem like an eternity when you are separated from someone you love. My Essie, she's been lying in that bed for almost two years. Her eyes see, but they don't recognize. Her ears hear, but she doesn't understand. Her mouth moves, but her sweet voice doesn't come out. If I could travel back to the day before she had that stroke, I would not have spent one second working. Time is a blessing and a curse."

"Daddy, why don't you go and check on Mama for me? I'm going to give Symphony and Amburgey a ride back into town before it gets dark. We sure did enjoy your visit. Didn't we Daddy?"

"We did indeed. I like meeting pretty young ladies who will

listen to me talk. My clocks are a part of who I am, like an arm or a leg." Isaiah rose from his chair. "I don't think I caught your names." Isaiah began to walk toward the door.

"I'm Symphony and this is Amburgey."

Slowly, Isaiah turned around. He tilted his head and thought for a moment.

"Amburgey. That's a name you don't hear every day."

Isaiah left the shed. They could hear him chuckling to himself while walking away.

"Okay, girls. I don't think he will come back in here anytime soon. But, he will, if he doesn't see me leave in that car. So, you best be getting on with your business. The old man doesn't leave just anyone in here with his clocks." Olivia watched out the window for her father to enter the house.

"Maybe you should step outside while we do this, Olivia."

"What? And miss seeing someone time travel? You have got to be kidding. I'm staying right here. After it's done, I'm going to go for a ride and convince myself I'm not crazy." Olivia doubled over laughing. "I'm sorry, girls. I shouldn't be laughing. I know this is serious business."

"We sure do appreciate this, Olivia. It's a brave thing for you to do." Amburgey reached out to give Olivia a hug. "Even though, I know you don't like me."

"I like you just fine. What you said to Daddy earlier was true though. Trouble does find you." Olivia sat down in a chair near the door. "I'm going to sit right here where I can make a quick exit, if need be. I'm going to pray to Jesus that you two have a safe trip."

Symphony and Amburgey stood in front of the clock together. With one hand, Amburgey held her photograph and grasped the handle of her suitcase. Symphony dared not mention the piece of luggage. She knew there was significance to it beyond her knowledge. Symphony held her pendant firmly with one hand.

"Are you ready?" Symphony took a deep breath.

"I guess so. No goodbyes. Only, I'll see you soon." Amburgey winked.

"I think Mr. Johnson's reaction to your name wasn't a coincidence." Symphony pulled Amburgey into a hug.

"What do you mean?" Amburgey drew back and looked Symphony in the eyes.

"I think this is your clock." Symphony whispered. "Now, you know his name. Let's go.

Symphony pulled Amburgey toward the clock. Their bodies touched the clock's frame; Symphony felt she was being pulled in a dozen directions. She smelled smoke and felt cold. A bundled child came falling toward her. A man raised his hand to inflict harm. All those images filled her mind in swirling motion until everything went black.

Chapter Sixteen

"OPEN YOUR EYES, SYMPHONY! Please open your eyes!"

"Did she hit her head when she fell, Garon?"

Symphony felt like she was in a deep dream. The kind of nocturnal experience where you know you are dreaming, yet everything seems so real. She must have taken a nap before her evening shift.

"Number, please. How can I connect you this evening, Chief Norman?" Symphony mumbled.

"Thank heavens! She's waking up. Symphony! Can you hear me? This is Garon. Wake up, darling."

"Garon, I thought you were the Chief. What are you doing in 1924?" Symphony continued to mumble while her eyes opened.

"Ut oh." Garon was the first to speak. "I think our girl was travelling again."

"Do you smell smoke?" Marcella knelt down beside Symphony,

and then helped her sit up. "Garon, you might want to check upstairs. I'm smelling smoke."

"I think it's our girl here. She was at the Great Fire."

SYMPHONY OPENED HER eyes and yawned. She was not sure how long she slept, but her body felt rested and tired in a way that was beyond explanation. After returning to the present, Marcella and Garon brought her home to face the disapproval and loving care of Nadia. Their conversations were brief and functional. It was now time for her to tell her grandmother all she experienced.

Finding Psycho at the foot of the stairs, Symphony sat down on the bottom step so that he could give her some slobbery licks, and she could welcome her friend with ear scratches.

"You know what this feels like, don't you, buddy?" While Symphony had not yet met the canine on her trips through time, she'd been led to believe that his first home was in another era.

"You're finally up." Nadia came around the corner. "I was getting worried. You must be hungry. What would you like to eat?"

"What time is it?" Symphony stretched and followed Nadia into the kitchen.

"It's about eleven."

"Would quiche be a possibility?" Symphony thought she smelled something baking.

"I had a feeling you might say that. There's a ham and cheese one in the oven. It's got another half hour to bake. How about a bowl of fruit salad to tide you over?" Nadia pulled out a large bowl from the refrigerator.

"Perfect. I've missed fresh fruit."

"What? There wasn't any fruit in 1924?"

"Not much. I was there during the winter. Grocery stores with large produce sections were scarce."

"I never thought of that. But why would I? *I've* never been to 1924." Nadia poured Symphony a cup of steaming coffee. "I suppose that about all the members of my present and past family have now."

"Guilty." Symphony took a small sip of the hot coffee. She never had much taste for the beverage until she moved to Wytheville. It now seemed to be a daily ritual. "I spent more time with Amburgey."

"That does not surprise me." Nadia's voice was void of emotion.

"I saw Tyler again and Cecelia."

"Tyler's sister?" Nadia looked up from the counter where she was chopping vegetables.

"Do you want to hear about it?"

"As a person who has endured far too many of these 'mornings after,' my answer is no. As your grandmother who loves you, and wants this to someday be over, I will say yes."

"I know you don't approve. I completely understand why. I would have thought that curiosity would get the best of you, especially where Amburgey is concerned."

"I've spent the better part of my life waiting for people to come home. It's like having a family member in a foreign war only the war never ends. I've become numb to curiosity. As interesting as the stories may be, there is no happy ending for me."

"Okay. Then I am going to ask you to listen, and to help me try to figure out what I should do next. I feel like I am closer to finding out what happened to Amburgey."

By the time the oven timer buzzed indicating that the quiche was done, Symphony had recounted a large portion of her experiences to Nadia.

"I never got to meet Cecelia." Nadia placed a plate of quiche with a green salad in front of Symphony. "When he brought her to this time, Tyler thought that bringing her into our home would be too confusing for her and too disruptive for us. He put her up in one of those extended stay type motels. He would take her food every day and gradually got her to go out. He showed her around the city where we lived at the time. We had started to explain a little about who she was to Amburgey, telling her that her aunt was coming to visit that she had been through a bad ordeal and was trying to get better. One morning, Tyler went to see Cecelia, and she was gone. She'd packed up the few belongings she had, and left a note that said she didn't want to be a burden to him. She would make it on her own."

"Wow. That had to be shocking and scary."

"Tyler was crazy with worry. He couldn't really contact the police. Cecelia didn't exist in this time. He didn't even have a photograph of her."

An image of the Cecelia she met passed through Symphony's mind, she wished for the ability to take her memory and print it out on paper.

"I think, at that point, Tyler would have been done with time travel were it not for Cecelia disappearing. He seemed to have hardness to it. I don't think that he had any real proof that she could travel through time on her own. But, since she was his sister, Tyler thought that perhaps she could figure out how to do so, if she wanted."

"It's like chasing a ghost." The words came out of Symphony's mouth before she realized what she was saying. "Amburgey was as real to me as you are when we were together. Now, it seems like she was someone I met in a dream."

"That is normally a feeling that is more likely to come when you have lost someone in death and many years have passed." Nadia took a long sip of coffee. "I had a sweet friend in school that passed one night in a car accident on the way home from a basketball game. All these years later, Sherry seems more like a character from a television show that I once watched than a person I really knew. Maybe it's our brain's way of helping us cope. It softens the memory around the edges so that we can bear to remember it."

"That's a lovely way to look at it." Symphony reached across the counter and took Nadia's hand. "I've come to the conclusion that the hardest part about spending time with Amburgey is not the fact that she was my biological mother that I never knew. The hardest part is that in the time we are together, she doesn't even know that I exist."

Tears well up in Symphony's eyes; they were matched by Nadia's.

"That's sort of how I felt about you all those years you were growing up somewhere else." Nadia wiped tears from her eyes. "For this tiny brief moment, you were real in my arms. Then, you were whisked away. It was like you were a dream. Then, one day, I woke up, and there you were." Nadia smiled and choked back more emotion. "Sitting next to me in a little café. It was like magic."

"Maybe one day we can both have that moment with Amburgey. Right here in our own time."

A few minutes of silence passed. Nadia cleaned up the kitchen while Symphony finished eating. A feeling of tiredness still hung over her like a weight on her body.

"I haven't dared to let this thought cross my mind in decades." Nadia sat down on a bar stool next to Symphony. "Do you think there is any possibility that Tyler is out there somewhere? Lost in another time? You understand more about time travel now. Could he be alive in another time? Could he still come back here now?"

"I really don't know how to answer that. To me, he was alive just days ago. But almost a hundred years passed since that time. He obviously came back from that trip because you know he brought Cecelia. Tyler was aggravated and scared about interacting with Amburgey. He didn't know who I was. It troubled him that he encountered me in two different times with his daughter. I saw genuine fear in his reaction to us."

"I remember that he was quite different when he returned with Cecelia. Looking back, I can see that it was more than her being with him. Tyler was happy that he got her out of that abusive relationship. A couple of times, I overheard him having conversations with Amburgey. She talked to me about them later. She didn't understand what he was trying to tell her. She thought he was away on business trips."

"Did you ever do any research to see if he might have died in another time?"

"What?" Nadia furrowed her brow.

"We could search death records and obituaries online to see if we could find anyone named Tyler Gibboney."

"I never thought of that. I'm not sure I want to know."

SYMPHONY RESTED THE remainder of the day; waiting to see the person she missed the most. Jason left for a business trip before her latest adventure. As far as she knew, he had no idea where she had been.

"I brought enough takeout from Peking Restaurant for all of us." Jason greeted Nadia with two large brown paper bags and a big smile when she opened the door.

"It smells delicious. Maybe, I can have some leftovers tomorrow. For now, I'm going to leave you two alone for the evening. I have a historical society board meeting followed by a bridge club game at Millie's house. You know what happens when we senior ladies get together." Nadia winked at Symphony.

"Anything can happen. I've witnessed it." Jason kissed Nadia on the cheek while helping her put on her jacket.

"Don't wait up! Psycho likes those crunchy things that come with the Chinese soup." Nadia waved before closing the door.

"How's my favorite girl?" Jason walked into the kitchen and set the bags on the island counter.

"She missed you with all her heart." Symphony came up behind Jason and engulfed him in a tight hug. Pent up feelings from too many emotional moments came gushing out.

"Hey. What's wrong? I was only gone for two days. What happened while I was away?" Jason turned around and pulled Symphony into his arms, kissing her on the forehead while she cried.

"I went on a trip, too." Symphony sheepishly looked up into Jason's eyes.

"I didn't know you were going anywhere. Did something suddenly come up?" Jason paused, continuing to stare into her eyes. After a few moments, he pulled away from the embrace and held her at arm's length. "Wait. You don't mean—"

"Yes. I was working with Garon on the new exhibit about the Great Fire. I lost my footing and fell back into the clock in the Rock House foyer, and that was my ticket to 1924."

"1924! Symphony? That's almost a hundred years ago! What were you thinking?"

"I wasn't thinking. I was working. It was an accident, I guess." Symphony rolled her eyes and started to talk faster. "Who am I kidding? Nothing is an accident with me. It was scary and tragic. I saw the downtown burn in a horrible blaze. I caught a baby in the air. I spent more time with my mother. The bank burned where the clock was. I met my grandfather's sister, and the most interesting man who fixed clocks."

"Slow down. Slow down. You caught a baby in the air? I don't understand."

"The whole time I was gone. You were there with me, in my heart, on my mind. All I could think about was getting back here to you. I'm probably crazy for saying this. It's too soon. But, I love you, Jason. I love you with my whole heart. It terrified me to think that I might not be able to come back here."

"Well, I'm glad that you were scared. I hope that makes you stay put in your own time. Stay right here with me, Symphony, because my whole heart loves you, too."

SYMPHONY TRIED TO put 1924 behind her as summer turned to fall. It was slightly difficult considering that the theme of the temporary exhibit at the Boyd Museum was the Great Wytheville Fire. It gave her a unique perspective as she put the information together for the exhibit panels. Stories were being told within it that Symphony experienced firsthand.

"I feel like I'm seeing the Great Fire through your eyes, Symphony." Allison Emerson viewed the exhibit in the moments before it was opened to the public. "I'm hesitant to give you any further assignments that have to do with the past though. Nadia gave me a dirty look at the last historical society meeting."

"Oh, she did no such thing." Symphony laughed. "Considering that my position is curator and we operate historical museums, you are basically putting my job in jeopardy when you say something like that."

"You have plenty of job security. Don't worry about that." Allison looked around before she whispered. "I wonder if I am the only museum director in the world who has a curator that goes back in time to do research."

"I sure would like to know if there are others. We could form a support group."

"It's about time for us to open those doors." Allison glanced at her watch. "Marcella said we had about forty RSVPs for the opening."

"I can see a line outside. I'm ready if you are."

The next two hours flew by. Symphony gave tours of the exhibit and answered questions. Many of the attendees had ancestors who experienced the Great Fire with stories passed from generation to generation.

One elderly man seemed to linger in the exhibit area looking at the photographs over and over again. Symphony approached him when she saw that Allison was about ready to close up.

"Do you have any questions about the exhibit, sir?"

"No, young lady. I am just reliving what my parents told me about that day. They owned a building that was destroyed. It was a devastating time for them. But, they persevered." The man turned to Symphony and smiled. "That is a very unusual pendant you have on. May I see it more closely?"

"Certainly."

Symphony lifted up the pendant so that the man could see the detail. She felt a jolt when he took it in his hand and rubbed the smooth surface. The strange feeling continued. He turned the pendant over and saw the unique engraving on the other side.

"I have touched this pendant before. I am certain of it." The man released it and looked Symphony squarely in the eyes. "You look familiar to me. Did you have family who lived here during the Great Fire? I am told that I was saved by a beautiful young woman who wore an unusual necklace."

Symphony turned away and pretended to cough to conceal the sudden emotion she was feeling.

"Excuse me." Still choked up, Symphony tried to form the thoughts that were racing through her mind into a sentence. "May I ask your name, sir?"

"I am Melvin Alper. The story on this panel." The man pointed. "It is my story. That was my parents' store. I was the baby that was caught during the fire. I was almost three years old. I cannot say that I truly remember it. Yet, I still can see flashes of something in my mind. When I took hold of your pendant, I had such a flash. You must be a granddaughter of that woman. I remember my mother used to speak of her. Unfortunately, I do not remember her name."

"You have lived a long life, sir. What has it been filled with?" Symphony stared at him in awe.

"Happiness, mostly. Hard work. My family. Medicine."

"Medicine?"

"I was an ophthalmologist. Some people say a famous one. I enjoyed helping people to see." Mr. Alper looked at his watch. "I have stayed too long. You are closing. Thank you for listening to the ramblings of an old man."

"It was my pleasure, Mr. Alper. I'm so happy you were able to come to see this exhibit. We are honored to have you here." Symphony led him into the main lobby and motioned for Allison to join them. "Allison, I would like you to meet Mr. Melvin Alper. Mr. Alper, this is Allison Emerson, our Director of Museums."

"It's nice to meet you, sir. I hope you enjoyed the exhibit."

"Allison, Mr. Alper experienced the Great Fire. He was the child who was thrown from the window and caught by someone on the street."

"A beautiful young woman who wore an unusual pendant like this lady is wearing."

"How wonderful! We are so honored to have you with us today." Allison gave Symphony a wide-eyed look.

"If you will excuse me, Mr. Alper. It was lovely to meet you. I will always remember your story."

"THAT'S INCREDIBLE, SYMPHONY. You met the man who you saved as a child. What are the odds of that happening?"

Nadia and Symphony huddled under a huge blanket in front of the fireplace. Despite that fact that it was still a rather warm season, Symphony returned home chilled to the bone.

"Probably a zillion to one considering that it happened almost a hundred years ago. He touched that pendant and I felt a jolt of something. It was incredible."

"A jolt of magic, no doubt. You can study all you want to about the science behind the theory of time travel. There are some things in this life that we must give in and attribute to magic. I'm not talking about wicked witches and cauldrons or wizards flying on brooms. I mean the magic of the universe that for most people is beyond what they are willing to believe. I think we see subtle examples of it every day. And then, there are some times, like you have described that challenge us to pay attention."

"I'm exhausted." Symphony took a long drink of the hot chocolate Nadia prepared them.

"It sounds like the exhibit opening was a success."

"It would have been a success if Mr. Alper was the only person there." Symphony laughed. "I can't wait to get to work tomorrow to hear what Allison has to say. I didn't have an opportunity to talk to her after Mr. Alper left. She was busy talking to one of the donors for the next exhibit."

"What's the next exhibit going to focus on?"

"Hotels in early Wytheville. There were quite a few of them. One of the specific features will be about the Boyd Hotel that was first on Main Street and, then later, at the railroad depot."

"They were owned by Thomas J. Boyd, I assume."

"The Father of Wytheville himself. Apparently, one of them has a notorious incident that took place in the mid-1800s." Symphony paused and took another slow drink of the hot beverage. She thought she tasted a hint of peppermint in the concoction. "That reminds me of something. I believe that you told me that Tyler only traveled back beyond his own time once. Tell me about that again."

"Yes. Tyler did not like going back before his own time. He was much more interested in the future. His first time travel journey took him back to the mid-1800s, as a matter of fact. It was a frightening experience for him. He witnessed a murder. A murder because of a young girl's fickle heart."

"A murder. It didn't occur in a hotel, did it? That would be quite a coincidence."

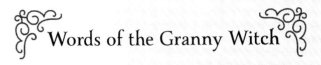

Words of the Granny Witch

"Sometimes the smallest acts have the biggest impacts. A smile given freely to a stranger might give him the will to live another day. A kind word to a child might be the only one she hears that day. We go through life concentrating on the big things, when it is the small ones that mean the most.

"I once met a man who chased time. It was his obsession to experience eras that did not naturally belong to him. In the end, he lost himself in time, and became a stranger to all who loved him. He traded a myriad of small moments for a big goal that only brought him heartache.

"There are secrets left to be told, but only to those who will listen with a heart that is open, not a mind that is already made up. The child has walked through fire. The burn will linger long after the smoke is gone. A broken piece of glass cannot be whole again. But, it can be created into something even more beautiful with patience and understanding."

Acknowledgements

I believe there are times in all of our lives when we are haunted by something. Perhaps, it is a decision we did, or did not, make. It might be a word spoken and forever regretted. Maybe, it was the path we chose when we came to a fork in the road of our lives. The second book of this series contains situations that haunt the characters. I believe we can all find parallels in our own lives. That's one of my favorite aspects about the journey of telling a story to my readers. Within the pages of this book, you find the tale of lives imagined. My hope is that you also find a little of yourself and grow in your understanding of how all our lives are entwined in this collective journey we travel.

As I've mentioned previously, I find inspiration in a variety of ways. For this particular series, a sizable portion of the inspiration came from the creative fingertips of my dear friend, Amanda Slaughter—the owner, designer, and creator of BloomSpoons jewelry (www.BloomSpoons.com). Her creative soul with its mixture of magic and honor to nature is the epitome of the characteristics personified by the original Granny Witches—the true Queens of Appalachia. The pendant Symphony uses to travel through time was created by Amanda and adorns the cover of this book.

While this is a work of fiction, much of the historical information contained within is factual. The setting of this series is Wytheville, Virginia. Wytheville is a real place. As the story tells you, there is only one community with such a name in the whole world. Most of the businesses mentioned in this book are real. A Great Fire did indeed occur in the small town in March, 1924, with devastating effects for its downtown district. Wytheville rose from the ashes after that fire, as well as subsequent ones in the decades thereafter. By the end of the second decade of the twenty-first century, it had undergone another revitalization, as this story describes, and Downtown Wytheville is a vibrant, growing area. To learn more about this wonderful community, look it up on the World Wide Web at www.VisitWytheville.com.

As any true writer knows, there comes a time when you have to let go of your words and allow others to help you edit and improve them. There are four talented and patient women who are the first ones to read my stories and give me the careful critiques needed. These ladies also happen to be dear friends: Pam Newberry, Marcella Taylor, Donna Stroupe, and Carole Bybee. They each see aspects and errors in my writing that I cannot see and lovingly give the suggestions I need to hear. I am eternally grateful.

Every book should be wrapped in a beautiful cover. I am so blessed to work with a creative soul who has the ability to read my mind even though we have never met. I fall in love with each cover that Cassy Roop of Pink Ink Designs (www.pinkindesigns. com) creates for me. I'm continually amazed at the little details she just seems to know to add. Her talented fingers are also behind the formatting of the pages within.

My humble thanks to all of you who invest your time and money to take this journey with me. It is because of you that I have the bravery to put my stories on paper. Thank you for going on this adventure with me. I welcome the opportunity to hear what you thought of my stories with a message via my website at www. RosaLeeJude.com or through a review on Amazon or Goodreads.

About the Author

Rosa Lee Jude began creating her own imaginary worlds at an early age. While her career path has included stints in journalism, marketing, hospitality & tourism and local government, she is most at home at a keyboard spinning yarns of fiction and creative nonfiction. She lives in the beautiful mountains of Southwest Virginia with her patient husband and very spoiled rescue dog. Learn more about her other books and writing journey at www.RosaLeeJude. com.

Want more?

Sign Up for Rosa Lee Jude's mailing list. It's for new releases and fun giveaways only, no spam.

www.rosaleejude.com/newsletter-sign-up

Other books by Rosa Lee Jude can be found on her Amazon Author Page www.amazon.com/Rosa-Lee-Jude/e/B00E6TYRGE

Please consider following her to keep up-to-date on new releases.

Or connect with her on her Facebook page
Rosa Lee Jude, Author
www.facebook.com/rosaleejudeauthor/

Did you enjoy this book? You can make a big difference by leaving a short review. Honest reviews help convince prospective readers to take a chance on an author they do not know. I personally read each review and appreciate the time that the reader has taken to tell me why he or she enjoyed it. Thank you.

.

Made in the USA
Middletown, DE
29 October 2023

41503275R00182